THE CREOLES SERIES

The Tapestry

Gilbert Morris
&
Lynn Morris

WestBow
P R E S S
A Division of Thomas Nelson Publishers
Since 1798
visit us at www.westbowpress.com

Published in Nashville, Tennessee, by Thomas Nelson, Inc.

WestBow Press books may be purchased in bulk for educational, business, fund-raising, or sales promotional use. For information, please e-mail SpecialMarkets@ThomasNelson.com.

Scripture taken from the King James Version.

Publisher's Note: this novel is a work of fiction. All characters, plots, and events are the product of the author's imagination. All characters are fictional, and any resemblance to persons living or dead is strictly coincidental.

Library of Congress Cataloging-in-Publication Data

Morris, Gilbert.
  The tapestry / Gilbert Morris & Lynn Morris.
    p. cm.—(The Creoles series ; 4)
  ISBN 0-7852-7005-1 (pbk.)
    1. Women—Louisiana—Fiction. 2. New Orleans (La.)—Fiction. 3. Creoles—Fiction. I. Morris, Lynn. II. Title.
  PS3563.O8742T37 2005
  813'.54—dc22

2004028699

Printed in the United States of America
05 06 07 08 09 RRD 9 8 7 6 5 4 3 2 1

I am not a fan of beauty contests, so I have decided to select my own Miss America and dedicate this book to her.

And the winner is . . .
MISS SARAH ANDRUS of Farmington, Minnesota.

You are *my* Miss America, Sarah, and I wish that every young woman in our country had your character, sweetness, and dedication to Jesus Christ.

Your family deserves to be included in this dedication, for I know that it was their love and commitment that has formed you into the fine young woman that you are. My warm congratulations to your parents and your brothers.

My prayer is that God will open up doors of service for you and that you will be a handmaiden of the Lord all the days of your life.

The Creole Heritage

In the early nineteenth century, the culture of New Orleans was as rich and widely varied as the citizens' complexions. Pure Spanish families, descended from haughty dons, still dwelt in the city, and some pure French families resided there, but many were already mingled with both Spaniards and Africans. Acadians—or "Cajuns," as they came to be called—lived outside of the city. This small pocket of Frenchmen had wandered far from home, but, like many groups in New Orleans, they stubbornly kept much of their eighteenth-century heritage intact and ingrained.

Of course, there were many slaves, but there were also the *gen de couleur libres,* or free men and women of color. Some of these were pure Africans, but most of them were the mulattoes, griffes, quadroons, and ocotoroons who were the result of French and Spanish blending with slaves. There were Americans, too, though they were strictly confined to the "American district." And there were Creoles, people of French and Spanish blood, who were born outside of their native countries. Creoles born in New Orleans were Louisianians, but they were not considered Americans.

All well-born Creole families sent their children to receive a classical education at the Ursuline Convent or the Jesuit schools, and both institutions accepted charity children.

This series of novels traces the history of four young women who were fellow students at the Ursuline Convent School:

- *The Exiles:* Chantel
- *The Immortelles:* Damita
- *The Alchemy:* Simone
- *The Tapestry:* Leonie

PART ONE

· April 1831–September 1833 ·

Chapter one

Simone d'Or stared at the paper in front of her, and then suddenly, without warning, reached out and crumpled it up. Throwing it across the room, she said loudly, "I can't stand this any longer, Damita!"

Damita Madariaga, who sat across the room from Simone, stared at her roommate, taking in the long blonde hair, the dark blue eyes, and the full lower lip. Damita had always admired Simone's beauty, although she herself was recognized for being one of the most attractive girls at the Ursuline Convent. Damita took the book that she was reading and threw it across the room with all her force. The pages fluttered, and the book struck a picture on the wall and knocked it to the floor. It fell with a crash, and the glass shattered.

"Good!" Damita said viciously. "I'd like to tear the whole building down!" She got up abruptly, went over to the window and stared outside. "I'm sick of this room!" she exclaimed. "It's like being in a prison."

Actually the room was much nicer than most of the others in the convent. Both Simone and Damita came from wealthy families who had spared no expense in fixing up the bare room. The floor was carpeted with an expensive Persian rug. Silk hangings decorated the walls, and the furniture was mostly of polished rosewood gleaming from the sunlight that streamed through the large window. The two half beds, each of which occupied one side of the room, were comfortable and covered with well-chosen and attractive coverlets.

"I'd like to take Sister Agnes and dump her in a well," Simone muttered darkly. Rising from her desk, she threw herself down on the bed, put her hands behind her head, and stared up at the ceiling. "She's too mean to be a nun."

"She's worse than the rest of them. If it wasn't for her, we wouldn't be confined to quarters. I think it's a shame, and I'm going to tell my papa to take me out of this place."

"He won't do it."

Damita started to argue, then shrugged. "No, he probably won't, but I'm going to get even with her somehow or other."

Simone closed her eyes and was quiet for a time. The two girls were perfect roommates, for both were spoiled beauties. The Ursuline Convent was not designed for such proud young women, and the two had been a problem for the sisters who were responsible for their training for their entire stay.

As Damita stared out the window, her mind worked quickly. She had known little discipline at her home—she was the spoiled pet of the family, and although the discipline was somewhat stricter at the convent, neither Damita nor Simone had allowed it to interfere greatly with their lifestyles. Damita watched as one of the servants washed clothes beside a well. A young man had come to flirt with her, and Damita felt a twinge of envy. "Marie can have men flirt with her, but we can't."

Simone got up from the bed in a smooth, easy motion and walked over to stare out the window. "She'd better watch out. If Sister Agnes catches her with Juan, she'll be sorry."

The two girls watched as the young man reached out and smoothed the golden-brown cheek of the servant girl. The laughter of the two floated up to them, and Damita exclaimed suddenly, "Let's do something *wicked*, Simone!"

"Do something? Like what?"

"I've got to get out of this room, or it's going to drive me crazy!"

Sister Agnes had confined them to their room for a week until they brought their work up to standard. She was a stern taskmaker with no respect for the power the girls' families had. She had even required them to take their meals there, and both young ladies were furious. They were the same age, seventeen, and the confinement had been the worst punishment they had known in their lives.

"I mean it," Damita said, her lips growing tight. "Let's just get out of here for a while."

"And go where?"

"We can go see that play in town. It's Shakespeare."

"Oh, *Romeo and Juliet*. I'd love to see that!" Simone exclaimed, but a doubtful look crossed her face. "I don't see how we could do it."

"Sister Agnes is gone for the day. She went over to one of the villages to take some food to a needy family. We can go to the matinee. I saw it in the paper."

Simone was caught by the daring idea. "All right," she said, "let's do it. But if we get caught—"

"So what if we get caught? What can they do to us—beat us with a whip?" Damita laughed and shook her head, her glossy black hair catching the spring sunshine. "All we have to do is sneak out when nobody's looking and sneak back. It'll be almost dark when we get back. It'll be easy."

"We can't go through the gate. They'd see us."

"You know where they're repairing the wall over on the south side? It's not quite finished yet, and the men aren't working on it. We could slip through that gap that's still there. Come on, get ready!"

"Do you have enough money for us to get in?"

"Yes. I've got plenty. Hurry up, now!"

"Let's go see if Chantel wants to go with us, and maybe Leonie."

"I doubt if they will, but we'll give them a chance."

The two girls left their room and moved cautiously down the hall. They knocked on a door, and then without waiting, Simone opened it, and the two girls slipped inside.

Leonie Dousett was sitting at the desk, writing industriously. She was a petite young woman with a good figure. Her waist was the smallest of any of the girls, the envy of the rest of them. She had a heart-shaped face, auburn hair that had recently darkened to a lustrous deep brown, and well-shaped gray eyes. Her complexion was olive, very smooth. She had a widow's peak and a dimple in her right cheek when she smiled.

"What are you two doing here?" Leonie asked.

"Where's Chantel?"

"She went down the hall to the washroom." Leonie was very plainly dressed compared to the other two. She was one of the girls that the sisters at the convent took in as an act of charity. Leonie was an orphan and had made her way, when she grew old enough, by working for the sisters and sewing for some of the students. "If Sister Agnes catches you out of your room, you'll be sorry."

"I'm not afraid of her," Damita said defiantly. "She didn't have any business confining us to our room anyway."

Even as Damita spoke the door opened, and Chantel Fontaine came in. She was a tall young woman with striking green eyes. "What are you two doing out of your room?"

"Never mind that," Simone said. Her eyes were glowing with excitement. "Damita and I are going to sneak out and go see *Romeo and Juliet* in town."

"Yes," Damita said, "there's a matinee that starts at three o'clock, I think. We'll get back about dark."

"You can't do that," Leonie said. "You'll be in trouble if you get caught."

"We won't get caught." Damita shrugged her shoulders. "We're going to go sneak through that place in the wall they're repairing. Come on. You can go with us."

Leonie shook her head. "No. I'm not going."

"I—I don't think I'd better," Chantel said. She came from a good family but one not as wealthy and influential as Simone's and Damita's families. She was a much milder girl and more amiable in every way.

"I told you they wouldn't go," Simone said.

"Well, *we're* going."

Leonie and Chantel tried to dissuade their friends, but both knew it was useless.

"Come on. I've got to get out of this place!" Damita said. She grinned roguishly and winked at Leonie. "You're going to miss a good time."

Leonie didn't answer, but as soon as the two girls left, she turned to Chantel and said with a worried expression. "I wish they wouldn't do that. They could get in serious trouble."

"That's never bothered those two," Chantel remarked. "I just hope Sister Agnes doesn't catch them. I think she'd really take a cane to them this time, no matter how important their families are."

Simone and Damita made their way down the hall. Both of them, of course, knew every nook and cranny of the convent, and they silently threaded through several corridors usually vacant. Finally they stepped outside, and Damita looked cautiously in both directions. "There's nobody in the courtyard, and the workmen are gone. Come on."

Simone followed Damita as they ran lightly across the grass and reached the wall. The wall, an ancient one, had been crumbling, and now only one small gap remained unfinished. Avoiding the pile of stones and the mortar boards and other tools of the trade, the two slipped quickly through the gap. As soon as they were outside, Damita laughed. "Now, let's go to town!"

The play was not the first Shakespearean play that the two girls had seen; both were lovers of drama. Damita had paid for the best seats in the house, and although Simone was worried that someone, somehow, from the convent might see them, Damita had shrugged. "Who from a convent would want to go to see actors? They think all actors are demons straight out of the pit."

"They'll think we are, too, just for going." Simone managed to smile.

When the play concluded and the actors came out for their curtain call, the two girls applauded until their hands ached. "I'm going to be an actress," Damita said firmly. "They get to travel everywhere."

"I don't think that would be a very good life. Besides, your parents would never let you do it."

"I suppose not. They never want me to have any fun, and yours are about the same."

The two left the theater and set their minds on a meal before returning to the convent. "If they're going to starve us at that old convent, we've got a right to eat out. Come on," Damita ordered.

The two girls found a café and filled up on shrimp, fish, and gumbo. They both laughed a great deal, feeling rather proud of their exploit.

Finally, however, the meal was finished and Simone sighed. "Come on. We'd better get back."

"I wish I didn't have to go to that place. It's like going to Devil's Island."

"Oh, it's not that bad!"

"It is too!"

"How do you know? You've never been to Devil's Island."

"I've read about it, though."

"Well, they don't throw us in dungeons and whip us with whips."

The two girls argued all the way back to the convent. The sun had already dipped below the horizon, and darkness was beginning to fall as they approached the gap in the wall. Damita whispered, "You'd better be quiet now. Sister Agnes may be back by this time."

The two girls tiptoed through the wall and no sooner were they inside than they were startled by a shadowy figure that appeared to their right. Damita, for all her boastfulness, gave a little cry, for she knew that to be caught by Sister Agnes was not far removed from being sent to Devil's Island.

"Damita—Simone—is that you?"

A gust of relief passed through Damita. "Leonie," she said when the young girl stepped forward. "What are you doing out here?"

Leonie moved closer and put her finger to her lips in a sign. "You can't go back the way you left," she whispered. "Sister Agnes is back, and she's patrolling all the halls."

"Does she know we're gone?" Simone said.

"I don't think so. Not yet. But you know how she is."

"How are we going to get in? We can't go to the front door," Damita said.

Ordinarily Leonie Dousett was not one to give orders. But now she saw that both girls were frightened. "Come around to the back," she directed.

"Those doors are always locked."

"I know, Simone, but the windows aren't. There's a window up over the shed."

"We can't get to that window."

"Yes, we can. There's a ladder, and we can climb in and get on the shed. From there we can reach the window. I checked on the ladder, but we'd better hurry."

It was typical that neither girl thought of thanking Leonie for the risk she was taking. They took it for granted as they took everything else for granted in their lives. The three girls followed the shadows until they had rounded the building, and at the back Damita made out the shed that protruded from the outer wall of the convent building.

"Climb up on that ladder," Leonie said. "You go on in. I'll climb up the ladder last. No one will know how you got in."

The two girls scrambled up. Leonie was about to mount the ladder herself when suddenly a light shone directly in her face.

"Who is that? Girl, stop right where you are!"

Leonie had no chance to run. The light had blinded her, but she recognized Sister Agnes's harsh voice.

Sister Agnes appeared, holding the lantern up to Leonie's eyes. "Leonie, what are you doing out here, and who's that with you?"

Leonie could not think of a single thing to say. She remained quiet, and suddenly Sister Agnes's hand took her arm. "Speak to me. I know that there was someone out here with you. Who was it?"

Leonie did not want to lie, so she couldn't say she was alone. At the same time she knew with a sinking heart that she could expect nothing good to come of this.

"I'm surprised at you, Leonie! I wouldn't put it past some of the other girls. You've been sneaking out to town, a group of you, haven't you?"

"I haven't been to town."

Sister Agnes stared at her. "Well, you can explain all this to the mother superior. Come along."

Leonie was a meek, quiet young woman who had never been in trouble in all her years at the convent. As she trudged heavily behind Sister Agnes, her heart was beating rapidly, and she had a sudden impulse to turn and run away—but there was nowhere to go. She had no home where she could take refuge. She began to pray as she entered the building. "Lord, don't let them throw me out of here."

∽

"That was Sister Agnes's voice," Simone whispered. She peered out the window, but it was too dark to see.

Chantel, who had met the two girls to help them through the window, asked, "What about Leonie?"

"I think Sister Agnes got her."

"She'll tell on us," Damita said, and fear showed in her eyes.

"No, she won't," Chantel said. She knew Leonie better than the other two girls. "She'd let them pull her fingernails out before she'd tell on anyone."

"I hope you're right," Damita said. "If she tells the mother superior about us, we'll probably be expelled. My family will have a fit."

"Mine too," Simone said.

"You don't have to worry. Leonie won't tell. She's not that kind."

The mother superior of the Ursuline Convent had rarely known such uncertainty. She was a small woman of fifty with hazel eyes and hair that was turning silver. Although one of the most petite of the nuns, her determination was by far the most firm. She had gone to the convent as a novice and stayed in the service until she was in authority over all the other nuns.

"I'm surprised at you, Leonie. What do you have to say for yourself?"

"Nothing, Reverend Mother."

"Do you admit that you were caught and that there were others with you?" She waited for Leonie to reply, but the girl did nothing but stand before her. The mother superior could see that Leonie's hands were trembling and that fear was in her face. She had formed a great affection for this young woman who had never given her a moment's trouble. She said quietly, "I have every confidence in you, Leonie. I know you wouldn't do anything that was wrong. Others might, but you won't—still, I can't let this pass."

"I know, Reverend Mother." Leonie's voice was barely audible.

She shook her head. "This is your last year here. It would be a shame if you lost your place before you graduated."

The implied threat frightened Leonie, but still she could say nothing.

"I believe you are protecting someone," the mother superior said. "You might think that's a noble thing, but I'm not certain it is. Those who were with you aren't helping you in the least, and I don't think they will. They'll let you take the blame and the punishment while they get off scot-free."

"I—I'm sorry, Reverend Mother. I hate to disappoint you."

"If that's all you have to say, I will have to punish you. All your privileges will be suspended, and you'll spend one month on rough cleaning detail." The mother superior saw relief come into the young girl's eyes, and she added, "And no evening meal."

"Yes, Reverend Mother."

"You may go now."

Leonie left at once, and as soon as she was out of the room Sister Agnes bustled in. "Did she tell you who the others were?"

"No, she didn't. You didn't think she would, did you?"

"If she had any sense, she would."

The mother superior smiled. "She's got more than sense. She's got character."

"Character!" Sister Agnes snorted. "What good does it do her to protect those others?"

"I took away all her privileges, including the late meal, and put her on rough cleaning for a month."

"And those who snuck out with her get away with it. Is that the way it has to be?"

"I can't think of anything else to do."

The two women stood regarding each other, and finally the mother superior said, "I've always had a soft spot for Leonie."

"Well, so have I, for that matter. She's had a hard life. I was an orphan myself."

"I know you were. Actually, we don't know that she was an orphan."

"I understand you were the one who found her, Reverend Mother."

"Yes. Most of the time, when people leave infants we meet the parents, but I found Leonie in a basket outside the door early one morning."

"You were never able to find out who her parents were or anything about her background?"

"We tried," the older woman answered, "but we had no success." She shrugged her shoulders and said, "She's a good girl."

"Yes, she is," Sister Agnes said. Then her features hardened. "But it does her no good, her friendship with those rich, spoiled girls. I wouldn't be surprised if they weren't the ones who were into this thing with her."

"I have no doubt that you're right, but you'll never get it out of Leonie."

⌒

As soon as Leonie stepped inside her room, she was greeted by all three of her best friends.

"What'd they do to you, Leonie?" Chantel demanded.

"Nothing very bad."

"I'll bet it was," Simone said. "What did she say?"

"Did she try to get you to tell her who was with you?"

"Yes, she did."

"But you didn't," Chantel said.

"No. I couldn't do that."

Damita expelled a breath of relief. "Well, what punishment did you get?"

"Nothing too bad."

"Come on and tell me," Chantel said. "I know it wasn't pleasant."

"Reverend Mother was very kind. I do without supper and have rough cleaning detail for a month."

Damita went and put her arms around Leonie. "Don't you worry about it. We'll make it right with you. You'll have a better supper in your room than you'd have in the hall. You'll see."

"Are you mad at us, Leonie?" Simone asked, studying the girl's face.

"Why, of course not. You'd do it for me."

Chantel shook her head but said nothing. "You'd better get back to your rooms now. I think probably Sister Agnes and Reverend Mother know pretty well who was in on this."

The two girls left, and for a while Chantel tried to pry more secrets of the interview out of Leonie, but the girl said little. Finally the two girls studied their lessons and went to bed. Their huge black cat with golden eyes, Louis, who was an expert mouser, was curled up on Leonie's bed. She had found him when he was just a tiny ball of black fur, and after much wheedling, she had obtained permission to keep him. That night Leonie was glad for his fellowship. Louis's purr was like a tiny motor that often made her sleepy. She went to sleep finally thinking of all that had happened and praying that God would take care of her.

⁓

For the first week Damita did well getting food to Leonie at night. She bought the best that money could buy, and it had become a game sneaking it into Leonie. But eventually she tired of the extra chore or forgot. Chantel did not, however, and she saw to it that her roommate got at least the same food that the rest of the students received.

As for Leonie, it was not a terrible burden for her to lose privileges, for she had no visitors. She put it out of her mind and had already begun to look forward to the day when she would finish her studies and leave the convent. The other girls all had families to go to, but she herself had no one, and every night she asked God to provide a place for her.

Chapter two

The days passed quickly after Leonie had completed her punishment, and as her graduation date was rapidly approaching, she seemed to have more freedom than ever before.

She had thought more and more about what she would do when she had to leave the convent, and it still frightened her to think of her future.

A bright day on the first of May brought her out of the convent on a pleasant errand. She had always enjoyed roaming the streets of New Orleans, and having been assigned a few errands by Sister Agnes, she moved through the city, taking it all in.

New Orleans in 1831 was perhaps the most multiracial society in the United States. It was a rich mixture of occupations and activities with a population composed of Spaniards, Americans, Germans, Indians, and Africans. The blacks, both slave and free, made up about half of the total.

As she walked along the streets, Leonie was as usual fascinated by the streams of people who crowded each other. She passed an older woman wearing a *tignon*, a madras handkerchief. The woman was clasping her prayer book and obviously on her way to the cathedral.

Indians were still a common sight even at this late date, and she watched them with interest, especially a couple who had three small children. The children were silent, absorbing the sights in the streets, and it struck Leonie that she had never seen Indian children laugh, and she wondered why.

She passed black nursemaids in Lafeyette Square, some of them wheeling their small charges in buggies, others leading them by the hand.

A woman passed by carrying an enormous wooden bowl on her head, filled with *calahs*, coarse rice fritters. The woman cried as she walked, "Fine fritters, just made!" Leonie used some of the money she had saved to purchase a few.

Other women, mostly black, carrying their wares, shouted out their virtues. Leonie approached the woman who cried, "Blackberries, very fine!" and bought a small sack full of the rich, juicy berries and munched them as she went along. Another vendor shouted about her own delicious products, browned pecan and pink or white coconut pralines. Leonie bought a few from her as well. Then she passed through the market house situated on the levee near the Place d'Armes, an enormous sale market with more than a hundred stalls and over three hundred feet long that extended along the levee.

She wandered along its arcaded sides under its low-pitched roofs and marveled at the babble of languages—English, French, German, and Spanish—that filled the place with a perfect hum. Though it was still early, the market was crowded with sellers and buyers. She stopped at the different vendors to buy items according to Sister Agnes's instructions. From the ceiling hung numerous spiderwebs, flies, and much dirt. The flies made a relentless buzz as they moved about.

Finally, when Leonie had bought all the wares Sister Agnes listed, she wound her way along the crooked streets until she reached one of the poorer sections of town. She had not gone far when a brutal-looking man lurched out of the alley and lunged toward her with a loose grin on his coarse features. He grabbed Leonie's arm, mumbling, "Hello, honey girl. Come along with me. We'll have us a good time."

"Please let me go!" Leonie cried.

"Come on. Don't be shy! You need to know what a real man is like, a real Kaintock."

"Kaintock" was the term many dwellers of New Orleans applied to all Americans, regardless of their points of origin. They were a rough, rowdy bunch for the most part. Many of them were the river boatmen, the roughest of all the men. They fought with huge knives, guns, or fists and filled the jails up in New Orleans regularly.

"Here. You be on your way."

The Kaintock turned quickly to see a tall naval officer frowning at him.

"I don't take orders from no sailors."

The officer had a sword at his side. He drew it in one smooth motion. "Fine," he said. "Which arm do you want removed: your right or your left?"

Leonie backed away from the scene. For one moment she thought the Kaintock intended to challenge the officer. He put his hand on the sheath of the large hunting knife he carried—and then turned and stumbled away.

"I thank you, sir," Leonie said, relief filling her voice.

"Why, you're welcome, miss," the officer said. His skin was bronze and he spoke with an accent she did not recognize. That was not unusual, however, because ships came from all over the world into the port of New Orleans. "You'd better let me escort you to where you're going."

"It's just down the street a ways, but I thank you."

The officer insisted on walking along with her, and she offered him some of the blackberries. He sampled one and said, "I'd like to have some of these to take to sea, but they wouldn't last long. Sailors eat everything good first and wind up with nothing but salted meat."

"It must be exciting to be a sailor."

"It's a hard life, miss." The officer shook his head. "You couldn't think how hard it is."

"And where are you from, sir?"

"I come from Scotland. Glasgow, that is."

"That's far away, isn't it?"

"Very far away. Many a time I wish I'd stayed there with my old pa and been a farmer. Too late now, though. He's gone. Nothing left for me but the sea."

The two reached the house, a mere shack, and Leonie said to the officer with a smile, "You take the blackberries. There are plenty more."

"Why, I thank you, Miss. You're a bonnie lass. Be careful now. There are lots of bad characters roaming the streets of New Orleans."

"I will. Thank you, sir."

The house that Leonie stopped in front of was a poor one indeed. It was unpainted and made of weathered boards, some of them rotten. Gaps showed between some of the flimsy boards, holes large enough to admit a bird.

Leonie knocked on the door and thought with pleasure of the tall sailor. She had a romantic imagination, and, for a moment, she stood thinking how it would be if such a man came courting her, but she realized that was not likely to happen. Scottish sailors didn't go to convents looking for sweethearts!

"Why, Leonie, you're here!"

The door had opened, and Susan Barnes was wiping her hands on her apron. She smiled. "Come in. You're just in time for tea."

"Hello, Susan." Leonie stepped into the house and was at once swarmed by four small children: Billy, Henry, Annie, and Dora. She put her baskets down but reached in and withdrew the pralines that she had bought for each. "Here are sweets for you."

"Now then. What do you say, children?" Susan elicited the thank-yous from those old enough to talk.

Susan busied herself with the tea, and shortly the two women were seated at the rickety table. They sipped the rich tea and nibbled on the fritters that Leonie had brought.

The Barnes family was poor, and matters had gotten worse when William Barnes, who was from Kentucky, had been injured in a fall from a building he was working on. He had broken both legs, and the family had become destitute. William was now just beginning to get around using canes, and during all of their trouble it had been Leonie who had been consistent in her care of them. She had begged food from the kitchen at the convent and even money from the wealthier girls to keep the family going.

The children were quiet as long as they had their sweets to suck on, and Leonie asked about William.

"He's out looking for work. Of course he can't do manual labor, but he thinks he can find something until he's well enough to work."

"That was a terrible accident."

"I don't know where we would have been if it hadn't been for you, dear," Susan Barnes said fondly. She reached over and took Leonie's hand and laid it against her cheek. "You're a sweet girl. Not many would show interest in a poor bunch of Kaintocks."

"Oh, it was little enough."

"No. It was more than that. The children adore you. Can you stay a while and tell them some of your stories?"

"For a little while, Susan."

The "little while" turned out to be more than two hours. William came home and greeted Leonie with a glad smile, adding his thanks for the food she had brought and the small bit of money that she had been able to raise. "I got a little something to do that'll maybe last until my legs get well enough to go back to work."

"What is that, sir?" Leonie asked.

"I'll be in a booth down at the French Market. All I have to do is hand out a few items and take the money. I can do that sitting down. It doesn't pay much, but every little bit helps."

The small family pleaded with her to stay, but she said, "No, I've got to get back." She hesitated, then said, "I'll be leaving the convent in about three weeks."

"Leaving!" Susan said with dismay. "You told us this would come, but I'm surprised it arrived so quickly."

"Will you be leaving New Orleans?" William asked.

"I don't really know, sir. Most of the girls have families they'll be going to, but I'll have to find work myself somewhere."

"Well, the good Lord will take care of you," William said. "He put you to taking care of us, and He'll find someone to take care of you. You're such a fine Christian girl that He'll not let you suffer want."

"I don't mind telling you I'm a little bit worried. I know that's a lack of faith, but I don't have any family at all. But I still hope to find work in New Orleans."

"You'll be coming by to see us, won't you, dear?" Susan said.

"Oh yes, I will. I don't have enough friends that I can afford to do without you."

"I think we ought to pray right now that God will open up a door for our sister," William said. "Come here, children, we're going to pray for sister Leonie."

The children scrambled around, all of them trying to get as close as they could to Leonie. She sat in her chair with their hands touching her, and she felt William's hand on her head. It gave her a strange feeling. She felt Susan's hands on her shoulders, and William began to pray.

Such a prayer! William Barnes prayed for Leonie's physical well-being, for her financial needs, for friends, and for God to open every door until finally he ended with, "This is Your daughter and Your handmaiden, Lord, so we're believing that You are going to open every door for her for good and shut every door for evil. In the name of Jesus, amen."

"Amen," Leonie whispered. She got up with tears in her eyes. "Thank you, William. That was a beautiful prayer."

"And God will answer it," Susan said. She embraced the young girl, then all the children had to have a hug, and finally William himself gave her a squeeze and said, "Don't forget. The Lord God never let any of His children go hungry. I've never seen the righteous forsaken nor His seed begging bread. That's what the Book says. You must believe it, sister Leonie."

Leonie said her good-byes, and as she left the Barnes house, she was thinking how much happier those poor people were than many of the wealthy people that she encountered. She was impressed by their faith in God, and somehow, for a moment, it was easier to face her unknown future.

The grounds of the Ursuline Convent were crowded with parents, grandparents, and friends of the graduates. The bright sunshine of May lit up the gloomy corners of the convent, and the sound of laughter and loud talk made a counterpoint against the bells as they rang announcing the ceremony.

Most of the graduates had purchased new dresses for the ceremony, and Leonie had put her skills with a needle to work and made dresses for three of her classmates. This had taken so much time that she had not been able to make anything for herself, so she simply wore a modest dress that she usually wore to church.

The excitement that filled the girls' rooms somehow depressed Leonie. She still had no idea where she would go, and soon she expected Reverend Mother to question her on her plans. The possibilities for work in New Orleans were slender for a young woman indeed, even one with the good education the convent provided.

Simone d'Or suddenly burst into the room Leonie shared with Chantel crying, "Leonie, you have to help me fix my hair!"

"Of course," Leonie agreed and at once followed the young woman down the corridor. When she entered, she was taken aback, for Simone and Damita had made no attempt to clean up. The room was a wreck with clothes, presents, paper, and food in a wild array.

"You're not going to leave your room like this, are you?" Leonie asked Damita.

"Why not?" Damita grinned. "Let the next student clean it up."

"That's right," Simone laughed. "We'll be through with this place by four o'clock this afternoon."

"It won't be a minute too soon," Damita said. "I'll be so glad to get away from here I could scream."

Damita and Simone talked rapidly about their gifts, which they hoped would include travel outside the country. Leonie felt more and more left out. It was as if she were another species. The gaiety of the two girls only caused her to worry more about what she would do with herself.

The girls were interrupted when their parents came in. Leonie felt out of place, so she went back to her own room where Chantel's parents were visiting with her. "Oh, Leonie, Reverend Mother wants to see you before the ceremony," her roommate told her.

"What does she want?"

"She didn't say. She just sent for you."

Leonie walked to the office, which was on the second floor. She found the mother superior looking out of the window at the crowd milling around below.

"You sent for me, Reverend Mother?"

"Yes, Leonie. Come in and sit down. It's quite an exciting day, isn't it?"

"Yes, I suppose it is."

The mother superior looked carefully at the girl and saw that she was not happy. "Is there anything wrong, Leonie?"

"Oh no."

"You're not ill, are you?"

"No, ma'am. Not at all."

The mother superior had gotten to be an expert at reading the faces of young women, and she saw something was vastly different about Leonie Dousett. She was usually one of the most cheerful young women at the convent, but now an air of disappointment and almost dismay hung about her. "Here, come and sit down. We have a few minutes."

Leonie took her seat, but no matter how hard she tried, she was not able to enter into the spirit of gaiety that floated through the window.

"I'm sorry to say that the position I had hoped to find for you has already been filled."

Disappointment seized Leonie. She had been hopeful to get the position as companion to a wealthy young woman in Baton Rouge.

"I wish it had been different," the mother superior said. "You haven't been able to find anything here in the city?"

"Not yet."

"Well, you'll find something, I'm sure."

"Yes, ma'am, I know I will."

"It will be harder for you than for Simone and Damita and Chantel. It helps to have wealthy parents."

"It would be nice to have parents even if they weren't wealthy," Leonie noted.

The mother superior was surprised. It was the first time she had ever heard Leonie voluntarily mention such feelings. She knew the young girl had determination and courage, but she knew how hard it must have been on her with the other girls having parents, grandparents, and friends coming to wish them well while she herself was all alone.

"I'll keep on looking, of course, and something will turn up," the mother superior assured her.

"If nothing else, I can always work as a seamstress."

"Oh yes, you're very good at that! I've never seen better." She waved at the tapestry that was on the wall. It was one of the two that Leonie had made, and she had offered it as a gift to the mother superior for all of her kindnesses. "That is a beautiful piece of work. Somehow it cheers me up. I don't know why a tapestry should do that."

"What a nice thing to say."

"Well, it's no more than the truth." The mother superior, seeing Leonie's depression, felt uncomfortable, wondering if she had failed the young woman. "I'll keep looking for a place for you."

"Thank you. I know that God will take care of me."

"That's the right attitude, Leonie." The older woman took her hands and said, "You have a very special gift, Leonie."

"Me! A gift?"

"The gift of faith. I've noticed it in you before. You've had a harder life than almost any of these girls here with not knowing your parents and being alone, yet you've not let it sour you. I know that God is going to honor you somehow or other."

Leonie felt the warmth of the woman's words and smiled. "Yes. God will take care of me."

⁓

The graduation ceremonies were long, and Chantel Fontaine won the award for the best scholar. This came as no surprise to anyone; she was a bright young woman. Leonie applauded as hard as Chantel's own family when she walked up to receive her award.

Finally the speeches and the ceremonies were over, and the four girls went to their rooms for the final time—at least for three of them.

"Do you have any more prospects, Leonie?" Chantel asked as she was packing the last of her clothing.

"I'll keep on looking until I find a position."

"I told my parents about you, and the other girls have done the same. We'll find you something."

"Thank you, Chantel. That's like you."

"We must keep in touch," Chantel said.

"Yes, of course," Leonie said, knowing it was not very likely. Chantel, Simone, and Damita moved in the upper regions of society of New Orleans. She herself would be somewhere in the lower order.

The three girls were in a flurry, parents urging them on, and each embraced Leonie. She walked out to the gates and waved as they left, all of them laughing and excited. When she turned back, despondency filled her. She was a young woman of great faith, supposedly, but still the future looked dark. She straightened her back, and her mouth tightened in a stubborn expression. "I'll find something," she murmured. "God won't let me down."

Chapter three

The days passed slowly after graduation, turned into weeks, and finally stretched into two months. New students were coming to take their places in the rooms, and Leonie felt more and more uncomfortable. The mother superior had not said anything about her leaving, but a larger enrollment than usual put rooms at a premium. Desperately she had gone throughout the city looking for work and found nothing, and she knew that the older woman had been active on her behalf as well. It had been a disappointment to her that she had not heard from any of her friends who had left the convent, but she knew they were busy with their families and plans.

It was midmorning, and Leonie was working on a tapestry. She was putting all of her skills into it, for it was larger and more ornate than anything she had attempted before. Leonie had spent the last two months trying to more fully develop her faith, and she decided to make something that would glorify God. Having decided to sew into the tapestry the miracles of Jesus, she was working now on the feeding of the five thousand, which was a challenge to her talents. How to give the impression of a multitude of people on a small bit of fabric was harder than she had expected.

From time to time, she looked outside her window, interested in the purple martins that were building in the house the custodian had put up for them. It had eight separate compartments, and every one was filled, and the birds were busy bringing food to the young ones. They were such a happy breed of bird, and the sounds they made were so cheerful that Leonie stopped often to watch them.

She also paused that morning to read the Scriptures and pray that God would put a way of making a living in her path. She was unusual in that she possessed a Bible, and even more unusual in that she read it. Most religious folk left the reading of the Scriptures and the explanation of them to certain authorities. Leonie had become fascinated with the Bible when she was but a young girl. More than one nun had warned her about the dangers of reading the Bible without guidance, but she could not seem to agree with that.

A knock on the door sounded, and without waiting for an answer Sister Agnes opened it, popped her head in, and said, "You're wanted in Reverend Mother's office, Leonie."

"Me? What for?"

"I don't know, but you'll find out when you go. Hurry now."

Quickly Leonie put her sewing away and looked into the small mirror to be sure that her appearance was suitable. She made her way swiftly to the second floor and knocked on the office door. When she heard the woman's quiet "Come in," she opened the door and stepped inside. "You sent for me, Reverend Mother?" Her eyes went to the leader of the convent first and then to a couple who were seated in chairs across from the large desk.

"Yes, I did, Leonie. This is Monsieur Gaspar Millard and his wife, Matilda. They own an inn in the city, and they are looking for a young woman to work for them. I thought you might be interested."

"Oh yes, I would!" Leonie said quickly. She turned to face the couple. The man had risen, and she saw that he was a tall, bulky man of some forty years. He had blunt features and a pair of quick, black eyes that took her in all at once. His wife was also a tall woman but very thin. She had iron-gray hair and was obviously at least ten years older than her husband. Her eyes were small and close-set, and she had a steel trap of a mouth.

"We cannot pay much," Madam Millard spoke up at once. "You must understand that at the beginning."

"Yes, that is true," her husband said quickly, "but we will offer you room and board. There will be plenty of food and a nice room."

"At least it's a beginning, Leonie, and I know you're anxious to get on with your life," the mother superior said.

"What sort of work would I be doing?"

"The same sort that needs to be done at an inn," Madam Millard said sharply. "Cleaning, helping the cook. I expect all of our help to work hard."

"I think you'll find Mademoiselle a very hard worker. She has set the example for others here for all of her years," the mother superior said quickly. She turned to Leonie, and her eyes expressed her lack of pleasure. "Leonie, it's not necessary for you to go. We will make a place for you here if you would rather do that."

Leonie understood that the woman was offering a way out. The couple did not seem to be particularly pleasant, but Leonie was anxious to start a life away from the convent. She turned to the Millards and said, "I have a cat."

"We do not allow animals," Madam Millard said sharply. "They're nasty creatures."

"Louis is very clean. I couldn't leave without my cat." She saw the anger rise in the woman, but Monsieur Millard spoke up at once. "Oh, let the girl have her cat. He can catch some of those pesky mice."

Madam Millard wanted to argue, but one look at her husband caused her to say, "Very well. You may keep the cat. We need help immediately. The last girl ran away without giving notice. When can you come?"

"I can come today, Madam."

"Good. Get your things. We have a carriage outside."

Leonie packed her few belongings and then put Louis in a basket that she had designed. She closed the lid, latched it, and he protested vehemently with loud, guttural cries.

"It's all right, Louis. We're leaving here, but we'll be together."

Picking up the basket, Leonie looked around the room she had lived in all of her life. As anxious as she was to make a living, it gave her an uncomfortable feeling to be leaving to go live with strangers. She was standing in the middle of the room uncertainly when the door opened and the mother superior came in. She had concern written on her face, and she said, "Leonie, you do not have to go with these people. They don't seem particularly agreeable."

"Oh, it's all right, Reverend Mother. I need to work, and this is what has come. Maybe it's God's will."

"Perhaps, but if you do not like it, you come back here. We will take you in. We'll find a place and work for you to do. You know we can't pay, but we love you, and you will always be welcome here."

Tears came to Leonie's eyes. "Thank you, Reverend Mother. You've always been so kind to me."

"I'll have George take your chest down. Remember, I expect you to come back often to visit with me and let me know how you're doing."

"Of course I'll do that, Reverend Mother."

On the way out, several nuns met Leonie to say good-bye. She had been popular with all of them. Sister Agnes stood before her and said, "Now, you behave yourself and be a good girl."

"Yes, Sister Agnes."

"I'll miss you."

Leonie blinked in surprise, for she had not thought Sister Agnes would ever miss anyone. She saw, however, that the woman actually was sorry to see her leave, and she put her hand out, saying, "You've been very good to me, Sister. I will miss you too."

When she stepped outside the building, the old gardener came to her with a small posy of flowers. "Ah, you're leaving us," he said. "You've been the light of my life."

"Why, Pierre, what a nice thing to say! And thank you for the flowers."

She made her way to where the carriage was waiting. By that time, George had brought her chest down. He waited until he had put it into the back of the carriage, then he turned and gave her a hand in. She put Louis's basket on the seat, and Louis protested vehemently.

"I hope that cat doesn't make that racket all the time," Madam Millard said querulously.

"No, ma'am, he's very quiet usually. He's just a little bit nervous."

"Natural enough. I'd yowl if somebody put me in a basket," Gaspar Millard said. "Well, here we go."

A small crowd, including the mother superior, was there to wave good-bye, and Leonie put her head out the window and waved, trying to smile. When they went out the gate, she turned and sat back, holding onto the basket with her arm.

As they traveled toward the city, Gaspar kept asking her questions, and she answered as well as she could. She was filled with a nameless fear, for she knew little of the world.

"I suppose you'll be glad to get out of that place, eh?" Gaspar said, twisting his head around and winking at her. "Not much going on there, I would guess, in the way of fun."

"No, but I'm sad, sir."

"Sad! Why would you be sad to leave a place like that?" he said with genuine surprise.

"It's the only home I've ever known, sir, and they—they were very kind to me, the sisters."

Gaspar shrugged and said nothing.

"Is it far to the inn?" Leonie asked.

"Not too far."

"Can I come back for a visit, do you suppose?"

"On your day off. Why not? I could bring you myself," Gaspar said with a smile.

"You don't have time to be hauling servants around," Madam Millard said.

There was a sharpness between the two, and Leonie could not help but wonder what sort of situation she was getting into. She said no more and sat back listening, whispering from time to time to Louis in his basket.

Gaspar followed a familiar route at first and then pulled off onto a route she did not know. It was close to the waterfront, and she saw the Mississippi from time to time through the trees. The houses were all poor, and there seemed to be an inordinate number of inns. More than once they passed men who were the worse for drink. It was a section of New Orleans, known for its roughness, where many Kaintocks lived.

Finally Gaspar said, "Well, there it is. The White Horse Inn."

Leonie looked quickly and saw a dilapidated-looking inn wedged in between two other structures, one a warehouse of some sort and the other a three-story dwelling with iron railings around the balconies. The White Horse Inn had a sign bearing what had once been a white horse but now was faded to a sickly green. Gaspar drove around and arrived at the back of the inn where there was a court of sorts with a stable. He got down, and a tall, scrawny young boy came at once. Gaspar spoke to him harshly, and the boy flinched as though he had been struck. "Take this young woman's chest up to Emily's old room," he said. "Be quick about it."

"Yes, Monsieur."

Leonie stepped out of the carriage, holding onto Louis's basket, and waited until Gaspar Millard helped his wife down. "Come this way," Madam Millard said.

Leonie followed the pair up a set of rickety steps and was greeted by an unpleasant smell of boiled cabbage and the ancient odors that any house will accumulate. They passed through the kitchen, which she saw was filthy. A large woman spilling out of her clothes with her hair tied up with a rag was cooking. "This is Gemma. She's the cook. Gemma, this is Leonie. She'll be helping you out."

"About time. I need a little help." Gemma's face was hardened by years of hard work, but her manner was not unkind.

Gaspar said, "Come. I'll take you up to your room."

"Thank you, sir."

Gaspar led her through the area that served for eating and drinking, and she saw that quite a few men were in there and even a few women, all looking more or less disreputable. The smell of strong liquor and other worse smells made her wrinkle her nose.

"Up this way. Watch your step."

The steps indeed were steep that led to the second floor where they turned and climbed to the third floor. "This is the attic. I made a room out of it," Gaspar said. There was a short hallway with only one door at the end. "You'll have lots of privacy up here if you want to entertain your gentlemen friends."

"I won't be doing that, Monsieur."

Gaspar laughed and opened the door. "You got your own window, you see."

The room was a disaster. It was filthy, and the covers on the bed were so awful that Leonie knew at once that she would have to wash them before she could sleep on them. She didn't know what she would do about the mattress. Whoever had occupied the room had never thought of cleaning it. The paper was peeling off the walls, what little paper there was, and the one window was coated with grime so that the sun could hardly force its way in.

The furniture consisted of a single bed with the filthy covers, a chair that looked ready to collapse, and a washstand with a chipped basin and a pitcher even more so.

"You'll have to haul your wash water up here," Gaspar said. "It'll take a little cleaning up, but you'll make out fine here."

"Yes, sir. Thank you for bringing me."

Gaspar suddenly moved forward and put his hand on her shoulder. It startled Leonie, and she quickly looked up at him. He had a peculiar expression in his eyes. "You and me are going to get along fine. If you want anything, you let me know." He squeezed her shoulder with a caress and Leonie, horrified, pulled away.

"Thank you, sir," she said quickly. "I'll be fine."

"Too late to do much today. Supper will be in a couple of hours. You can work on your room until then." He turned and stared at her, and she felt something unclean in his look. He laughed harshly then turned and left.

What a horrible, horrible place! How will I ever live here? The words did not escape Leonie's lips, but they were true enough. She was used to cleanliness and quiet, and already she could hear the boisterous yells and shouts and raucous laughter coming from the bar downstairs. She had a feeling it would be much worse at night.

For a moment Leonie thought of leaving, of going back to the convent at once, but there was an innate determination in this young woman for all her mildness and meekness. "I can live here," she said aloud, then straightened her back. She reached over and opened the basket, and when Louis jumped out, she picked him up and hugged him to her breast. "We'll be all right, Louis. You'll see."

⌒

For the rest of the day, Leonie threw herself into a frenzy of cleaning. She hauled up hot water and soap in buckets until she had scrubbed the room, including the ceiling. She had gone out and bought fresh blankets out of her own slender store of money and had exchanged the mattress, such as it was, for a better one. Gemma, the cook, had helped her, saying, "This ain't much of a place for a fine young lady like you."

"It'll be all right, Gemma. I'm used to hard work."

"It ain't the work." Gemma closed one eye in a wink, and her mouth twisted upward in a wry grin. "Watch out for the master. He likes young girls."

"It'll do him no good."

"You watch what I say. Don't ever let him get you alone. He's gotten more than one girl in trouble here. Have you got some kind of a knife?"

"A knife! Of course not."

"Here. Take this one." Gemma reached over into a drawer and pulled out a short but obviously very keen weapon. "Here. Keep this with you all the time."

"Oh, I couldn't use that."

"You could if it kept him from harmin' you, couldn't you?"

"I won't need that. The Lord will take care of me."

"Well, the Lord helps them that helps themselves. You watch out for him. You mind what I say."

"I'll be sure and watch, and thanks for the warning, Gemma."

⌒

The noise from the inn downstairs rose up to the third floor and seemed to fill the room. There were shouts, curses, laughter, and music of a sort. Leonie could even hear the words of some of the coarse songs. She had bathed as well as she could and gotten into bed, but not before she had knelt beside her bed and asked God to protect her.

As she lay there, suddenly the bed bounced as Louis leaped upon it in the light way that cats had. She nuzzled up against his purring, and soon she could feel the heat from his body. It was nice to have a warm cat on cold winter nights, but the little room was stifling in the summer heat with only the window for fresh air. Nevertheless, Leonie was glad to have Louis close at hand. She reached over and stroked his silky fur, and he purred loudly and kneaded the blanket with his claws, occasionally touching her skin.

"That hurts, Louis. Be easy," she whispered. She closed her eyes and tried not to listen to the noise from downstairs. Finally when Louis dropped off to sleep with a steady purr, she found herself exhausted. She dreaded to waking the next day, for she knew that this life was not going to be pleasant. When she drifted off, she prayed a final prayer to God that He would watch over her and keep her safe from all harm.

Chapter four

A sense of despair gripped Leonie as she straightened up with a grimace, putting her hands on the small of her back. She arched her body backwards and felt her stiff muscles protest. She was exhausted, as she was every day, for the work at the inn had been far worse than anything she could have imagined. She worked from dawn to dark cleaning, washing soiled bedding, emptying the chamber pots, scrubbing the greasy dishes, and helping Gemma, the cook, prepare the meals.

As she walked downstairs, the morning light barely penetrated the grimy windows, and Leonie stared at them doggedly. She had been commanded to wash them all, every window in the inn, that day. First she had to scrub the floor in one of the guests' rooms.

Slowly she got her bucket, wash water, soap, and a rag and began to scrub the floor, which was filthy as usual. She sometimes wondered if human beings or pigs kept the rooms there; no one ever made the slightest attempt to keep his or her room clean. Evidently the man who lived in this room was worse than usual. The floor was littered with cigar butts, beer that had soaked into the ragged carpet, and every sort of smelly garbage imaginable.

With a sigh Leonie remembered the convent and how clean and

neat everything had been. It was the only life she had known, and the relentless grime of the inn was a continual drag upon her spirit.

Wearily she scrubbed the floor and for that one moment wished desperately that she was back in the convent. Involuntarily a prayer rose deep in her breast, and although she did not speak it, it was an effectual cry: "Oh, God, help me to survive this nasty, dirty place!"

"Stop your lagging there, girl!"

Madam Millard had suddenly appeared in the doorway, her eyes angry and her lips drawn tight. "You're going to have to work harder. Do you hear me?"

"Yes, Madam, I hear you."

"Mind what I say then. Hurry up with that room. I want you to go down and help muck out the stable."

Before she could think, Leonie responded, "Why, that's not a maid's job!"

Madam Millard seemed to explode with fury. Her eyes seemed to be flickering points of fire. "What did you say?" she screamed. "Don't you talk back to me! You'll do anything I tell you to!" She advanced quickly and stood over Leonie, who had not risen from her knees. Profanity and anger mingled in her screams, and she drew her hand back suddenly and struck Leonie. The blow caught her on the cheek, and Leonie nearly fell prostrate from the force of it. "You'll get some more of that if you don't do what I tell you. Now hurry up!"

Leonie was a meek young woman, milder by far than most, but the blow did something to her. An overwhelming desire to get away from the place seemed to mushroom inside her breast. She got to her feet slowly and stared at the doorway from which Madam Millard had disappeared. Anger was such a rare thing with her, but the place had become intolerable. It was not only Madam's cruelty—Gaspar Millard's constant pursuit was even worse. He was always finding some way to put his hands on her, and Gemma's warning had proved true. Once he had trapped her in her room when Madam was gone to market, and Leonie had barely managed to squeeze by and flee downstairs to the kitchen.

Now tears formed in Leonie's eyes, and she returned to scrubbing the floor. She had nowhere to go except the convent, and she knew that there was really no place for her there.

She had almost finished the room when suddenly a shadow fell across her, and she turned to see a tall, bulky man standing there framed in the doorway. Startled, she said, "I'm through with the room, sir."

"Why, don't be in a hurry." The speaker was a blunt-faced individual with twisted lower lips as if he had tasted something sour. There was an unhealthy look about him, and he advanced toward Leonie, saying, "You don't have to worry about the room, a pretty little thing like you."

Instantly Leonie was on her guard. The male guests at the White Horse Inn took it for granted that a young female servant was there for their convenience. She dropped the rag and attempted to move around him, but he grabbed her arm with his hand and put his other around her shoulder.

"Please, sir, let me go."

"Not a chance."

Leonie wrenched her arm away, and the unexpected suddenness of it caught him off guard. The man moved quickly enough, however, and put himself in the doorway. "You can't run anywhere," he said, smiling dreadfully. "Come on now. Be nice to a chap, can't you?"

Leonie wished desperately that she had kept the knife that Gemma tried to get her to carry, but she hadn't. There was no weapon available, though her eyes searched frantically around the room. The big man stepped forward, and as he did, Leonie took the only thing close at hand: the full chamber. With one swift move she bent over, picked up the chamber pot, and without even thinking, dashed the contents of it into the face of the big man.

He let out a wild scream, clawing at his face, and as he did, Leonie ran out of the room. She ran lightly, hearing his cursing and knowing that it meant trouble for her.

The trouble came in the form of Madam Millard's visiting her in the attic and screaming as usual. "What do you mean, soiling a guest like that?"

"He was trying to put his hands on me. I was afraid of him."

"Well, you've done it now. He left, and I can't say as I blame him. But you're not as good as you make out to be!" Madam Millard screamed and cried and shouted, and all Leonie could do was stand and listen.

"Let me tell you this. He's left his room, a good lodger. Paid every week. And the cost of his room comes out of your wages until we get another lodger."

Suddenly Leonie knew she could not stand the place any longer. "I won't stay if you do that."

Madam Millard stared at the girl in disbelief. She was accustomed to being obeyed—she ruled by fear. "You'll do whatever I say!"

"No, I won't! It wasn't my fault."

"What's going on here?"

Gaspar Millard had come up the stairs and was staring at the two women. "What are you shouting about, my dear?" He listened while she told him the story, and he said, "Well, after all, it wasn't so bad."

"Not for you. You'd do anything to get a young girl to stay here, but she's not staying," Madam hissed in a sudden reversal. "I've had enough of your ways!" she shouted at Leonie. "Get your things and get out of this place now!"

"Now, my dear, don't be hasty."

But Madam Millard was out of control. She fumbled in the pocket of her apron, pulled out some bills and peeled off a few and threw them on the floor. "There's your pay! Be out of this place in ten minutes!"

Gaspar Millard gave his wife a desperate glance. "But my dear, who will do the work?"

"You'll do it until you find somebody else!" Turning back to Leonie she shouted, "Now you leave!"

The two left, and Leonie, who was trembling so badly she could barely stand, knew that there was no choice. Quickly she dragged her chest out and began throwing her belongings in it. It did not take long, and she closed it and then pulled the basket out and went at once to Louis, who was lying on her bed, alarm showing in his round, golden eyes. "Come on, Louis, we've got to go."

Louis was agreeable enough. He was almost limp as she put him in the basket, and she was glad he didn't protest. Putting on her cloak and bonnet, Leonie went down the stairs. From the back of the inn she could hear Madam Millard screaming and her husband trying to talk and failing.

Stepping outside, she looked desperately down the street. A cab pulled by a large, gray horse was coming down the street, and she shouted, "Please, can you help me?"

The driver, a small man in his late sixties with bright blue eyes, pulled the horse up at once. Snatching his hat off, he said, "Why, of course I can, miss." He was bald as an egg, but he had almost as much facial growth as he would have had on his head. His mustache was fierce, and he tugged at it proudly, saying, "Where can I take you?"

"Please, could you get my chest? It's upstairs in the inn there."

"You just show me, Miss."

Five minutes later, after the cab driver had gone upstairs and brought the case down and placed it in the back of his vehicle, he turned and looked at her. He was birdlike in his motions, and his eyes were avian, too, sharp and moving quickly. "Where can I take you?"

At that moment Leonie realized she had absolutely no idea where she might go. "I don't know," she said.

"You don't know? That's strange. I've got to take you someplace."

"I've got to find a place to stay, and I've got to find a job."

"Well, that's two pretty tall orders. Which shall we do first?"

Leonie was weak. The scene had unnerved her, and the cab driver saw her distress. "Look, you get in," he said, "and we'll just get away from here. Then we'll talk about it, all right?"

"Yes. Let's do that."

The cab driver helped her in and asked, "What's in the basket?"

"My cat."

"Oh, I like cats myself. By the way, my name's Jean Larue."

"I'm glad to know you, Mr. Larue. My name is Leonie."

Larue jumped into the seat with a sprightly motion and said, "Get up, Caesar," and the horse began ambling down the street. He drove for a block before he said, "What kind of job would you be lookin' for now?"

"I was a serving woman at the inn."

Larue turned back to stare at her. "A serving woman, is it? Well, that was pretty rough. The White Horse Inn ain't no place for young ladies, I'd say."

"It was terrible."

"What about your family?"

"I—I don't have any family, Mr. Larue."

"Oh, I'm old enough to be your grandfather. You can call me Jean. Everybody does. No family at all?"

"No. None at all."

"What about friends then?"

Suddenly the words came pouring out of Leonie. She found herself telling Jean all about her life, how she had never done anything but live at the convent and how cruel her life had been at the White Horse Inn. "I just couldn't stand it anymore, Jean."

"I should think not. Well," he said, "the good Lord has a place for you. He feeds the sparrows, don't He? And we're worth more than sparrows. That's what the Good Book said."

"The Good Book? Which Book is that?"

"Why, the Bible, Miss!"

"Oh yes, it does say that!"

"Well, you believe the Bible, don't you?"

"Yes, indeed!"

"I'd think so." Jean Larue nodded vigorously. "Now, why don't we just ask the Lord to open up a door for you?"

Leonie stared at the small man, not understanding his meaning. "You mean—pray right now?"

"You got a need right now, don't you?"

"Well, yes, but . . ." All of Leonie's praying had been one of two kinds: either a formal prayer she memorized and spoke by rote in public or the prayers in which she bared her heart to the Lord, which she always said in the privacy of her room. The idea of praying for a specific thing in the presence of another person was uncomfortable to her. "I don't know how to pray like that."

"Don't know how? Let me teach you." Larue looked up into heaven as if he expected to see the Lord leaning over one of the black iron balconies that lined the houses. "Lord," he said, "this young woman has a need. She needs a job and a place to stay. Now, Lord, You know that I don't know anything about either one of those, but You know all about both of them. So I'm asking You right now to do what You promise. Give this young woman a place to work and a place to stay, and I'm asking it in the name of Jesus because, Lord, I know You can't refuse a prayer in that name. Amen."

Jean turned to her and broke into a smile. "There. That's done now."

Leonie was a bit dazed. It was so foreign to her experience that she could not speak for a moment. Finally she said, "Thank you, Jean."

"Now I know what you're thinkin'."

"How could you know that?"

Larue tapped his head and grinned at her broadly. "I'm not a mind reader, but it's what we all think when we've asked God for something. As soon as we ask it, the devil comes and says, 'Well, you don't think you'll get it, do you?'"

Leonie had to smile, for that had been her exact thought. "I believe you are a mind reader," she said.

"No, not a bit of it, but you just begin to tell me now a little bit more about yourself."

Leonie was at a loss but feeling desperate. She spoke briefly about the kind of work she had done, then said, "Really, aside from that the only thing I can do well is sew."

"Ah, you're a seamstress, are you?"

"Yes, I'm a very good seamstress."

"Well then. We'll go knocking on the door of every seamstress in New Orleans until we find the one God wants you to work for. There's one right down the street here. I know nothing about it, but God knows all about her and all about you. We'll try there first."

Leonie had absolutely no confidence in asking for a job as a seamstress. It was true she was very skillful, but her experience at the inn had left her fearful and shaken. She thought about the tapestry that was packed in her chest and thought it might be good to take it inside any place she asked for work. Hope began to grow in her. Jean pulled up in front of a small building with the sign "Madam Belleau, Seamstress."

Leonie said, "I've never done this before."

"Well, you're about to go your first time, then. Shall I go with you now?"

"No. I'll go alone." She got out of the carriage, and with Jean's help, she opened the chest and pulled out the tapestry. It was not finished, but at least it showed the kind of work she could do. She walked inside the shop and was met by a short, fat woman who smiled at her, asking, "Can I help you?"

"Please, I need work. I'm a good seamstress."

"Well, I'm sorry, Miss. I just don't need anybody. This shop just about produces enough work for me."

"I'm sorry to bother you."

Leonie turned to go, but before she got to the door, the woman said, "Wait a minute! Not so fast." When Leonie turned, she saw the woman was thinking.

"I know of another seamstress. She might need help."

"Oh, please, could you give me her address?"

"It's three blocks down the street to your right. It's on the second floor. You'll see the sign."

"Three blocks to the right. Thank you so much."

Leonie ran outside with a light in her eyes. "She didn't need anybody, but she said there's another seamstress that may need help."

"Did she now? Well, let's be going to it."

"It's three blocks down the street and to the right."

Leonie climbed up into the seat, holding the tapestry to her breast. Excitement flickered faintly in her, and she said nothing as they made their way along.

"Now then. Maybe this is just the place the good Lord wants you to stay, and He used that other woman. Ain't it marvelous the way the good Lord arranges circumstances?"

"I suppose it is."

"There's no supposin' to it," Jean said, nodding vigorously. He drew the horse around the corner and at once pointed with his whip, which he never bothered to use. "There it is right there: 'Madam Honore, Seamstress.' You hop right in there, and I'll stay out here and pray that you'll get just what you ask for—the desires of your heart—a place to work and a place to stay. This could be the place to work anyway."

"Thank you, Jean. I'll be right back." Jumping to the ground lightly, Leonie stepped quickly up the stairs. When she left the landing on the second floor, she saw that the entire floor, apparently, was made up into a dress shop. Models hung on frameworks, and the smell of cloth was strong in the air. She saw no one, so she called out, "Madam Honore?"

A door opened to her right at the back, and a woman emerged. "Yes, I am Madam Honore. Can I help you?"

"Madam Honore, I stopped down the street and was told that you might be able to use help."

Madam Honore stepped forward. She was a small woman, almost petite, with silver hair and lines in her face. There were traces of earlier beauty there, however, and her eyes were kind. "It is true I do need some help, but I was hoping for an older, more experienced person."

"Please, would you give me a chance? I'll work very cheaply. Look. Here is a sample of what I can do."

Madam Honore took the tapestry. She moved over to the light that came flooding through the window and ran her fingers over the material. "Why, this is fine work, child! But you understand we do dresses, not tapestries."

"I have been at the Ursuline Convent all my life, Madam. I have made dresses for myself and for my fellow students for many years now. I had a very fine teacher. Sister Abigail was a seamstress herself in Paris before she came to this country as a nun."

"Well, this is a beautiful piece of work. It's not finished, I see."

"No, ma'am, not yet."

Desperately Leonie held her breath as the older woman fingered the seams. "These are very fine stitches indeed. Do you have any of your other work?"

"Just this dress, which I made myself."

"Let me see." Madam Honore studied the dress and even took a seam between her fingers and felt it. "Very nice. You must understand, I cannot pay much."

"Oh, that doesn't matter. I do need work badly."

"I have a room you could have. It's small, but it would be handy to the work here. If you can cook, perhaps you can even help me with the cooking and the housecleaning." She held up her hands and said, "My hands are very stiff, you see. It's difficult. You would be doing most of the fine work under my direction."

"Oh, that would be wonderful!"

"When could you begin?"

"Today—right now, Madam."

Madam Honore smiled. "Well, you are eager enough. Let us see if you can keep up."

"I must go down and get my chest. Where is the room?"

"Come. I will show you."

Madam Honore led Leonie through the shop. At the rear was a door, and when she opened it and stepped back, Leonie went inside. She took one look around and sighed with delight. "Why, it's a beautiful room!"

"It was my daughter's room before she left New Orleans. She took great pride in fixing it up."

It was indeed a beautiful room. The room was very large, almost twelve-by-twelve-feet square. The walls were painted a light pink with a white ceiling and two floor-length windows covered in sheer white curtains. The furniture was large and well built, with a lustrous dark shine showing the pure beauty of the mahogany. The bed had a pink, blue, and green coverlet on it with overstuffed pillows, and on the floor was an enormous gray and blue area rug.

"Well, if the room is satisfactory, we will work out something with the wages. Go get your things. Oh, what is your name?"

"Leonie Dousett."

"Well, Leonie, go get your things."

Leonie practically flew downstairs, and her face was alight. Before she could say a word, Jean Larue laughed and said, "You don't have to tell me. God's dropped a gift in your lap, ain't He?"

"Oh, it's so wonderful, Jean! A very fine lady, so kind, and I'm to live in a beautiful room, and she needs me almost as much as I need her. Her hands are stiff with rheumatism."

"Well, ain't that a wonder now! God had His eye on an older lady who needed a young woman and on a young woman who needed work and a place to stay. Praise God. He puts it all together as He always does! Shall I carry your chest up?"

"If you will, please."

Jean shouldered the chest, and Leonie picked up Louis's basket and led the way. Jean carried the chest into her room, put it down, and smiled. "Now, it's a lovely place."

"Oh, I forgot to ask Madam if I could have a cat. I've got to keep Louis."

"Well, if she won't, I'll take him myself."

"No. He's my best friend. I have to have him." Worry furrows spread across Leonie's smooth brow. She went at once outside the room and found Madam Honore waiting. "I forgot to tell you I have a cat. I hope you don't mind. He's really very quiet and no trouble at all."

"Well, let me see the fellow."

She led the older woman back to the bedroom and undid the top of the basket. Louis hopped out in all his glory, his golden eyes gleaming. Madam Honore went closer, put her hand out, and he butted against it with his head in the manner he had with those he liked. "What a handsome chap you are! You and I will get along fine."

"This is Jean Larue. He's been a great help to me, Madam."

"I'm very happy to meet you, Jean."

"You take good care of this young woman now. I've taught her how to pray, so she ought to be all right."

"How to pray?" Madam Honore raised her eyebrows. "Are you a preacher then?"

"No. Nothing like that. Just a child of the King."

"Here. Let me pay you, Jean," Leonie said, opening her purse.

"I wouldn't take a penny, Miss. It was all the Lord's doing and glorious in our sight. Just a little service for the Lord Jesus. I pass here pretty often. You give me a wave from the window once in a while and shout 'Hallelujah!'"

"I may do that, Jean. Thank you so much. I wish you'd let me pay you."

"No." Larue shook his head. "A pleasure to be of service to a lovely lady and to the lovely God of heaven and earth."

⌒

Leonie had worked all day on a dress that had to be ready for a wealthy customer. She finished it by five o'clock, and when the lady came by, she was pleased. "This is good, fine work, Madam Honore."

"My new assistant finished it up. She does very skillful work, don't you think?"

"Why, yes." The woman smiled. "I'm glad you found someone. Here, I'll put a little bonus in here for such a fine job."

"Thank you, Madam."

After the customer left, Madam Honore said, "Come. While you were working I fixed us a good dinner. I hope you like Creole food."

"Oh yes, I like it very much. We had a cook at the convent who was a Creole lady. Her meals were always the favorite."

"Well, come along. It's hot, and I'm hungry." Madam Honore led Leonie back to her apartment, which was as neat as the woman herself.

"Your apartment is beautiful."

"Thank you. Here, you sit down, and I'll do the serving this time."

The meal was delicious. It included lamb-okra gumbo and a delicious asparagus salad, and the main dish was beef bordelaise. There were delicious, tiny rolls that melted in Leonie's mouth, and for dessert, fresh apple trifle. After the two women had eaten, Leonie could only say, "You're a wonderful cook!"

"If you'd like to learn how to cook Creole, it would be my pleasure to teach you."

Leonie accepted the offer with pleasure. Then she began to speak of the cab driver who had brought her there. "Just think: if any other man had come along, he wouldn't have been as willing to help me. You know," she said, her eyes wide, "I think Jean Larue may be an angel."

"That's possible."

"Do you believe in angels, Madam?"

"Oh, I think angels are all about us. We need to keep our eyes open for them."

"Well, he doesn't look much like an angel, but I think God sent him. I wouldn't have found you, Madam Honore, if it hadn't been for him."

"Then we'll fix him a very special treat. Something good to eat. The next time we see him going down the street, we'll call him in."

Madam Honore noticed that exhaustion was filling Leonie's face. "You go to bed, my dear. I'll clean up."

"Oh, let me help."

"Not tonight. Tomorrow you can do it all. Cook the supper and wash the dishes and wait on me. We two are going to suit each other very well."

"I—I thank the Lord for you, Madam. I'm going to work very hard to please you."

"I'm sure you will."

Leonie barely managed to wash her face and hands, get into her nightgown, and climb into bed before drowsiness stole over her. Louis crawled up on her chest and sat down. When she closed her eyes, he reached out and touched her eyelid gently with a soft pad. It was something he usually did in the morning as if saying, "Open your eyes. Let's see if you're in there."

"You can't sleep there, Louis. You're too heavy." She rolled over, and Louis snuggled in beside her. She wanted to say a prayer but had said only a few words when suddenly sleep seized her, and she knew no more.

Chapter five

September had come, and as Leonie sat sewing the collar on a dress, she thought of the two months she had spent with Madam Honore. It gave her intense satisfaction to think how well the two had suited each other. The older woman had been kinder than any employer she might have dreamed of, and Leonie had thrown herself into the work with all of her strength.

She listened as the traffic passed on the street below and once went over to the window, hoping to see Jean Larue. They had become good friends. Madam had insisted that they have him for supper and fixed baked Creole red snapper fresh off the dock. The old man apparently had no family in New Orleans, and now a week scarcely went by but that he came to bring them some food he had picked up from the market, and they always had a special treat for him.

She had seen the Millards in the marketplace twice, and both times Madam had glared at her as if she were a criminal, and her husband had acted as if he was afraid to see her.

She had been back to the convent twice, carrying glowing reports of her new place, and the mother superior had been very happy for her. The convent had given her a strange feeling. Although she had been there all of her life, already her life among the sisters seemed to be something that had taken place many years ago instead of only a couple of months.

Leonie went to Mass every Sunday. She got up early every weekday and more often than not made breakfast for herself and Madam. She had worked steadily, her skills improving under Madam Honore's teaching. The customers had been more than satisfied with her work. Madam said once with a smile, "They like your work better than mine. They will begin to ask for you instead of me!"

Leonie had gotten to know the shop owners on the street. She did most of the shopping for Madam, and it had given her great pride to think she had learned how to buy wisely. She mused over all the changes in her life in such a short period of time.

Madam Honore interrupted her thoughts. "Mrs. Wilson will be in for her dress tomorrow. How's it coming, Leonie?"

"Oh, it will be finished in plenty of time. This is such beautiful material. I've been afraid I'd spoil it."

"You wouldn't do that." Madam Honore smiled. She sat down across from Leonie and humor sparkled in her eyes. "You've made a conquest."

"A conquest? What do you mean?"

"Monsieur Guignard has asked permission to call on you."

Leonie stared at her employer. "You mean the butcher?"

"Yes indeed."

"But—he's an old man."

"Why no. He's only forty. That may seem old to you, but it seems young to me." Madam Honore studied the young woman carefully. She had become quite fond of her in the weeks that she had been there, and she asked, "What shall I tell him?"

"Why, tell him no. I don't want him calling on me."

Madam Honore smiled. "You better think it over. He's quite prosperous. His butcher shop is a moneymaking business, I understand. And he likes you."

"I'd rather not."

"I think you should at least allow him to call."

"Is that what young women do? I have no experience."

"It can do no harm. He's actually a very respectable gentleman. He holds to the old ways, and of course, I do too."

"Well, if you think it's best, I suppose it'll be all right."

Aubrey Guignard was a very respectable man indeed. His suit was respectable; his words were respectable. Even his shoes were respectable. Everything about him was respectable, including the attention he paid to the two women.

"The supper was very fine," he said. "I recognize the meat."

"Yes, you should," Leonie said. "We bought it from you just this morning."

Aubrey Guignard was enthusiastic about one subject, and that was meat. He launched into a long discussion of meat that lasted almost until time for him to leave. Finally, when he did rise to leave, the two women rose with him. "It was so nice of you to have me in your home, Madam Honore, and you, Mademoiselle."

"It was a pleasure, Monsieur. We must do it again some time," Madam answered.

"Yes. We certainly shall." Monsieur Guignard put his respectable hat on, turned, and left.

As soon as the door closed, Madam began to laugh. "Well, did you fall madly in love with him?"

"No! I certainly did not!"

"I am not surprised. He's the most boring human being I ever heard. All he knows about is meat. I will admit he is a fine butcher."

"I wish him well, but I hope that we don't have to have him in again."

"Well, we need to be careful."

"Careful about what?"

"About how we treat him."

"I don't understand you."

Humor danced in Madam Honore's eyes. "As long as he thinks you consider him a possible husband, he'll give us good buys on meat."

"Madam, you don't mean that!"

"No, I don't. That wouldn't be fair."

"You must tell him I'm not the woman he needs."

"You don't have to worry about the butcher anymore."

As the two women were cleaning up, Madam said, "Leonie, you've done so well. We're almost out of work."

Leonie agreed, "We are, aren't we? But I think I may help with that."

"What do you mean, Leonie?"

"I have three very good friends. They come from wealthy families. Why don't I take a day off and go visit them? They are always buying fine, expensive clothing."

"I think that would be excellent. What are friends for, if not to make us prosperous?"

Leonie laughed. "You don't believe that."

"No, I don't, but if you could get some business, it would be good."

"I'll go tomorrow," she said.

⌒

Damita stepped into the parlor, her eyes alight. "Why, Leonie, how wonderful to see you!"

"It's good to see you, too, Damita."

"I've just gotten back from a long trip."

Leonie listened as Damita spoke of her travels, and finally Damita asked, "Well, what have you been doing, Leonie? You left the convent, I suppose?"

"Yes. I'm working as a dressmaker now."

"A dressmaker. Well, you always made beautiful things for all of us. Do you like it?"

"Very much, but I'm afraid I've become a beggar."

"A beggar? What do you mean?"

"I've come to ask you if you would consider letting me do some work for you."

Damita's eyes flew open. "Certainly! Why not? And we must go to Simone and Chantel."

"Oh, I've already been to see them. They're both coming for fittings."

Damita smiled. "What time shall I come?"

"You set the time, Damita. You're the customer." The two chatted for a moment about meeting times. Leonie then left the house and returned to Madam Honore's shop. When she entered, she was bubbling over. "We have three new customers, all rich!"

"Wonderful! I love rich customers. Now, sit down and tell me about them."

Leonie was excited, and Madam Honore listened. Finally she said, "Are you ever jealous of these young women?"

"Why would I be?"

"Why, because they're rich. They don't have to work. They can buy whatever they want, and you have to work for a living."

Leonie stared at the older woman. "No. I never thought of such a thing."

Madam Honore's eyes grew soft. "You're a wonder, Leonie Dousett. Most girls would be eaten up with envy."

"God has been good to me, Madam. I am content."

"That is good. I hope you always will be."

Chapter six

"Reverend Mother, there's a gentleman to see you."

The mother superior looked up from her desk, which was covered with documents. A frown crossed her forehead. "I'm not expecting anyone."

Sister Agnes shook her head. "I didn't think you were, and I don't believe you want to see him."

"Why not, Sister?"

"He's not respectable."

Humor glinted in the mother superior's eyes. "Jesus wasn't considered respectable in His day." She loved to tease Sister Agnes, but she saw that she had gone too far. "I'm sorry," she said. "I didn't mean to put it like that. What is he, a tradesman?"

Sister Agnes's mouth tightened. "I don't know what he is. He's almost like a beggar, his dress, anyway, and he has a—well, a rather rough look about him. He looks like a criminal."

"Well, criminals come under the gospel decree, I suppose. Did he say what he wanted?"

"Only that he had to talk to you, and it was private." Sister Agnes sniffed with disdain. "Be best to send him on his way."

For a moment the mother superior drummed her fingers on the desktop, then shook her head. "I'm afraid to do that."

"Why?"

"A few times in my life I missed opportunities to serve our Lord with people. I wouldn't want to miss another one. Just think, Sister, what if Jesus didn't stop at the well to talk to the Samaritan woman? Her life wouldn't have been changed, and you remember the story in the Bible. It says that the whole village pretty well came to know Jesus because of her testimony. No, I don't think I'll take the chance. Send him in. I'll get rid of him if necessary."

"As you say then." Sister Agnes was miffed as she turned and walked outside the door.

When the man entered, without meaning to, Reverend Mother thought, *Sister Agnes was right. He does look like a criminal.*

"My name is Blaise Mignon."

"Won't you sit down, Monsieur Mignon?"

"Thank you." Mignon took his seat. He was a small man, his face was lined and burned with the sun, and his hands, Reverend Mother noted, were callused and twisted. He had dark eyes almost hidden by heavy lids, and there was a sinister air about the man.

"What can I do for you, Monsieur?"

"I want to inquire about a young woman who, I understand, was one of your pupils here."

"Which young woman would that be?"

"Her name is Leonie Dousett."

A slight alarm went off in the mother superior's head. She had spent a great deal of time years before trying to find something of Leonie's history, all to no avail. Though two years had passed since the young lady had left the convent, she still kept in close contact with her. The woman's protective instinct arose. "Why are you interested, may I ask?"

Mignon hesitated. "I understand you can't give information about your pupils to anyone who walks in here." He grinned. "Especially to a rough-looking fellow like me."

"It's our policy to be very cautious about giving out information."

"Very commendable, Reverend Mother, but you may rest assured I mean the girl no harm."

"I'm afraid I'll have to have a little more assurance than that, Monsieur."

"Of course. I understand completely." Mignon leaned forward. His eyes were almost hooded, yet there was a glitter in them of intelligence and even audacity. "I was not always as you see me now. Many years ago I was a man rising in my profession—the law, if you can believe it—but misfortune overtook me." He hesitated for a moment, then said, "I have been in prison. You probably guessed that."

"I'm sorry to hear it, sir."

"So am I," Mignon said almost solemnly. Then he managed a grin. "Like all the others, I was totally innocent."

The mother superior didn't respond.

Mignon said, "I cannot give you the name of the family I worked for, but I think you would know it if I did." He leaned forward and clasped his hands together. "I have reason to believe that the young woman that you know as Leonie Dousett is the daughter of a very wealthy, indeed, a noble family."

"You astonish me, sir!"

"I would give you more details, but let me ask you, Reverend Mother, were there any clues to the infant's identity when she came to this place?"

"Sir, there was very little. I found the child myself."

"You did? Where?"

The mother superior decided there could be no danger in revealing the details of Leonie's arrival. "It was very early in the morning, when I left to go to the village. A basket was on the doorstep and an infant was in it."

"And the basket, was there anything in it that would lead to the child's identity?"

"Only a locket and a book."

"No names? No letter explaining the infant's arrival?"

"Nothing like that."

"No doubt. Well, what about the locket?"

"It had a man's picture in it. It was an expensive locket."

"Could I see it?"

"I do not have it, sir. I gave it to Leonie on her twelfth birthday. It was all she had of her family."

"The picture inside—had you ever seen the individual?"

"It was perhaps the child's father—but who could say?"

"I must see this young woman, Reverend Mother. If I am right, and she is who I think she is, she will be very fortunate indeed. She would be an heiress to a very large fortune."

"Of which you would expect a liberal reward, Monsieur?"

Blaise Mignon laughed. "You are right indeed. But I will do all things aboveboard. The crime for which I was sent to Devil's Island was not theft but violence. I killed the wrong man in a duel. He was very prominent. But I will not rob the girl. You yourself will know all the details as soon as I discover them myself."

The mother superior said, "Let me see your face. Look me in the eye."

Mignon lifted his head, his eyes open wide. He did not speak, and for a long moment the two were totally silent. "There's no art to find the mind's construction in the face," Mignon said. "I believe that comes from *Macbeth*, and he was right. Some of the most angelic-looking men I've ever seen were villains at heart. You can tell nothing by my face."

"I do not agree, but I cannot ignore your request. Monsieur, return tomorrow at this same time."

"Ah," Mignon said with a smile. "That means she is in New Orleans or very close. You wish to contact her and tell her about her odd-looking benefactor."

Ignoring Mignon's words, the mother superior nodded a dismissal. "You may come back tomorrow at this same hour."

Mignon rose, bowed, and left without another word. As soon as he was gone, the mother superior got up and began to pace the floor.

She was excited but at the same time cautious. *What can the man want? It could not be money, at least not from Leonie, because she has none. If he's telling the truth, I have no right to withhold it from her.* She walked to the door, opened it, and called out, "Sister Agnes, have someone take word to Leonie that I wish to see her immediately."

⌒

As soon as Leonie entered the mother superior's office, she saw that the older woman was nervous. "Is something wrong?"

"I'm not sure. Sit down. I want to talk with you."

Leonie sat down at once and felt a tension growing. The mother superior was usually a calm woman who showed little strain.

"A man came to see me yesterday, Leonie. His name is Blaise Mignon. Have you ever heard the name?"

"Why, no. Never."

"I didn't think so—nor have I. He had a very strange claim." The mother superior fixed her eyes on the young girl. "He said that he knew something about your background."

"My background? Is he related to me?"

"Don't get excited. It may all come to nothing. No, he's not related to you."

"Well, who is he then? What does he want? How does he know about me?"

The mother superior slowly explained every detail of Mignon's visit. She saw that Leonie was pale and paused to warn her. "He spoke of your family as being wealthy and prominent, but why would a wealthy, prominent family abandon a baby?"

"Perhaps—perhaps I was stolen."

"That sounds like a fairy tale or a romance novel."

Leonie looked down at the floor for a moment, and her voice was almost inaudible. "I've always longed to know who my family was and why they gave me up. I assumed it was because they were poor and couldn't take care of me."

"Leonie, I must beg you not to build your hopes on this. The man may be a scoundrel. Indeed, he appears to be one, at least to the eye."

"That may be, Reverend Mother, but I must talk to him! I would do anything to find out who my parents were and if I had brothers and sisters."

"I thought you might say that, and in fact, I would say the same thing myself. Very well, Leonie. I will give the man your address, but I must caution you, child: be very careful. You are young and inno-cent, and this man has a terrible background. I ask you to come and see me as soon as you have talked with him. Perhaps I can give you some counsel."

"Oh, I will, Reverend Mother. Will you tell him to come as quickly as you can?"

"I assure you, child, he will be knocking on your door almost by the time you get home. He made no secret of the fact that he expects to be well paid if he's the agent of reuniting you with your family."

"That would be only fair."

"Come and see me immediately after you have met the man."

"I will. I promise."

As soon as Leonie walked out, the mother superior shook her head and murmured, "I hope I've done the right thing. But who is to know about things like this?"

Chapter seven

Leonie's heart beat more rapidly as the man who called himself Blaise Mignon stood before her. She had been waiting for him, and when he appeared at her door, she escorted him to the parlor that she shared with her employer.

"Madam Honore is working in the shop," she explained. "Will you have a seat, sir?"

"Thank you, Mademoiselle." Mignon took his seat and kept his eyes fixed on the young woman. "It was kind of you to agree to see me. I know Reverend Mother warned you that I was not particularly presentable."

Leonie smiled. "I am not particularly interested in fashionable clothes. What I am interested in is what you told Reverend Mother—that you may know something about my parents."

"Perhaps you need to know something about me first. I know my appearance is against me. I was at Devil's Island for many years. I was only relieved a year ago."

"I've heard about that place. It must be terrible."

"It is indeed, Mademoiselle, and as I told the mother superior, I was not sent there because I stole but because I killed a man. Oh, it was in a duel, in a fair fight, and he was a very wealthy, prominent man—a nobleman, as a matter of fact—and I was only a lawyer."

"What was the duel about?"

"Foolishness, as they always are. I wasted my life because of a moment's anger."

Mignon's face changed, and she saw a sadness there. He was shabby, and she could tell that he had been drinking, but there was a hope in her as she looked at the man. "Would you please tell me why you think I am related to a noble family?"

"I served a family called Augustine. Sir Ancel Augustine was my employer. He's dead now, I'm sorry to say."

The three canaries that Madam Honore kept were singing, and the sun was streaming in through the windows. The cheerfulness of the scene contrasted with the tension in Leonie. She waited patiently for Mignon to continue.

He began to speak again. "Sir Ancel and his wife, Maria, had a son named Ives. They were very proud of him. He was the male heir, and he was the only child, and they had great expectations, of course. But as such things sometimes happen, Ives Augustine fell in love with a woman who was unacceptable to the family." He paused to look at Leonie and said, "Her name was Lila Moran."

The sound of people passing on the street below came faintly into the drawing room, but Leonie shut them out. "I have never heard the name."

"Likely not. She was a beautiful woman. I met her only once. It was a rather painful scene. Sir Ancel met with his son, Ives, who had brought Miss Moran in to meet his parents. They wanted to be married, but Sir Ancel wouldn't hear of it. Sir Ancel was a hard man. He told his son that if he married the woman, he would be cut off forever and not even allowed to come back to the house."

"What did his wife say?"

"A good question. She tried to take the woman's part, but Sir Ancel was a headstrong man. He always was, so he had his way about it."

"Did they get married?"

"They did. I heard about it indirectly."

"How did you find me, Monsieur?

"A trick of fate, I think. I was walking down the street and saw a painting in the window of a run-down shop. I recognized it as the woman that Ives fell in love with. Naturally I went into the shop and inquired about the painting." He shook his head, adding, "The owner told me that his father had bought the painting years ago."

"Did he say who sold it to his father?"

"Better than that, Miss Dousett: he found the slip that gave the name and the date of the sale. The woman who sold the painting was named Zuri Vidette."

"What a strange name. I don't recognize the origin of it."

"She's a gypsy. She owned a boardinghouse years ago, but she's fallen on hard times. I found her in a workhouse. I think you should go with me and listen to her story."

"Yes, Monsieur, let us go at once!"

〜

As Mignon led Leonie up the steps, he warned her, "She's a gypsy, as I told you. Looks like one, too, and rather a foul old woman, so you'll have to be prepared."

The two entered the house and were greeted at once by a slatternly woman who appeared not to have bathed for years. "We'd like to see Zuri Vidette, Madam."

"What for?"

"I think I'll keep that to myself, if you don't mind. Where is she?"

"Out in the back."

"Thank you for your kindness."

Mignon led the way through the house, which had terrible odors and seemed to be held up mostly by dirt. "Do your best to bear it, my dear," he said. They went out onto a wide porch that circled the house, and Mignon murmured, "There she is over there." He led the way over to where a tiny figure was seated in a chair. She had snow-white hair, and when she turned to face them, her dark eyes were alive though the rest of her was shriveled up, and her voice was a shrill cackle. "Well, the lawyer man is back."

"Yes, Zuri, I am, and I brought a guest. This is Miss Dousett."

Zuri Vidette locked her dark eyes on Leonie but spoke to the lawyer. "What do you want now?"

"I want you to tell this young woman the story you told me."

"You'll have to pay again."

"I'll pay. Don't worry."

"The same amount?"

"Yes. The same amount. Now, you tell Miss Dousett your story."

The old woman turned to face Leonie. "Be careful of this one. He's got the devil in him."

"I'd like to hear the story, Miss Vidette."

"Ah, she's got manners, this one! Not like some I could mention." Zuri gave a malevolent glance at the lawyer. "Like I told the lawyer here, a young woman came to me for a room. She was expecting very soon, and she had almost no money. She had a little jewelry and a painting. She stayed with me until the child was born. She pawned everything, including the painting."

Leonie leaned forward. "Did she ever tell you anything about herself?"

"Not much, but I knew a lot. She talked about her husband. Not by name, of course, not to me. And I found out."

"What did you find out?" Leonie demanded.

"I found out his family didn't want him to marry her. She wrote letters to someone. I posted them."

"Letters to whom?"

"I don't know. I can't read."

"What was the woman like?"

"Well, she was a good one, I'll have to say. Of course it's been a long time. You could tell she had seen better days. She was sick when she came to me, and she didn't get no better."

Leonie took in every word as Zuri rambled. She got off the

subject often, but then Mignon drew her back to speak of the young woman.

"And finally the baby came. Born right in her room, it was. She had a hard time, and she was dying." The old woman's eyes glittered like a bird's. "She made me promise to take her baby to the holy sisters. I took her out to the convent early the next morning and left her there."

Mignon stood to one side listening as Leonie asked many questions about the young woman who had died and left her baby in Zuri's care. Finally the old woman grew sullen. "Give me my money. That's all I'm saying for now."

Mignon reached into his pocket, pulled out several coins, and handed them to her. "We'd best be going, Miss Dousett." After saying good-bye to the old woman, Mignon gently guided Leonie out of the house. "I have something to show you, but it's in my lodgings. I can bring it by tomorrow or later today even."

"Couldn't we go by now?"

"I don't live in the most respectable part of town, but we can go if you'd like. You'll be safe enough."

"Yes. I'd like to go now."

Leonie got into the carriage that had waited for them, and all the way to Mignon's quarters she was thinking about the old woman and the strange story that she had told.

"Are you convinced?" Mignon quickly asked, breaking into her thoughts.

"There's not enough evidence."

"Not yet."

They spoke no more until they got to his quarters. She got out of the carriage, and Mignon told the driver to wait. He led her inside and asked her to sit down in the drawing room that all of the boarders used. No one was there at that time, and he left her for a moment. When he came back, he was carrying what she had expected, a painting. Without comment he handed it to her.

Taking the picture, Leonie examined it. It was a portrait of a woman. Leonie stared at the features. "She's very beautiful. She couldn't be my mother." Leonie could not take her eyes off the picture. "She seems so—so gentle."

"She was. I liked her very much."

Leonie pulled out a locket out from where it hung next to her flesh. She removed it and unsnapped it and handed it to Mignon without comment. He looked at it and said, "This is Ives Augustine, your father. I see the resemblance."

"There was also this. I brought it to show you." She pulled out a small book and handed it to him. He looked at the title: *The Imitation of Christ.*

"It was in the basket with you when you were found?"

"Yes."

He opened up the book and stared at the writing that filled the white spaces around the print. He fluttered through the pages. "All we have to do is match this handwriting with a sample of your father's."

The words "your father" sent a sudden thrill through Leonie. "You really think it is my father's book?"

"I think there's no doubt of it, my dear." He gave her the book back and said, "I have learned that your father died at very nearly the same time as your mother did. They both were very ill. And now, your grandfather is dead, but your grandmother, Maria Augustine, is alive. She would have to receive you as part of the family. You would, in fact, be an heiress, for you are the only child of Ives Augustine."

"There were no other children?"

"No. There are two cousins, a man and a woman, children of Ancel's dead brother."

"What do we do now, sir?"

"I think it's time for us to present you to your family."

Suddenly Leonie looked at the man and asked, "Why are you doing this?"

"For two reasons," Mignon said. "When I was arrested, your father did his best to help me. He did everything in his power, but it was hopeless. But he tried, and I always admired and liked him."

"And the other reason?"

"We've already talked about that. If we come into a fortune, I would expect to be rewarded for my efforts."

"Are you a scoundrel, Blaise Mignon?"

"I am a half-scoundrel, but then all of us are."

"I think you're right."

"Good," Blaise said. "Now I will need to disguise myself as a respectable man. Your grandmother, of course, will remember me, but I need to be a bit more presentable. Do you have enough money for a new suit to clothe a respectable man?"

"I will make it myself."

Blaise Mignon laughed and reached out and put his hands on her shoulder. "The Augustines," he said, his eyes sparkling, "are in for a shock!"

PART TWO

· SEPTEMBER–OCTOBER 1833 ·

Blaise

Chapter eight

Leonie paused to look around her room briefly and for a moment was overwhelmed, an emotion that confused her. Ever since she had heard of the possibility of finding her family, she had been thrilled with excitement, but now, for some reason, fear brushed its fingers across her spirit, and she stood bolt upright and stared blankly at the wall.

What if it's not true? What if it's all part of a moneymaking scheme on the part of Monsieur Mignon?

The thought of losing the only hope she had ever had of touching her past loomed large in her mind. Especially now, since Madam Honore had mentioned possibly giving up the shop. Her arthritic hands continued to worsen, and the woman could sew less and less.

But that worry for was another day. Today Leonie must marshal her strength and go face the people who might be her blood relatives. Taking a deep breath, she picked up her purse, petted Louis, and left her room. *It will be well!* she told herself.

Taking one last look in the small mirror on her wall, she tucked her hair in under her bonnet and left her room. She found Blaise Mignon talking with Madam Honore, and both of them turned quickly to look at her. She saw that Madam Honore was anxious and said quickly, "I don't think we will be gone for long, Madam."

"Take all the time you need."

"I can't say when we will be back, Madam Honore," Mignon said, "but rest assured I will take good care of Mademoiselle."

Madam Honore turned and fixed her steady eyes on the lawyer. "I will expect you to do exactly that."

"You do not trust me, I see."

"Not one inch!"

Suddenly Blaise Mignon laughed. "I am accustomed to that. Prisoners in Devil's Island get little trust, and as I was a lawyer before that part of my life, I was already used to this response from people."

"Make sure that Mademoiselle Leonie returns safely and soon, or it will be the worse for you."

"You forget one thing, Madam. She is my meal ticket. If anything happens to her, why, I would make nothing out of this. And we all understand that I am a very mercenary creature."

Suddenly Madam Honore laughed. "You are a scoundrel, sir, but I think you have touched on it. You would do nothing to endanger your opportunity of making a profit."

Mignon smiled and bowed slightly. "Exactly right." Turning to Leonie, he said, "I think we are ready."

The two left the shop, and Mignon handed Leonie up into the carriage. Leonie was somewhat surprised at the gesture and gave him a small smile. "Thank you, sir."

"You're not accustomed to being treated like a fine lady," Mignon said with a grin, "but I expect you will have to get used to it." He walked around the carriage, got inside, nodded, and picked up the lines. "I rented this carriage for a day since I wasn't sure how much time we would need. Besides it's cheaper, and I'm short of funds."

Leonie turned as Mignon drove the carriage away from the curb, and she gave him a close look. He was wearing a new suit that she herself had made for him. *It was a good job I had done of it*, she thought with satisfaction. It was a rich brown color with a matching shirt, and somehow he had found himself a pair of shoes that glistened with polish. "You look almost respectable, Monsieur Mignon."

Mignon found this amusing. He spoke to the horses as they picked up their pace, and he said, "*Almost* respectable. That is quite a compliment, coming from you." He fingered the sleeve of his suit and said, "You are a fine seamstress. Madam Honore showed me the tapestry you have been working on. Do you enjoy such work?"

"Yes, I do."

"Most women consider sewing a chore."

"I do not find it so, Monsieur."

"Why do you not just call me Blaise? I would like it better. Why would you enjoy the work?"

"Making a tapestry is a little like making a life, I think."

Surprised, he turned to her and lifted one eyebrow quizzically. "And how is that?"

"When I make a tapestry, I put in the very best that I have. I make it a matter of pride to do the most elegant, the most perfect work that I can. Once you have put in a seam, it is there to stay, and I find life is a little like that. If I do the best I can, each deed is a seam that will stay there. If I do good things, then my life will be a good tapestry. If I do shoddy work, my life will be the same."

"I would hate to see the tapestry that you made of my life. It would be a very ugly thing, I fear."

"But it is possible to start again with a piece of tapestry. Throw the old one away and start again."

Blaise turned to stare at her. "I believe you are preaching at me. You got that from the sisters at the convent, I assume."

"They taught me many things. Most of all, they taught me how to trust in the Lord."

Blaise handled the lines well and did not speak until they were clear of the city. Finally he turned to her and picked up the conversation as if there had been no intermission. "You really believe that, that we can start over?"

"Why, of course."

"I do not."

"How can you say that?"

"Because once I committed murder and was sent to Devil's Island, I could never pick up my career again. No one would ever trust me. I would have been a rich, successful lawyer by now. Obviously, if there is a God, He does not favor me."

"It was not God who caused you to fight the duel. You made that decision yourself."

Blaise turned and stared at her, his eyes wide. She was a meek, mild young woman, gentle in spirit, but she had spoken straight-forwardly, and he found it difficult to meet her gaze. "My heaven!" he exclaimed. "That's speaking right out."

"Are you an atheist, Blaise?"

"I was at one time. When I was in prison, life was so terrible I could not believe in the goodness of God."

"Bad things happen to good people," Leonie said simply.

"Yes. The patriach Job in the Bible proves that."

"You have read that story?"

"Many times. Why, I felt like Job. He lost everything: his family, his money, his position, his health. I thought about him often when I was suffering on Devil's Island."

"You must not let your bad experiences poison your life. You are yet a young man. You can do many things."

"A young man? No one has called me that for a time." He laughed shortly and shook his head. "I find it hard to believe that God would be interested in a criminal like me."

"Jesus died to save criminals."

Once again Blaise was stopped short by the bluntness of her words. "I have thought of Jesus Christ so often. He's the only thing I could not answer."

"What do you mean?"

"I could not find a reason why an innocent man should die for sinners like me."

"That is the great mystery of Jesus, that He could do such a thing to prove He is God, for no man could do that."

The two rode along in silence, and strangely enough Leonie felt compassion for Blaise Mignon. He had endured much, and she knew that he was not a good man, yet somehow she had hope for him. She knew she would pray for him every day from that point onward.

Finally she asked, "If what we're trying to do works out, and we get some money, you'll be able to change your life. What would you do if we got a great deal of money?"

Blaise laughed and shook his head. "Something foolish, no doubt."

"What," she asked, "will you do if we don't get accepted?"

"I will live life one day at a time. That's how I made it at Devil's Island." He turned and said, "What about you, Leonie? Will you be crushed if Madam Augustine and the family reject you?"

"It will be painful." She looked out over the countryside. September brought the cool air, and the trees were beginning to lose their green. Already tints of golds and red in the hardwood leaves were beginning to show. "It will be very hard for me. All I've ever really wanted out of life was to have a family."

"Well, having a family isn't everything. Many people are disappointed in their relatives."

"Do you have a family, Blaise?"

"I had one once. I had a wife, at least, but when I was sent to Devil's Island, she divorced me."

"Do you ever think of going back to her?"

"She remarried and has three children. That door is closed to me."

"Well, another door will open," she said and smiled.

He studied her face. She had a fair, smooth complexion—rose-colored—and now a summer darkness lay over her skin. He was struck again by the beauty of her eyes. The color was a deep gray that he had never seen in any other human being. It seemed impossible that anyone would have such clear eyes. Her lips were fixed with determination, and he noted that she had a long, composed mouth. The sunlight touched her dark hair, which lay rolled and heavy on her head, and the dove-colored dress she wore seemed to deepen the shade of her hair. "You are an attractive young woman," he said.

Her face colored. "Why, no, I'm not particularly. I know that because I grew up in the convent with three very attractive women. I was like a sparrow among beautifully colored birds."

"Well, we shall see. We will be at Belle Fleur soon."

"Belle Fleur? What is that?"

"It's the name of the Augustine mansion. You will be impressed with it, I think." He said no more until finally he pulled off the main road and gestured with his buggy whip. "There is Belle Fleur."

The mansion was indeed impressive. It was a three-story white house with four columns in front, two on each side of the large front door. It had eight windows across the front on the top floor, six on the second, and six on the first, all flanked by green wooden shutters. The stairs to the first floor were shaped in a half circle and led up to a very impressive porch. The estate grounds had large, old trees everywhere, almost obscuring the view from the road, and the driveway made its way to the front of the house and back again through a circle with gardens of elegantly shaped shrubs and rose-bushes on each side and in the center, surrounding a massive water fountain.

"It is a beautiful place," Leonie said. She was overwhelmed by the magnificence of the house. There were other buildings, but the house seemed to fill her eye.

Blaise stared at the mansion as they approached. "Old memories," he murmured. "I used to come here often. Just a ways beyond the garden are the bayous. I'm told your father spent many hours there, walking, fishing, thinking. I wonder what would have happened if I had grown up in such a place? I was going to be a great lawyer and then go into politics. Why, I might have been governor. Who knows what I might have been? And I wind up at Devil's Island. Life takes odd turns, Leonie."

Blaise pulled the carriage up in front of the house, and a black man came and said, "Take your horses, sir?"

"Yes, if you please." Blaise stepped down out of the carriage, walked around, and handed Leonie out. He saw her eyes were wide and thought that she seemed intimidated. "Don't be afraid, Leonie," he said. "Never be afraid of anything."

The two went up the steps, and Blaise reached out and grasped the brass knocker. He struck it firmly, and when the door opened, Leonie saw a tall, stern-faced woman. Her eyes were fixed on Blaise Mignon, and Mignon said at once, "Well, do you remember me, Mrs. Danvers?"

"I remember you well enough, sir." The woman was in her sixties, and her eyes were cold. She had brown hair speckled with gray, and she stood staring at Blaise.

"We need to see Lady Augustine, Mrs. Danvers."

The woman at first shook her head slightly, but then she changed her mind. "I'll see if she will receive you. You may come inside, I suppose."

The two stepped inside, and Mrs. Danvers said, "Wait here." Her voice was icy, and when she disappeared down the wide hallway, Blaise said, "That's the housekeeper. She was married to the manager. Poor devil. She led him a horrible life."

"She obviously was not glad to see you."

"No. She never cared for me. I think she was suspicious of everyone whose name wasn't Augustine."

The two stood until the woman came back and said in a spare tone, "Madam will see you now."

Leonie's heart seemed to close for a moment, but then it began to beat faster. She felt a touch and saw that Blaise was offering his arm. She took it, and he smiled and whispered, "Courage. This is your home. These are your people. I know it!"

They followed Mrs. Danvers down the hallway. Without a word, she gestured at the door, then turned and walked away.

"And thank you, Mrs. Danvers," Blaise smiled. He led Leonie through a pair of tall French doors into a lavish parlor. As soon as they were inside, Leonie's eyes were drawn at once to the woman who stood at the far end of the parlor. She had risen from a couch and stood facing them.

"I did not expect to see you again, Monsieur."

"I'm sure you didn't, Madam, but I felt I had to come."

"What do you want?"

"May I introduce Mademoiselle Leonie Dousett? Mademoiselle, this is Lady Maria Augustine."

Leonie curtsied but could not say a word. She felt the woman's eyes on her, and the thought that she might be her own flesh and blood was overwhelming. Lady Maria Augustine was a tall woman with dark hair mixed with silver. She was in her sixties, Leonie guessed, and she had the most direct gaze that Leonie had ever seen. Her eyes were brown, a rich color, well shaped and widely spaced. Her complexion was pale, and her figure was straight and trim.

"How do you do, Mademoiselle?" she murmured. Then she turned and said, "State your business, Monsieur."

"I can understand your attitude, Lady Augustine," Blaise said quickly, "but I have something that you need to hear."

"State it briefly."

A silence fell across the room, and Leonie's eyes went to Blaise. She knew that he was weighing his chances, and she had no idea how he would bring up the subject that they had come to present to Madam Augustine. She saw him take a deep breath. Then he said abruptly, "Does this young lady look familiar?"

"Familiar?" repeated Lady Augustine, and her eyes went back to Leonie. "No, not particularly."

"She is your granddaughter, Madam."

Shock washed across Maria Augustine's face. Leonie could see it. The older woman turned and stared at her, and Leonie could tell that she was shaken and even distressed by the news. She shook her head firmly and said, "What game is this? Another of your lawyer tricks?"

"If you would give us ten minutes, Madam, that's all I ask."

For a moment Leonie thought Lady Augustine would order them out of the house. She felt the woman's gaze seemingly envelop her, and finally she was relieved to hear her say, "You may have your ten minutes but no more."

Blaise spoke quickly of his release and his finding the portrait that had led him to Leonie. He held out his hand and said, "The locket, please." When Leonie handed it to him, he in turn stepped forward and said, "You may recognize this."

Lady Augustine took the locket and stood holding it. She was silent. Then, without lifting her eyes to the two visitors, she opened it. She stared at the picture on the inside for a long time. "Anyone could have found this."

"You'll admit that it is your son, Ives."

"Of course it is. You knew that, Mignon. Well, is this all you have?"

"No. We have this." Mignon handed over the copy of the book, saying, "This book was found with this young woman when she was left as an infant. I think you will recognize the handwriting."

Lady Augustine took the book and opened it. She turned the pages over slowly, and Leonie noticed that her face was pale. She looked up and her voice was different. She was shaken by the experience. "Anyone could have found these items."

"That is true, but if you will examine this young woman, you will see the resemblance she has to Ives. I knew him well. Not as well as you, naturally. He was your son, and you will notice that this young woman has the same dimple in her cheek. She has the same· widow's peak. Her eyes are the same shape. She resembles him greatly."

"That means nothing."

"Lady Augustine, I know you think I'm a cad," Mignon said. "You have had reason to think such, but I have two reasons for being here. One is that when I was arrested and put on trial, your son, Ives, did all he could to help me. I have never forgotten that."

"He did so against my judgment and against my husband's."

"His heart was gentler than yours, Madam."

Color rushed into Maria's face. "Yes. You are right about that. He was always a tenderhearted boy and a gentle man." Suddenly she turned and said, "Tell me about yourself, Miss Dousett."

Neither of them had been asked to sit, so Leonie began speaking, standing firmly in front of the woman who so filled her eyes. "I know very little to tell you. I was at the Ursuline Convent from the time of my earliest memories. The mother superior herself found me there in a basket with this locket and with this book."

"The kind reverend mother will bear witness to that, Madam Augustine," Blaise put in.

"They were very kind to me at the convent, Lady Augustine," Leonie said quietly. "They gave me an education, and I had many friends there. Naturally I often wondered about my parents, but I had no idea who they might be until Monsieur Mignon appeared and showed me the painting and told me the story. That is all I can tell you."

"You have no more to say?"

Leonie hesitated. "I know that Monsieur Mignon would like to make money out of this situation, but I hope you will believe me when I say that the only thing I want is to find my people."

Lady Maria Augustine stared at the young woman for a long time. The only sound in the room was the ticking of the large ormolu clock on the mantel over the fireplace. Finally she said to Mignon, "You said you had two motives for bringing this young woman, the first to pay a debt to my son. What is the other?"

"Why, to be rewarded, of course."

"At least you are an honest cad. I believe you always were."

Leonie stood stock-still; she saw that Lady Maria was weighing this situation that had walked in her front door.

Finally the woman said, "You may leave these things with me. I will send for you when I have had time to consider. Where are you staying?"

"At the Black Hawk Inn."

"You should hear from me in a few days. Now good day, sir."

"Good day, Lady Augustine. Thank you for your time."

Leonie curtsied and saw that the woman she hoped was her grandmother staring at her in a fixed fashion. She did not speak, so finally Leonie turned and followed Blaise out of the house. Mrs. Danvers opened the door for them and did not speak a word.

Blaise handed Leonie up into the carriage, gave the black man a coin, got in, and drove off. As they were leaving Belle Fleur, Leonie turned and took one last look at the mansion. Blaise said abruptly, "Well, that was successful. She could have thrown us out at once. Her husband would have."

"She certainly didn't like us."

"She doesn't like me, but didn't you see how she devoured you with her eyes?"

"No, I didn't."

"She loved her son, Ives, better than she loved anything else. I think she saw some of him in you. I wasn't lying when I said you resemble him greatly. You do."

"What do you think will happen?"

Blaise suddenly chuckled deep in his chest. "I think she'll tell the family, and all perdition will break loose."

"They wouldn't want me?"

"If you are who I claim you are, you would be the heiress of Belle Fleur. The rest of the family would be left out in the cold. Now, you know little of human nature, growing up around nuns, but I can tell you, my dear, in this world no one appreciates having a fortune snatched from their fingers. They will not receive you with open arms."

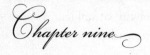

Chapter nine

Dinner at Belle Fleur was always an ornate affair. On this particular Thursday evening, Maria had insisted on everything being in order. As she entered the dining room, she looked around, remembering the times that she and her husband, Ancel, had chosen the decor for it. She had always liked the dining room and even now felt a sense of pride in the beauty of it.

The large room had a bright white ceiling and dark green wallpaper with golden flocked fleur-de-lis on the upper half of the wall. The lower half was painted a dark red. The large Persian carpet was green with hints of red and gold, and the highly polished wooden floor gleamed out along the outer edges. Two floor-length windows were covered with light, airy curtains that fluttered with the breeze, and the sun's evening glimmer of red, orange, and yellow found its way into the room, giving it an iridescent look. The table was long and wide and covered with a delicate, handmade lace tablecloth. Along with the buffet and chairs, the table was made of the best mahogany. Fine crystal, china, and silver covered the table and the buffet, where delicious and decadent food was served.

Taking her seat, Maria looked around the table, her glance touching every face. To her right was her brother, Hugh Langley, a trim man in his midforties with auburn hair and brown eyes. He smiled at her, and she had to struggle to return his smile. They all had had such great hopes for Hugh. He had started to gain recognition as a painter when his wife died, yet since that day he had given up.

"Good evening, Maria. You are looking well."

"Thank you, Hugh."

Next to Hugh sat Lowell Augustine, the nephew of Maria's husband. He was a fine-looking young man of twenty-five years. He nodded and spoke to her pleasantly. "Good evening, Aunt."

"Good evening, Lowell."

Zara Augustine, Lowell's sister, sat across from her brother. She was a beautiful young girl with the same wealth of brown hair and brown eyes. Next to her sat Julian Harcourt, a young man with fair hair and blue eyes. He seemed to be in love with Zara. Maria studied Julian for a moment. His father and grandfather had run through his family's money and had designs on the Augustine estate, Maria believed, and apparently planned to live on the Augustine fortune when he married Zara.

They all waited and bowed their heads, following Lady Maria Augustine's example. She insisted on grace before a meal and pronounced the simple blessing herself. "Thank You, Lord, for this food and for every blessing. We are grateful to You for all that You have given us, and we thank You in the name of Jesus. Amen."

A faint echo of amens went around the room and then the meal was brought in.

First came a large pot of delicious crawfish gumbo with hot bread and fresh butter. After this came a small salad of cucumbers and tomatoes with a zesty homemade dressing, followed by the main dish of baked pork with onions, a dish of buttery, spiced green beans, mashed potatoes with fresh garlic, warm applesauce, and for dessert, hot coffee with fresh slices of pecan pie covered in heavy cream.

Maria only half listened to the account Zara was giving of the trip abroad she planned to make. She was excited about it, and Julian laughed at her enthusiasm, saying, "You'll be bored to tears. Nothing is more boring than a long voyage on the ocean."

Zara reached over and slapped at her suitor's arm. "You're spoiled, Julian!"

"I will admit it, and I would like to be spoiled more."

Lowell said, "Lady Maria, I've been telling you about this mare that is such a great animal."

"You already have three horses, Lowell. You can't ride but one at a time, can you?"

Lowell laughed, "Not unless I was an acrobat, but this mare is going to win a lot of races, and she's going to produce some great foals."

"I think three horses is enough for any man, and I don't like that racing crowd anyway."

The conversation was amiable enough, but Hugh Langley noticed that his sister was very quiet. "Is something wrong, Maria?"

"There may be."

Silence fell across the table.

"What is it? You're not ill, are you?" Zara asked at once.

"No, I'm fine. But I had a visitor two days ago whom you all need to hear about."

"What sort of visitor?" Lowell asked. "He didn't come to court you, did he, Aunt?"

"No. It was Blaise Mignon."

"That rascal!" Zara exclaimed. "What did he want?"

"You remember him, do you, Zara?"

"I was just a child, but I remember he was arrested and sent to Devil's Island."

"That's right, he was."

"What did he want this time, money?" Zara demanded, her eyes indignant. "When did he get out of prison? I thought he was there for life."

"He was pardoned, I understand," Maria said. She took a deep breath and looked around the table. "He brought a young woman with him."

"A young woman? What sort of young woman?" Hugh asked.

"A young woman he says is Ives's daughter."

Zara gasped and her hand went to her breast. "Ives's daughter? Impossible!"

"Why should it be impossible? Ives was married. Why couldn't he have had a daughter?"

"Why, we would have known about it!" Lowell exclaimed.

"How would we have known?" Hugh said. "He was forbidden ever to come to this house. As far as I know, you and your husband never received any word from him, did you?"

"We may have."

Once again surprised faces met Maria's eyes. "You never told us that you heard from him," Lowell said. "What did he say?"

"I never saw any letters from him," Maria admitted, "but I think he wrote. Ancel let it slip once that he had heard from Ives, but he never let me see the letter, and there may have been more. It's very possible," she said slowly, "that Ives and his wife had a child. We may not have known because Ancel was very unforgiving. You all know that."

"Why, it's ridiculous!" Zara said loudly, her cheeks flushed. "Mignon's nothing but a criminal. How could you take his word for it?"

"There's a little bit more than his word."

"He has evidence, Lady Augustine?" Julian Harcourt spoke up. His eyes were fixed on his hostess, and he had a sharp, clear mind. He had studied law, and although he had not completed his work, he still had a lawyer's mind. "Was there any physical evidence?"

"Yes, there was."

"But who is this girl? Where has she been? How old is she?" Lowell demanded, leaning forward anxiously.

"She was left as an infant, only a few days old, at the door of the Ursuline Convent. The mother superior herself found her there."

"And when was this?"

"Nearly twenty years ago. The young woman is nineteen now."

"But about this evidence," Julian insisted. "What does it consist of?"

"This." Maria reached into the small reticule that she had brought and held up the locket. She handed it to her brother, saying, "You'll recognize it, Hugh."

Opening it, he said, "Why, this is Ives. No question about it."

As the locket was passed around, Maria said, "This locket belonged to my mother. I gave it to Ives myself, and I commissioned the picture. There's no question that it's genuine."

"But it could have been stolen. They could have found it," Zara protested.

"Yes, they could."

"What other evidence, if any?" Harcourt demanded.

"This book: *The Imitation of Christ*. I gave you and Ives copies at the same time, brother."

"Yes, I remember it." Hugh flipped through the pages and said, "Ives's handwriting." He passed the book on and looked at Julian Harcourt. "That's pretty strong evidence, Julian."

"That lawyer could have laid hold of these things a dozen different ways!" Zara protested.

"No. The mother superior says they were in the basket that the infant was left with. She's had them all of her life."

"But how did Mignon find out about all this? Where did he find the young woman?" Lowell asked.

Maria repeated the story of the painting and said, "There's one more bit of evidence."

"What is it, Aunt?" Zara asked quickly.

"The girl looks very much like Ives. There's a strong resemblance."

"Coincidence," Lowell shrugged.

"You're too young to remember Ives, but you're not, Hugh. She has his widow's peak, which we often commented on, and also the same dimple. She looks very much like him." Her voice seemed to grow unsteady then. "She resembles him a great deal."

"You're not believing this crooked lawyer, I hope, Aunt," Zara said.

"I haven't decided."

"I'll never believe it!" Zara exclaimed.

"Well, you'll have a chance to judge for yourself." Maria smiled slightly. "The two of them will be here tomorrow morning. You can ask either of them anything you like."

Hugh laughed. "Well, I must say this has been the most interesting dinner we've ever had." He picked up the locket again and said softly, "I miss Ives, sister, more than you can know."

Taking the locket from him, Lady Augustine looked down at the picture. "So do I, Hugh. So do I!"

"Keep your courage up, my dear," Blaise said taking Leonie's elbow. He had noticed that she was stiff with anxiety. "It'll be all right."

"I'm afraid, Blaise."

"They'll give you a hard time, but you're going to win out. Keep your eye on Lady Maria. Remember Ives was the sun in her heaven. To have even a piece of him back again would be beyond anything she could desire."

"But the rest of them—they won't accept me."

"We'll see," Blaise said. He knocked on the door firmly, and while they were waiting, he whispered, "You can bear the hatred of the others if you become mistress of Belle Fleur."

The door opened, and Mrs. Danvers stood just as she had on their first visit.

"Good morning, Mrs. Danvers. I believe we're expected."

Mrs. Danvers reluctantly stepped back. "They're waiting for you in the large parlor."

"Thank you."

As Leonie walked through the foyer, she kept a firm hold on Blaise's arm. All night long she had tossed and turned. Ever since the invitation had come from Maria Augustine, she had been tense. Actually it had been a summons more than an invitation. Blaise had showed her the brief note: "Come to Belle Fleur in the morning at ten o'clock. Maria Augustine."

Not exactly the warmest of notes! she thought. Still, Lady Maria had written, and now as Leonie glanced up at the portraits of Augustines, dead and gone, the thought came to her mind, *My picture may be on this wall one day, and someone may be looking up and wondering who I was and what I was like even as I wonder about these.*

Mrs. Danvers led them toward a large double door. "You may go in," she said, disapproval in her tone.

"Thank you, Mrs. Danvers," Blaise said pleasantly. He winked at Leonie, and she managed a smile. Blaise opened the door, and she stepped inside. Blaise followed, and the two stood just inside the doorway. Leonie glanced around the room at the strangers standing and staring at her, and it took all her courage not to show fear.

"You are prompt, sir, and you, Miss Dousett."

"I imagine you're not too surprised at that, Lady Augustine," Blaise said smoothly.

"Not at all." Lady Maria turned to face Leonie. "You may sit down. Indeed, let us all sit down."

Numbly Leonie took her seat in the wing chair that Maria Augustine indicated and was glad that Blaise sat down in a chair very close to her.

"Let me introduce you to the family. This is my brother, Hugh Langley. This is my nephew, Lowell Augustine, and his sister, Zara Augustine. And this is Mr. Julian Harcourt." Taking a deep breath, she said to the others, "And this young lady is Leonie Dousett."

"Well, after all, that's what we're here to decide, isn't it?" Blaise said quietly. "It's possible her name is Leonie Augustine."

Lady Maria gave the man a steely glance and said tersely, "You may tell your tale again, Monsieur."

"With pleasure, Lady Maria." He began telling the story of his finding of Leonie, and as he did, Leonie watched the young people in the room. Zara Augustine stared with a stark antagonism that she found difficult to meet. *Why, she hates me!* Leonie thought. Her eyes went to Lowell Augustine, and although he, too, showed no friendship, his stare was not as bitter. The young man, Julian Harcourt, was studying her clinically. She had no idea who he was. He wasn't an Augustine, and Lady Maria had not explained his presence.

The one encouraging sign was the man called Hugh Langley, who was Lady Maria's brother. He was watching her intently, but there was no antagonism in his look. He seemed curious about her, and when she met his eyes, he smiled slightly and nodded as if to say, "Keep a stiff upper lip, my dear." He was a fine-looking man, although his eyes were red the way drinkers' eyes get at times. He was careless in his dress, and although his clothes were expensive, they were rumpled and not at all in keeping with what she expected of an aristocrat.

When Mignon finished, he said, "Now you may ask anything you wish."

Zara said, "I don't believe a word of this."

"And why not, Mademoiselle Augustine?" Blaise asked calmly.

"It's obviously a twisted attempt at getting money."

"It's always possible, when a great deal of money is involved, that someone will come up with a way to get some of it."

Zara's face flamed, and she said, "What are you implying?"

"Why, nothing, Mademoiselle. I'm merely stating a fact. The question is, am I a charlatan? You have a right to believe it, but look at this young woman. She spent her whole life in a convent, she was found there a helpless baby, and in the basket she was found in there were two irrefutable items that belonged to Ives Augustine. Surely you don't suggest that she is involved in a plot."

"There are other ways. You could have found these things, and you may be lying!" Julian Harcourt said.

"All you have to do is go to the mother superior of the Ursuline Convent. She will vouch for this young woman's history."

"I'm afraid we'll have to accept the mother superior's word. I've already checked with her."

"You always were very careful, Lady Maria," Blaise said.

"It's likely that I would be careful where something like this was concerned." Lady Maria turned to her brother and asked, "What do you think, Hugh?"

"She has the Augustine look. Ives's dimple and widow's peak, and generally she resembles him."

"Why are you doing this, Mignon?" Lowell Augustine demanded. "You're not a member of our family."

"You are right; I am not. But your son was kind to me, and I would like to do something for his daughter in return."

"So you don't care about money."

"I would not say no to money," Blaise said.

Julian Harcourt remained silent while Lowell and Zara fired questions at Blaise and at Leonie. Finally he said, "I think you would be unwise to take any action on this, Lady Maria. After all, there is no actual proof. It's all circumstantial."

"Very strong circumstance would put Ives's locket and the book that he treasured in such a place."

"That may be true. Still, there is, as this man says, a great deal of money. She would be—"

"Yes. She would be the only living child of Ives and would stand to inherit under Louisiana law," Lady Maria said, her eyes fixed on Leonie.

"I do not care about the money," Leonie said firmly. She held her head high and said, "None of you, perhaps, understand what it is to have no family, to be completely alone. That's been my life. The sisters were kind to me, but all my life I dreamed of having a family. When Monsieur Mignon came to me, that was what thrilled me."

"So you're willing to give up the money?" Zara said quickly. "It means nothing to you?"

Leonie turned to face the young woman. "I understand little of legal things, but if I were taken into the family as the daughter of a man I can't even remember, I would promise that there would be no contention about money. If I were to inherit, all would inherit. All I want is to find my people and to love them."

"I suppose you learned all those noble sentiments from the sisters?" Zara sneered.

"I learned a great deal from them. Every one of those sisters gave up everything in order to serve Jesus. I would certainly give up anything to find a family."

"We mustn't be too hasty about giving up anything," Blaise said abruptly. "Time enough to settle that when the case is clear." He glanced at the two cousins and smiled, "I am sure that you would be well provided for, regardless of this young lady's status."

"I have decided what must be done."

Instantly every eye in the room went to Lady Maria. She was sitting bolt upright, and her mouth was drawn into a fine line. Her chin was held high, and her eyes were locked with those of Leonie. "I cannot say that I am totally convinced, but I cannot ignore even circumstantial evidence. If this is the child of my son, Ives, she is my granddaughter. I cannot ignore that."

A gust of relief ran through Leonie. "Lady Augustine," she said, "do you believe it is possible that I am your kin?"

"I cannot say, but I will know soon. Ives had certain qualities. I would see these things if you lived here. Therefore, you will come and stay here."

"Under what circumstances?" Blaise said quickly, his eyes sharp.

"For a time, as a guest. She will be expected to live here, to share in some of the duties perhaps, and in time I will know for certain. I must pray about this, Monsieur, you understand."

"I understand," Leonie said eagerly. "I will be happy to come. But I have a cat."

"You may bring your cat." Lady Augustine stood, and everyone rose with her. She walked over to stand directly before Leonie. Leonie's eyes were wide, and the older woman studied her. "Julius will come for you tomorrow morning." She gave Leonie the locket.

"Yes, Madam."

"Do not sever all your connections. I am not welcoming you into the family. I am saying we will look into this."

"Yes, of course," Leonie said.

Maria turned and faced Blaise. "You need not return anytime soon, Monsieur Mignon."

Blaise shrugged. "It shall be as you say, Madam. Come, I will take you back, Leonie."

After the two left the room, a battle of voices erupted in protest. Zara and Lowell were the loudest, but Julian Harcourt echoed them by saying, "It is a dangerous precedent. The law might come to believe that you are recognizing this girl as your grandchild."

But it was Hugh Langley's voice that prevailed. He went to Maria, put his arm around her, and said quietly, "You have done the right thing, my sister. I see Ives in her."

"I'm glad you approve, Hugh. I've always trusted your judgment."

"Why should you trust the judgment of a man who can't even stay sober?" Zara asked furiously.

"She has a point, I'm afraid," Hugh said, his eyes sad. "It is all a feeling with me."

Maria Augustine stood in the small circle, but her thoughts were on the young woman who had stood before her. "She looks so much like Ives," she whispered. "We will see if she has any of his goodness in her."

⌒

Pulling up in front of Madam Honore's shop, Blaise said, "You have said hardly a word all the way back."

"I'm afraid I'm a little bit overwhelmed, Blaise."

"You have a right to be."

"I don't know what to make of it all. I understand the enmity of the young woman and her brother. They think they will lose money. Why is Mr. Harcourt so much against me?"

"Because, my dear, he hopes to marry Zara. The Zara he hopes to marry, in his mind, is the heiress and the mistress of Belle Fleur.

If you are who you say you are, she is merely a poor relation. Quite a different thing."

"But I've said I don't care about the money," Leonie said. "I would share anything I received, in ample measure."

"That's a discussion for another day," Blaise said quietly.

"I don't know what to make of Lady Augustine."

"She has had a hard life. Her husband was not an easy man to live with," he said, shaking his head. "She has to make up her mind about you, and I'm afraid you must expect a hard time."

"I don't mind that."

Blaise got down, walked around the carriage, and handed her down. They went to the door, and Madam Honore opened it before they could knock. "Come in," she said. "I want to hear what happened."

The two went in and sat down in the small parlor. Madam Honore fixed tea for them and listened intently as Blaise told the story.

"I'm very glad for you, Leonie," she said, her eyes on the young woman.

"They don't love me," Leonie admitted. "Only one, the man Hugh Langley, seemed to have any warmth at all."

"Then they will have to learn," Madam Honore said firmly, "and they will. I have something to tell you, my dear."

"What is that, Madam?"

"As I told you might happen, I am leaving New Orleans. I have sold the shop. I simply can't sew anymore." She held up her arthritic hands and stared at them. "I really don't have any choice."

"I'm so sorry, Madam." Leonie looked sadly at her first kindly employer, her close friend for two years.

"I hope to leave in a few days. Now that you have a new home, I feel much better."

"They may not keep me," Leonie said.

"Don't talk like that," Blaise said. "It's going to be all right. I was watching the old woman, and I know her pretty well. She's hard and tough, but she's fair. And as I've told you several times, she loved her son dearly."

"We will pray that you will be accepted by your family, will we not, Monsieur Mignon?"

"Prayer is a little out of my line," Blaise said. He shrugged. "I will hope, and you may pray."

"That's the best: hope and prayer," Madam Honore said.

"Will I ever see you again, Madam? You've been such a friend to me."

"Baton Rouge is not a long journey. I think we will meet again."

"I hope so. I do not have so many friends that I can afford to lose one." Leonie tried to think of what life would be like at Belle Fleur, but she could not. Finally she said quietly, "It is all in the hands of God."

"Everything is," Madam Honore smiled. "Is it not so, Monsieur?"

"That is what I am trying to find out," Blaise said. "Maybe this will be the time for me as well as the time for this young lady."

Chapter ten

Leonie heard the knock at the door. When she opened it, she found a very tall, strongly built black man whom she recognized as the Augustines' groom. He removed his hat and said, "Mademoiselle Dousett?"

"Yes. I am Mademoiselle Dousett."

"My name is Julius. Lady Augustine says I am to take you to Belle Fleur."

"Yes. I'm all ready, Julius. Would you help me with my trunk?"

"Yes, ma'am."

Julius followed Leonie through the shop to her room. He picked up the trunk as if it weighed nothing and asked, "Is this all?"

"Except for my cat, but I can carry him." She picked up Louis and put him in his basket, ignoring his protests. "If you'll go to the carriage, I'll be there in a moment. I just want to say good-bye."

"Yes, ma'am. I will be waiting."

Leonie went to Madam Honore's door and knocked. When the door opened, she said, "It's time for me to go. A man has come for me."

Madam Honore embraced Leonie and kissed her on the cheek. "You're going to be fine. I've been praying much for you."

"You've been so kind to me." Tears came to Leonie's eyes. "I'm going to miss you greatly."

"And I shall miss you. You must write me regularly, and I will answer, and we will find a way to meet again."

Leonie hugged the older woman and said, "Good-bye for now." She turned and left the shop. She went down the stairs and found Julius standing beside a very large carriage. "All ready, Mademoiselle?"

"All ready." Julius handed her in, and she took her seat. When Julius got in and spoke to the horses, she turned and took one final look at the place where she had spent two years, happy ones at that.

"You'll be living at Belle Fleur, Lady Augustine tells me."

"Yes," she said, "at least for a while."

"I add my voice to welcome you, Mademoiselle."

"Why, thank you, Julius."

Leonie did not speak for a time, and finally when they were getting to the suburbs and the open country was beginning to appear, she said, "Have you been at Belle Fleur long, Julius?"

"Oh yes, ma'am. Many, many years." He turned and smiled at her. "I belong to Lady Augustine, but she allows me to be the pastor of a small church for my people."

"You are a minister?"

"One of God's poor servants."

"Is your church large?"

"About forty souls, ma'am, when we're all there." He was silent for a time, then he said, "I heard your story. Servants hear almost everything. I just wanted to say while we're alone, I remember your father very well."

Surprise swept across Leonie's face. "You knew my father?"

"Oh yes, Miss. I was just a boy, but I remember him well. I used to go with him and carry his gun when he went hunting. And more than once I paddled the boat when he fished in the bayou."

"What was he like, Julius?"

"Oh, Miss, he was a very fine gentleman. Fine-looking—everyone commented on that."

"I have a picture of him." Leonie took out the locket, removed it from her neck, and opened it. "See?"

Julius took the locket and stared at it for a long time. "It's him, Mademoiselle. He's just like life." He looked at her and smiled. "You have some of your father's looks."

"That's what Monsieur Mignon says."

"But it wasn't his looks that drew me to your father. It was the way he cared for people."

"Tell me all about it, Julius. Everything you can think of."

"Well, he was very kind to the slaves, to all of us. He was the one member of the family we could go to and be sure we'd get a fair hearing. And . . ."

Leonie listened with pleasure. She could picture her father based on his picture, and as Julius spoke and as she kept her eyes on the miniature, he seemed to come to life. "I wish I could have known him."

"I wish you could, too, Miss. He would have been mighty proud of you, I can tell you."

"Did you know my mother too?"

Julius nodded and straightened up in the seat. "I saw her twice," he said. "He brought her to Belle Fleur once, and then once when I went to carry a message to him."

"A message from whom?"

"From your grandmother, Miss. She sent a letter by me. You understand that Mr. Ancel, he was a very hard man and would have nothing to do with anyone who crossed his will. Hard man, indeed, but not your grandmother. She's very different."

"She's not sure that I'm her granddaughter."

"No. She's a careful woman, but she's a kind woman."

All the way to Belle Fleur, Leonie listened as Julius told her tales of her father's youth and young manhood. The groom had indeed been very close to him, and by the time they had arrived at Belle Fleur, she felt she knew her father much better. "It's so kind of you to tell me all these things."

"Why, it's my pleasure, Mademoiselle. Your father was very kind to me, and the least I can do is to be kind to his daughter."

Ten minutes later they arrived at Belle Fleur. Julius stopped the team, got down, and said kindly, "I will bring your trunk in, Mademoiselle."

"Thank you, Julius." Leonie picked up Louis's basket, got out of the carriage, and walked up the steps to the front door. She remembered how frightened she had been on her previous two visits and admonished herself, *Really, Leonie, you must have courage.* She knocked on the door, and Mrs. Danvers stared at her. "Come in, Mademoiselle."

"Good morning, Mrs. Danvers."

Mrs. Danvers merely nodded. "I will show you to your room." She lifted her voice and said, "Hurry along with that trunk, Julius."

"Yes, Mrs. Danvers."

"Come this way." Mrs. Danvers walked down the foyer to a staircase, and without a word she led Leonie and Julius up. At the top of the third flight she turned right and stopped before a door painted pure white. "This is your room."

She opened the door and Leonie walked in, curious as to where she would be staying. "What a beautiful room!" she exclaimed.

The walls were adorned with light purple and white wallpaper, the three large windows were covered with white, airy curtains, and the ceiling was painted pure white. The furniture was all highly polished rosewood, the bed having a canopy with ornate carvings on the posts and deep purple bedding and bed curtains tied back with white lace ties. The armoire was very large and was decorated with the same carvings as the bed. There was a desk between two of the large windows with paper and pens and books arranged neatly on the top and with a beautiful tapestry-covered chair on one side. A large, snowy-white area rug was centered in the middle of the room, and pictures of flowers and family members in gilded frames were arranged on the walls.

"Julius, put the trunk there," Mrs. Danvers said. When Julius put the trunk down, he smiled and said, "Welcome to Belle Fleur, Mademoiselle," and left.

"Lady Augustine is waiting for you. Come. I will take you."

"I hope I won't be any trouble to you, Mrs. Danvers," Leonie said as the two made their way. "I'll try not to be."

"That would be convenient."

The woman seemed continually angry, and Leonie made up her mind to make a friend of the woman. "I would be glad to help with any work that you find for me."

The offer caught Mrs. Danvers off guard. She gave the girl an astonished look. "You're here as a guest."

"I wouldn't be happy unless I had something to do. I'm a good seamstress. Anything you want mended, please bring it to me. Really, I want to be helpful."

Mrs. Danvers studied her briefly, and then nodded. "That may be," she said. "Come this way."

They found Lady Augustine alone in her bedroom. She was sitting beside the window as the two entered and did not get up. "Thank you, Mrs. Danvers," she said, dismissing her. "Come in. Come over here, Mademoiselle."

"Please. Everyone at the convent called me Leonie."

"Where did you get that name?"

"It was the name of the mother superior's sister. She named me after her."

"It's a most unusual name. Sit down."

Leonie took the seat but felt stiff and awkward.

"Do you find your room satisfactory?"

"Oh, it's a beautiful room! Much too nice for me."

"I'm glad you like it. You'll be expected to take your meals with the family."

"Yes, ma'am, of course." Leonie said, "I would like to be able to help with anything I could. I've worked all my life, Lady Augustine."

"There are always things to do in a place like this. I have a considerable correspondence."

"Oh, I would be glad to help with that! My handwriting is not as good as it should be, but I will do my best."

"Very well. Also, there are some small markets close by. You can help with that, I'm sure."

"Thank you, Lady Augustine."

Maria studied the young woman. She had slept little since this situation had exploded in her life. She saw the girl's innocence and humility, but still it frightened her to think that she might be Ives's daughter. She could not think why she should be afraid, for she had loved Ives deeply. Suddenly she said, "You understand, Leonie, I must be certain that you are Ives's child. We never had any word that Ives and his wife had a child."

"Oh, I understand that perfectly well. Do I really look like him, Lady Augustine?"

"There are several portraits. I will show them to you. You look very much like him, but that could be a coincidence."

"I will serve you as best as I can, Lady Augustine."

Lady Augustine looked at the young woman. "We will see about all this. We must get to know each other. Tell me again about yourself. Do you like to read? Have you been to the theater? I need to know as much as I can."

"There's really not much to know, but I will be glad to tell you, ma'am."

⁓

Later that afternoon, Leonie took a walk around the grounds. She had been introduced at the house to some of the servants, including Olan Winters, a short, strong man who served as overseer. She encountered him directing the digging of a ditch. "Hello again, Mr. Winters."

"Bless you, miss, it's just Olan." He was a balding man with a pair of sharp, hazel eyes.

"You've done a marvelous job on the grounds."

"Well, I've been here a long time."

"What's the ditch for?"

Olan explained the purpose of the ditch and waved over toward a bed that some black men were digging. "There's going to be a new bed of flowers there. Your grandmother loves flowers."

"My grandmother?"

"Why, I understood you were her granddaughter. You are Mr. Ives's daughter."

Leonie looked confused. "Well, no one has confirmed that yet."

"Why, all they have to do is look at you. You're the spittin' image of Mr. Ives."

"You knew my father?"

"Of course I knew him. I knew your mother, too—Miss Lila. Of course I didn't meet her but a couple of times. You've got her look about you too. Her hair was the same dark color as yours, and her face was shaped like yours."

"I'd like to hear all about both of them!" Leonie exclaimed.

"You drop by for a cup of tea after I get off of work; I'll be glad to tell you, Miss."

"I will. Thank you so much, Olan."

Continuing her walk, Leonie marveled at how she was in the presence of people who had actually known her parents. She herself was totally convinced that she was Ives Augustine's daughter. *That would make me Leonie Augustine,* she thought as she continued to walk along the garden. The flowers were mostly gone now, but she knew that they must have been beautiful in the spring—banks of color everywhere. She turned a corner and encountered Zara Augustine, who was hurrying out of the house.

"I've been looking for you, Leonie," she said.

"Yes, Miss."

Zara said, "I want you to help me clean my room. It's a mess."

This had not been one of the duties that her grandmother had mentioned, but Leonie was happy to oblige. She hurried to the room, and for the next hour she worked assiduously. Zara was a beautiful young woman but a terrible housekeeper. Her clothes were everywhere, and she had many of them. Zara made no attempt to help except to tell her where things were located.

Finally Leonie was done, and Zara said, "That will do for now. You'd better come by every afternoon and straighten things out."

"Of course. I'll be glad to."

"And about that cat—I'm afraid you'll have to get rid of him."

Dismay swept through Leonie. "Why, no, I can't do that."

"You'll do as you're told!" Zara snapped. "You're only a guest here. Remember that. I don't think for one moment you're a relation."

"I can't get rid of my cat."

"You do what I tell you!" Zara said. "Now leave!"

Leonie left the room with a sense of gloom. For over an hour she wandered the grounds, wondering what would happen if she refused to give up Louis. Finally she started toward the house, determined to speak with her grandmother, but she encountered Hugh Langley, who had been sitting on a bench in the garden. "Hello, my dear," he said. "Come and sit beside me. Let's get acquainted."

Leonie hesitated, but she liked the look of the man. She sat down, remembering how Lady Augustine had turned to him for advice. "I have a great problem, Monsieur."

"At your age, you couldn't have much of a problem," Hugh said, smiling. "What is it? Tell me all about it."

"It's Miss Zara. She tells me I have to get rid of my cat, and I can't do that, sir. I just can't. I've had him since he was a kitten."

"Why, I heard my sister say you could keep your cat."

"But Miss Zara says—"

"Rain on Miss Zara! My sister decides things like that. She told you the cat was all right. Don't worry about it."

"Are you sure?"

"I'm sure of one thing. Zara will do whatever my sister tells her. We're all dependent on her, you see."

"Sir, did you know my father?"

"Yes indeed! We were great friends. I was only seven years older than he. We hunted and fished together." He smiled. "He was a fine man, Leonie. So was your mother." He shook his head. "She was beautiful and good and fine. I expect you want to know all about them."

"Oh yes, sir, I do."

"Well, I don't know much about your mother, but I can tell you a great deal about your father."

"Olan said that he knew him well too."

"Yes. They were good friends. Ives liked people."

Leonie was entranced by the stories the man told about her father. The picture she had of him in her mind was becoming even more lifelike. She knew very little about her mother and probably never would know more, she thought sadly. To Hugh she said, "It's so kind of you to share these memories with me."

"Not kind at all. I was very fond of Ives."

"I understand you are an artist."

Suddenly lines formed over Hugh's forehead. "I used to be considered so."

"Don't you paint anymore?"

"I don't do much anymore except grieve."

"Grieve over what, Mr. Langley?"

"Why don't you just call me Hugh when nobody's around? Mr. Langley's so formal."

"If you wish."

"I grieve about my wife, Autumn. She was the brightest thing in my life, Leonie. She encouraged me, and I worked like a madman. Everything was fun when she was around. When she died," he said, and his voice quivered, "I lost everything. I just gave up."

"I don't think she would like that, sir."

Hugh Langley looked surprised. "What do you mean?"

"Your wife. She loved you, didn't she?"

"So she said, and I believed it."

"She wouldn't want you to just give up. Didn't she encourage you while she was living?"

"More than anyone."

"Then I'm sure she would love to see you go on now."

"It's too late," he said. "I lost whatever fire it is that artists are supposed to have."

Leonie reached out and put her hand on the man's arm. There was such a kindness in him, and he was so sad. "I'm sure your wife would want you to continue. It would make her proud. Who knows," she said, "maybe she's looking down from heaven right now."

"I've often wondered about that," Hugh said softly.

"I wish you would think on it."

"I will." He patted her hand, then rose and said, "It's time for dinner." He reaffirmed, "Don't worry about the cat. Don't worry about anything Zara or Lowell says. They're afraid they'll lose their inheritance. Come along, my dear."

They walked into the dining room, and the others came in shortly afterward. Lady Augustine came in, sat down with a terse greeting, and asked the blessing. The mood during dinner was strained, and Leonie said almost nothing except when spoken to.

After the dinner, Leonie was at a loss as to what to do. She wandered into the library and was looking at the books when she heard some footsteps. She turned to see Lowell Augustine come in. "I followed you here," he said cheerfully. "You didn't say much at dinner. Are you sad at leaving your old place?"

"I feel out of place," she admitted. "I knew my place at the convent and then later with Madam Honore. But everything is strange here."

Lowell walked over to stand opposite her. He had good looks— a firm chin and quizzical gray eyes. "Don't worry," he said. "We have to be nice to you. If we don't, you'll throw us all out when you become the mistress here." He saw the shocked look in her face, then laughed and said, "I like to throw people off guard, but after all, that's the way it is."

"No, it isn't. I would never do such a thing."

"I don't believe you would," Lowell said. "You spent most of your life in a convent. Haven't seen much of the world."

"That's true."

"Well, now you can afford to see some of it. I'll tell you what: why don't I take you to the theater?"

"I've never been to the theater."

"It will be interesting."

"I'm not sure that Lady Augustine would permit it."

"Oh, she won't mind. I'll ask her myself."

"I'm not sure that it would be proper."

"Well, I'm not a very proper young man, but you're a proper young woman," he said with a grin. "I expect you have enough properness in you for both of us."

"I feel very—awkward, Mr. Augustine. Please don't make it worse."

Instantly Augustine apologized. "Why, I'm sorry. I'm too flippant, I know. But I heard what you said the first time at our meeting—that even if you are accepted and become the heiress and the mistress of this place, you would be generous."

"That's right, sir."

"Look. I'm only twenty-five, Leonie. You don't have to call me 'sir.' Lowell is fine. And I'm just a cousin, not really a threat. Why can't we be friends?"

"I'd like that very much."

"Friends then?" He put out his hand, and she, with some hesitancy, took it. He said, "Fine. Watch out for my sister, Zara, though. She's not as nice as I am."

"She doesn't like me."

"Oh, she hates you," Lowell said cheerfully. "She's got her mind set on having the Augustine fortune and becoming Lady Augustine one day. That would have happened if you hadn't come along. You can't expect her to be too happy about that."

Leonie shook her head. "She doesn't have to be upset. I hope I can convince her I mean her no harm."

"You can try."

At that moment Lady Augustine entered the room. "Hello, Aunt

Maria," Lowell said. "I've just been asking Leonie if she wouldn't like to go to the theater. I offered to take her."

"Perhaps you can take us both."

"Why, that would be fine!?"

"Yes. We need to get out a bit more. Now run along."

"Of course. I'll see about the tickets."

As soon as the young man left, Lady Maria said, "I heard that Zara told you you had to get rid of your cat."

"Yes. She did say that."

"Don't worry about it. I said you could keep the cat."

"Thank you."

Lady Maria was studying the young woman so closely that finally Leonie said, "May I ask you something?"

"Of course."

"Do you see anything in me that looks like my father—or my mother?"

Maria did not answer for a moment, but then she nodded. "I see something, but I'm not sure if it's just the physical resemblance. I'm a lonely old woman, Leonie, and only time will tell. I will say this: nothing would please me more than to have a grandchild with Ives's blood in her. But I am not ready to say that yet."

"Of course, Lady Augustine."

"We shall see. I am praying that God will give me guidance."

"I will pray with you, if I may."

"You are a Christian then?"

"Oh yes, naturally. I grew up in a convent."

"That's right. You did. Well, you will learn our ways here, and we will learn something about you. Come now. I will show you the portraits of my son."

Chapter eleven

Lowering the newspaper, Lowell Augustine looked at his sister as she walked in and sat down heavily across from him at the breakfast table. He studied her carefully, then grinned. "You look terrible," he commented. "You stay up all night?"

Zara glared at Lowell and snapped indignantly, "That's none of your business!"

"Everything you do is my business, sister. Where would you be if it weren't for me?"

Zara ignored Lowell and turned to Nora, the maid. "Hurry up with my breakfast, Nora," she said, irritability flavoring her tone.

"My, you *are* in a foul mood," Lowell remarked.

"I'm not feeling well. That's all."

"There's nothing wrong with you. You're healthy as a horse." He picked up his coffee cup, drained it, then put it down with a wrinkle in his brow. "Our aunt isn't feeling well."

"What's wrong with her?"

"She's got a slight fever. I've tried to get her to call for the doctor, but you know how she is—stubborn as a mule. Want some free advice?"

"From you? No."

"Come on, sister of mine. Let me straighten you out here. When Auntie grew ill yesterday morning, Leonie began taking care of her. She sat up with her half the night while you were out doing depraved things with Julian."

"We weren't doing depraved things. We simply went to the Creole Ball."

"That's what I said. You know how those things are."

"Lowell, I wish you would hush."

"Those balls are nothing but a marketplace for men to find beautiful Creole mistresses."

"I don't want to talk about it."

"People usually don't want to talk about depraved things, but anyway, don't change the subject. Leonie has been caring for Maria, and you should be doing it."

"I'm not a nurse."

Lowell leaned back in his chair. He was very rarely serious. For him, life, as long as he had plenty of fine food, feminine companionship, and expensive clothing, was happy. Now, however, he grew concerned, and he leaned forward and lowered his voice. "I don't think you appreciate what's going on here, Zara."

"What do you mean?"

"I mean we could be out on our ear, and you don't seem to be aware of it."

Zara glared upward as if she could see through to the second floor. "You mean that girl?"

"I mean that young woman who is probably Maria's granddaughter."

"I won't believe it—not ever!"

"Unfortunately that's not the test. The question is, will Maria believe it? If she does, we're sunk. I'd have to go to work," he said, shrugging his shoulders, "and you'd have to marry somebody with money."

"Lowell, you can't be serious," Zara said. "Our aunt's got more sense than that. She'll never make that impostor the heiress."

"She might, Zara. You've got to remember. She loved Ives better than anyone, and once she makes up her mind for sure that Leonie is her flesh and blood, the daughter of her precious Ives, she'll deed this place and all that goes with it over to her quicker than you can blink."

Zara put her hand suddenly on her breast, and a look of fright came into her eyes. "We've got to do something, Lowell."

Lowell nodded. "That's exactly what I've been trying to tell you. Be sweeter to Tante Maria."

"You mean wait on her? She has servants for that."

"The servants aren't trying to get into her will, Zara. You'd better think about this, and by the way, if I were you, I'd be a little more pleasant to Leonie. If she inherits, we'll be totally dependent on her. Watch me. I intend to be as appealing and as charming to her as I possibly can, and I suggest that you do the same."

⌒

"Couldn't you eat just a little bit more, Lady Maria? I made it the way you like it."

"I can't eat anything else, Leonie. Take it away." Outside, October winds blew, whipping around the house.

Leonie had made a bowl of oatmeal spiced with cinnamon. She had found out from Opal, the cook, that Maria Augustine loved this. Now, however, she sighed and shook her head. "You really should eat something."

"I can't keep it down," Maria said. Her face was pale, and new lines crossed her forehead. "I don't know what's the matter with me."

"You need to see the doctor."

"Oh, I'll be all right. Don't fuss over me, Leonie." She threw the cover back and said, "I'm burning up."

"You have fever. Let me get some cool water."

"Oh, don't bother. I don't like to be fussed over."

"It will be good for you," Leonie said. She went to the nightstand

and poured water from the pitcher into the basin. She saturated the cloth, wrung it out, and then went and sat down on the edge of Maria's bed. "Let me just bathe your face."

Maria lay still and finally sighed, "That does feel good."

"If your fever gets any higher, we'll have to do something."

Maria Augustine lay still while the girl tried to relieve her fever pains. She studied the young woman's features and not for the first time tried to decide if the resemblance to her dead son was accidental or a matter of genes. *She looks so much like Ives,* she thought. She asked, "Are you happy here, Leonie?"

"Why, yes, Lady Augustine."

"Call me Lady Maria."

"If you wish. Yes, I'm fine here."

"Are you as happy here as you were at the convent?"

"That's hard to say. They were very kind to me there."

"And we haven't been kind here."

"Oh, I didn't say that. Everybody has been very nice."

"That's the first wrong thing I've heard you say," Maria said. "Zara hasn't been very hospitable."

Leonie could not answer that, for indeed, Zara had been snappy and even cruel to her. "She just doesn't like strangers, I suppose," she commented.

Maria began to cough and toss, and Leonie said, "You must see a doctor!"

"There is only one doctor that I have any confidence in, and that's Dr. Duvall."

"Then I'll go get him at once."

"It wouldn't do any good," Maria said faintly. "He doesn't make calls any longer. He's too old."

"Let me go to him, please."

Maria hesitated, but she felt terrible. "All right. Have Julius take you. He knows where the doctor's office is. It's all foolishness."

"No, it's not. I'll go down right away."

"Ask Zara if she will come in."

"Yes, I'll do that. I'll be back as quickly as I can."

Leaving the room, Leonie went downstairs and found Zara and Lowell still at the breakfast table. "Lady Maria would like to see you, Miss Zara," she said.

"Is she all right?" Lowell asked with something like alarm.

"I don't think she is. I'm going to get Dr. Duvall."

"Dr. Duvall? He's older than dirt," Lowell said. "He won't make a house call."

"Maybe he'll make an exception. I've got to try." She left the room at once, and Lowell said, "There's your chance, Zara. Go up and pamper Maria."

"All right. I will."

Leonie was leaving, bundled up in two coats, when Mrs. Danvers appeared. "Oh, Mrs. Danvers," she said, "I'm going into town to get the doctor."

"She's worse, isn't she?"

"I don't think she's any better. She wants Dr. Duvall."

"He won't come. I can tell you that now."

"Well, I have to try. If he can't come, I'll find another one."

Mrs. Danvers stared at the young woman. "Do you know any doctors?"

"No, but Reverend Mother at the convent will. I'll ask her."

Mrs. Danvers brushed her hand across her face in a futile gesture. "She has an affection for Dr. Duvall. He saved Master Ives's life when he was just a boy."

Although Leonie was in a hurry, she stopped. Anything about her father was fascinating to her. "What was he like as a boy—Mr. Ives?"

"A good boy and a good man." Something seemed to change in Mrs. Danvers. The sternness of her face broke, and she touched her cheek and said, "I—I haven't been too kind to you, Leonie, but there are some who try to take advantage of Lady Maria. I thought you might be one of those."

"Oh, certainly not."

"No. I can see you wouldn't." Mrs. Danvers looked upstairs and whispered, "She's very lonely now. If you can bring her any cheer, I'll say amen."

Lowell watched her go from the window. Julius drove up in a buggy. The black man got out and handed Leonie in, then took his seat again and drove off at a fast clip. *I'd give anything to know what Aunt's will says now, but Maria won't tell anybody.* He thought for a moment about his future, which seemed particularly bleak. *I'd hate to have to go to work for a living or marry an ugly, rich woman for her money.* He had no illusions about himself. He was a wastrel and lived totally for his own gratification. He thought about Leonie for a moment, and smiled. *I may have to court Leonie if she's going to hold the purse strings. Shouldn't be too hard. She couldn't have had too many handsome fellows such as myself chasing after her. She wouldn't be hard to handle, either.*

He began to whistle and then walked out to the stables and mounted his favorite horse. A few minutes later he was riding out over the fields of Belle Fleur, wondering what it would be like to actually own all of it.

◡

"Right there's Dr. Duvall's home, and his office is over there in that section built on," Julius observed. He pulled up in front of the office section of the home and said, "Let me go find out if the doctor's here."

Leonie watched as the tall, black man went to the office door and knocked. Nobody came, but the door to the house opened, and a black woman came out. Leonie watched as the two spoke briefly.

Julius came back, got up in the buggy, and said, "Dr. Duvall is able to see nobody. He's a pretty sick man himself. What'll I do now, Miss?"

"Go to the convent, Julius."

〜

"I'm so glad to see you, Leonie, and you look so well." The mother superior embraced the young woman. "You're happy there at Belle Fleur?"

"Well, I guess I am."

"You don't sound quite sure."

"I don't suppose I'll be sure until it's settled."

The older woman studied Leonie's face. "How do you feel about it?"

"I feel as if that's my place. All of the pictures of my father, that is, of Ives Augustine, look like me—or should I say, I look like him. I don't know, it just feels right to me. I've talked to so many people there who actually knew my father, and some knew my mother too. It's been so strange."

"And how does Lady Augustine feel?"

"She doesn't say much. She's very ill right now, and that's why I came to town."

"Not serious, I hope."

"I think it might be. I went to see Dr. Duvall, but he couldn't go."

"Oh no. He hasn't seen any patients now for six months."

"I thought that perhaps you could recommend someone."

"It's a bad time, Leonie. The scarlet fever is everywhere, it seems. It would be very difficult to get a doctor to make a call that far away."

"Don't you know anyone?"

The mother superior thought for a moment. "One of our girls grew very ill recently. We had to do something, so I called on a young physician who had just gone into practice in New Orleans. His name is Sheffield. He came, and it's a good thing he did. He had to operate on the young woman, and he saved her life."

"I'll go to him at once," Leonie said firmly.

The older woman took a piece of paper and wrote on it, saying, "Here's his address. Remember, I don't know much about him except that he helped us out a great deal."

"Thank you, Reverend Mother. I'll go at once."

Chapter twelve

A cold wind brushed across Leonie's face. October had brought the coldest temperatures she could remember. She was sure that in days to come, people would talk about the winter of '33 as one of the bitterest that they ever experienced. "There's a blanket in the back if you need to wrap up more, Miss Leonie."

"No, thank you, Julius." Leonie smiled. "Actually the cold feels kind of good after the hot summer we had."

"Yes, it does. The good Lord sends us hot summers and cold winters, so we won't get bored."

Leonie laughed. "You always think of something to say about the Lord, don't you, Julius?"

"I guess I do, Miss." Julius smiled. The sun lighted his dark face, and his hands looked huge as they held the lines guiding the horses. "The Lord is about all there is in my life. You know, I just live to praise the Lord."

Curious about that statement, Leonie sat quietly for a while. "How do you praise the Lord, Julius?"

"Why, Miss, you know how to do that. You're a Christian."

"I know, but when I hear you talk about praising the Lord, I feel as if there's something I'm not doing."

"Well, you read the Psalms."

"Of course I have many times, but that doesn't seem to help much."

"Well, let me ask you this. Do you remember the time when David brought the ark back to Jerusalem after it had been in the camp of the enemy for a long time?"

"Yes. I remember that."

"Do you remember what David did?"

Leonie thought. "I can't really remember. It's been a long time."

"The Bible says that David danced before the Lord with all his might. Ain't that somethin' now? Dancing with all his might! I sure would like to have seen old David do that!"

"We don't having anything like that in our services, I'm afraid. If anyone did it, he or she probably would be considered crazy."

"Well, I don't think they'd be crazy. If David did it, it must be all right. He was the man after God's own heart. But just think about the Psalms, Miss. Can't you just hear David when he shouted, 'The King shall joy in thy strength, O LORD; and in thy salvation how greatly shall he rejoice!' Can't you just hear him shoutin' like that? That's in Psalm 21. Psalm 33 says, 'Praise the LORD with harp. Sing unto him with a psaltery and an instrument of ten strings. Sing unto him a new song; play skillfully with a loud noise.' Ain't that fine, Miss? With a *loud* noise. That's the way I like to praise the Lord."

"But what do you say?"

"Why, I say what the Bible says: 'Praise the Lord. Glory to God in the highest. Blessed be the Lord, O my soul.' I just tell God how good He is and how much I love Him."

Leonie sat quietly listening to Julius, whose face shone with excitement. She felt a desire growing in her to be as close to God as he was.

"You'll have to come to our church sometime, Miss."

"Do white people ever come?"

"Not very often, but you'd sure be welcome."

"I'd like to do that, Julius."

"You come to my church, and then someday I'll get to come to yours."

Leonie could not help thinking, *He wouldn't get much in the way of dancing and loud shouting and singing at Mass.*

"There it is, Miss. That's the address written down on the paper. Sure is sorry, ain't it?"

Indeed, the section of town that Julius had brought her to was pathetic. The houses were leaning on each other so they almost appeared to be holding each other up. The yards were filled with trash and litter. Here and there a group of children tried to play but seemed almost too feeble to do it.

"This is awful!"

"It's pretty bad, but that's where the doctor's office is. Right there."

Stopping the horses, Julius got down and walked around. He reached up, and her small hand was lost in his. "Reckon I'd better go in with you?"

"No, I don't think I'll be long, Julius. All I need to do is ask the doctor if he'll come to Belle Fleur."

"He must not be a very successful doctor if this is his office," Julius muttered.

Leonie felt somewhat the same, but he was a doctor after all. She looked at the paper again. "Dr. Ransom Sheffield," she whispered aloud, then she went up to the door and hesitated. Taking a deep breath, she stepped inside. The warm air struck her, for a stove was burning at the far end of the room. Chairs lined the walls, and she saw at a glance half a dozen patients waiting—all poor people. She waited for a nurse or a receptionist, but finally an old man looked up at her and nodded. "You have to take your turn, Miss. The doctor will see you then."

"Thank you." Leonie stepped outside to invite Julius to come in from the wind. Then she took her seat and wondered how long she would have to wait. The room itself was bare except for a worn carpet, and there were several pictures on the wall. One of them was of two children about to fall through a dangerous hole in a bridge, but a bright angel above was reaching down to save them. Leonie smiled briefly and thought how much the angel looked like her earliest concepts of angels, bright and strong and powerful-looking.

After about twenty minutes, an older woman came out of the inner office, and a man got up stiffly and walked in to take her place without being told.

The door let in the icy breeze when the patient left, and a woman with three small children shook her head. "It's so cold out there," she whispered.

"Yes, it is," Leonie said. She looked at the woman more closely and saw the pinch of hunger on her face. She was a thin woman, not old, but worn by work and sickness apparently. One of the children was able to walk, but the other two were infants. The woman was trying to hold both of them, and Leonie said, "Let me help you." She got up, went over, and said, "I can hold this fellow right here."

"He's not very clean."

"That's all right." Leonie smiled. She took the baby and stood for a while, rocking him in her arms. The baby started to cry, but when she whispered to him, he opened his eyes and stared at her owlishly. She walked around the floor singing under her breath, and finally she went over to the mother and said, "He's a beautiful baby."

"Thank you."

"Is he sick?"

"No. That's Timmy. George here is sick." She nodded toward the infant she held in her arms. "And Leah there, she's getting whatever he has."

"I'm sure the doctor will be able to help."

"I hope so."

"Have you seen Dr. Sheffield before?"

"No, I haven't. Have you?"

"No. I've never met him."

The woman was staring at her. "You don't look like you belong here."

Leonie looked up from the infant and said, "What do you mean?"

"I mean nobody but poor people come here. I came because my neighbor told me that Dr. Sheffield would treat people that didn't have any money. I hope it's true."

"It's true enough," said a tall, skinny man who was leaning back with his head against the wall, his eyes shut. He had a deep bass voice that didn't seem to go with his emaciated body. "He ain't a society doctor."

"Why, I never heard of a doctor like that," Leonie said.

"Neither did I, but I hope it's true. I hate it when my children are sick."

Leonie held the baby until finally the room cleared out. The women and her three children were the last ones. As the tall, skinny man left with a bottle of medicine clasped in his hand, he said, "You can go in now."

The young woman struggled to her feet. "I'll take Timmy now."

"Oh, let me go in with you. I can hold him."

"That would be kind."

"My name is Helen Finch."

"I'm Leonie Dousett."

The two women entered the inner office, which was brightly lit with kerosene lamps. A tall man in a white jacket had his back to them, arranging a series of bottles on the shelf. He turned and smiled. "Well, ladies, what do we have here? I'm Dr. Sheffield."

"I'm Helen Finch, Doctor. My children. They're sick."

"Well, let's see what we can do about that. All of them?"

"Not this one but the other two are."

As the doctor came over and plucked the infant from Helen's arms, Leonie took a good look at him. He was tall and lanky with coarse, black hair that needed trimming. He had blue eyes widely spaced, and he was rather a homely man, not at all handsome. Still, there was a strength in his face, and his broad lips turned up at the corners in a smile. "Well, let's see what's going on here, young fellow."

For the next twenty minutes Dr. Sheffield examined all three of the children and finally turned to the mother. "Mrs. Finch, I don't think there's anything to worry about. There's a mild flu bug going around, but it doesn't seem to be serious."

"I thought—I thought it might be scarlet fever."

"No. I can tell you it's not that. I'm going to give you some medicine, and I want you to be sure that they get plenty to eat and stay warm. Keep them in for a few days."

Leonie saw the woman's face change when the doctor said to feed the children well. When Dr. Sheffield turned to fill a bottle with brown fluid, she reached into her reticule and pulled out a couple of coins. "Here," she whispered, "buy something good for the children to eat."

Helen Finch's eyes misted over. "I would like to be proud, but I'll take it for the children's sake. God bless you."

Dr. Sheffield overheard the exchange. He turned and handed the bottle to Helen Finch, saying, "There. A teaspoonful of this three times a day for all of them. Come back and see me if they don't get better."

"I don't have any money, Doctor."

"Well, in that case you'll have to pay me in something besides money."

Confusion swept across the woman's face. "What do you mean?"

"Why don't you just pray for me? I need it."

"I'll do that, Doctor. God knows I will, and thank you." The woman left bearing two children, with the third hanging onto her skirts.

Dr. Sheffield looked at Leonie with surprise. "Aren't you going with her?"

"No. I don't really know her."

"Why, I thought you two were together."

"No. My name is Leonie Dousett, Doctor. I live at Belle Fleur. That's a plantation about two hours' drive from here. Lady Maria Augustine is very ill, and she needs to see a doctor."

"Doesn't she have a physician?"

"Well, Dr. Duvall was her doctor, but he's not making calls anymore."

"No, I understand he's retired. Well, I'm sorry to tell you that I don't have any way to get there."

"Oh, I have a carriage outside. We will take you and bring you back if you'll just come."

Ransom Sheffield studied the young woman. "Are you related to Lady Augustine?"

Leonie could not speak for a moment. "It's—it's a little bit complicated, Doctor."

"It is? I think it'd be simple enough. But we can talk about it on the way. Let me put a notice on the door and then get my coat and my gear and my bag, and we'll be on our way."

Leonie waited as the doctor began to stock his bag, but even as he did, she heard a door slam.

"Another patient. You'll have to wait, I'm afraid," Dr. Sheffield said.

"That's all right, doctor."

Dr. Sheffield stepped to the door and opened it and exclaimed, "Man, what happened to you?"

Leonie stood back as a man came through the door. He had blood all over the shirt he wore and was holding his neck and his side. "I got cut up in a fight."

"Here. Lie down here, man. You're losing blood fast. When did this happen?"

"About—half hour," the man said and then collapsed.

Ransom Sheffield turned quickly. "Miss Dousett, is it?"

"Yes."

"I need your help. Can you hold this cloth right here on his neck? He's bleeding from the artery there. He'll die if it's not stopped."

Instantly Leonie moved forward and held her hand firmly on the wound. It was spurting so that it got on the front of her dress and the outer lapels of her coat, but that did not seem to matter. She watched as Dr. Sheffield cut the man's shirt open with scissors and gasped when she saw the terrible cut.

"This is going to be tricky. Can you hold on there?"

"Yes, Doctor."

"You won't be sick and faint?"

"I don't think so."

"Good girl."

Later, Leonie did not remember too much about the rest of her visit with Dr. Sheffield. She had never seen a doctor in action in such a case, but she watched as he sewed up wounds, and by the time he was through, both of them were covered with blood.

"There. I think he'll live, but he's lost a lot of blood."

"What will you do with him?"

"We'll have to take him to the hospital. That is, unless I stay with him."

"We can use our carriage. I'll go get the servant in the waiting room. He's very strong. I think he can carry the man."

Julius walked in at once at Leonie's urgent call. "What happened to you, Miss? You're all bloody!"

"I helped care for that wounded man who walked in."

"I seen him go in holdin' himself. Is he dead?"

"No, but we've got to take him to the hospital. Can you pick him up?"

"I expect I can."

Indeed, picking up the man was easy for Julius; he was a powerful individual. He put the man in the back seat, and then the three of them got in the front. Julius drove quickly to the hospital following Dr. Sheffield's instructions.

"I expect I'll have to go back and change clothes before we go tend Lady Augustine," he said. Dr Sheffield was examining Leonie carefully. "Most women would have panicked seeing a thing like that. Have you had any experience with nursing?"

"Just with girls. Never with wounds like that. I don't see how you did it, Doctor."

Sheffield grinned, which made him seem much younger. "That's what doctors do, Miss Dousett."

Chapter thirteen

The sun was going down rapidly as Julius drove the horses at a fast clip. He had mentioned that he wanted to get home before dark, and indeed, this was Leonie's wish also.

Dr. Sheffield looked more presentable since he had changed clothes, but Leonie still was wearing the bloodstained garments. She looked down and saw that the blood had dried into a brownish color and wondered at herself for functioning as she had.

Sheffield was watching the young woman. He asked, "Have you been living with Lady Augustine long?"

"Oh no. Only a few weeks." She struggled to find a way to explain her position and then said, "It really is complicated, Doctor."

"Don't tell me if you don't want to, Miss Dousett."

"I don't mind. Well, you should know that I grew up in the Ursuline Convent. I just left there two years ago. Since then I've been working as a seamstress."

"Do you have a family?"

"Well, that's the complication. I was left as an infant, only a few days old, at the convent. Only recently have I learned that I may be related to the Augustine family. As a matter of fact, Lady Augustine may be my grandmother."

"Sounds like a mystery."

"It is rather." She said, "What about you, Doctor? Are you from Louisiana?"

Sheffield laughed. "Can't you tell from the way I talk I'm not a Louisiana man? No, I was born in Kentucky. Lived there all my life until recently."

"Is your family here?"

"My family? Oh, I'm not married."

"I meant your parents."

"They're gone now. As a matter of fact, I'm here because of my mother."

"Was she from here?"

"Oh no. She was born in Kentucky. We were from the mountain country. Very poor. My father died when I was only eight. Mother had a rough time raising the four children. She had already lost three in miscarriages. It was hard living, Miss Dousett, very hard."

Leonie turned to study the doctor's profile. He was not a handsome man, but somehow he had a winsome quality that pleased her. "How did your mother cause you to be here?"

"She grew ill, and none of the doctors would come and look at her. I was just a boy, barefooted almost. I was only seventeen. I went to every doctor that I could find, and none of them would come without pay, so she died a slow, painful death."

"How terrible!"

"Yes, it was. So I determined I'd do something about it." He turned to face her, and she saw a warm light in his brown eyes. "I fought my way through school, working nights and going to school in the daytime. Finally I finished my medical training. I had a chance to go into practice in St. Louis, but I'd always said I'd try to do something for poor people if I became a doctor. So that's what I'm doing here."

"How long have you been here?"

"Not long. Just about six months. I know that's a pretty poor place, where I am now. Someday it will be different. I'll have a clinic.

Maybe there'll be a whole hospital that will take poor people when nobody else will."

"What a fine thing to do!"

Her compliment seemed to make Sheffield uncomfortable. He laughed shortly, "Well, I'm not nearly as noble as I make myself sound."

"I think you are."

The two talked all the way to Belle Fleur, and when Julius drew up in front of the house, Dr. Sheffield jumped out and helped Leonie down. "You're going to scare them, covered with blood like that."

"Maybe no one will see me," Leonie said hopefully. She turned and said, "Thank you, Julius. I appreciate it."

"Anytime, Miss."

Leonie led the doctor up the stairs to the porch. Before they reached the front door, it opened. Mrs. Danvers took one look at Leonie and exclaimed, "What in the world happened to you?"

"It's not my blood, Mrs. Danvers. I was helping Dr. Sheffield with a patient. It is the patient's blood. How is Lady Maria?"

"She's no better, I think."

"This is Mrs. Danvers, our housekeeper. She'll take you up to Lady Augustine while I go change."

"I'm not sure she'll see you, Doctor. She doesn't like changes."

Sheffield grinned. "We all have to change, Mrs. Danvers."

As quickly as she could, Leonie changed her clothes and hurried to Lady Maria's room. She stepped inside and saw Mrs. Danvers standing back in the shadows, looking anxious. Sheffield was standing beside the sick woman. He turned and smiled at Leonie. "You look a little better now."

"What's wrong with her?" Lady Maria said, her voice weak.

"Why, nothing, ma'am," Sheffield said easily. "She helped me with a patient and it got a little messy. She's quite a nurse."

"You're too young to be a doctor."

"Well, there's a cure for that." Sheffield smiled, reached down, and took her hand. He held her wrist, taking her pulse, and said, "I'll get older soon enough. Time always takes care of that."

"What's wrong with me?"

"Why, you have scarlet fever."

"Oh no!" Leonie said. Gloom filled her face. "I thought it was something less."

"You two need to get out of here. It's very contagious."

"I had to nurse the girls at the convent when they had it, and I never caught it."

"That doesn't mean you can't catch it this time."

"Mrs. Danvers, you leave now." Lady Maria's voice was weak. "We'll need you to keep the house running."

"I need to help you."

"No. You leave now. Mind what I say."

As soon as Mrs. Danvers left, Dr. Sheffield said, "You will need a great deal of care, constant almost. There's some danger of this disease spreading. I'd like to keep it confined to this room."

"I can do that, Dr. Sheffield," Leonie insisted.

Lady Augustine lay still. Her fever was high, and her face was crimson. She whispered to Leonie, "I don't want you to be exposed."

"I'm already exposed. Let's not argue about it."

"Really, Lady Augustine, I think it might be wise to let the young lady help. I'll stay until you're out of danger."

"You seem awfully young. Are you a good doctor?"

"Why, I'm the best doctor in this room." He leaned over and put his hand on her forehead. "Would you mind," he asked, "if I pray for you?"

Lady Augustine's eyes opened wide. "I suppose it would be all right."

"I always like to pray for my patients. God needs to be involved in any sickness."

Leonie's eyes met those of Lady Augustine, and the two women were speechless. Sheffield began to pray, and it was a simple enough prayer, asking that he be given knowledge and skill but most of all that the great Physician would take over the case. When he said amen, Lady Augustine said, "You are a strange doctor."

"You're probably right."

"Come with me, Doctor," Leonie said. "There's a room right next to this one. You can stay there. Julius can go get some of your clothes to bring here."

"Very well."

Mrs. Danvers had come to help Leonie fix the room for the doctor. The housekeeper commented, "I'm surprised that Lady Augustine would let him treat her."

"He took her by surprise." She related how the doctor had asked if he could pray for her, and laughed. "It caught Lady Augustine off guard. She said a doctor never did that before."

"I hope he knows what he's doing. He's so young."

"I think he does, Mrs. Danvers."

"This is Dr. Ransom Sheffield," Leonie said as the two of them entered the dining room. "He's been kind enough to come and treat Lady Augustine." She introduced the other members of the family and saw their curiosity.

"Are you new to New Orleans, Doctor?" Lowell asked.

"Very new, Mr. Augustine."

"How long have you been in practice?" Hugh Langley asked.

"The ink's practically dry on my certificate. Here, let me help you, Miss Dousett."

Leonie was surprised when he pulled her chair back. She took her seat, and when he seated himself next to her, she said, "Dr. Sheffield's going to open a clinic for the poor people of New Orleans. Isn't that wonderful?"

"You must be independently wealthy." Lowell grinned. "Most doctors are more interested in making money."

"I suppose I'll do some of that too. I may have this young lady as my nurse. She's quite handy."

"How do you mean that?" Zara demanded, her eyes on Leonie.

"Why, this man came in just as we were leaving, cut to shreds. She helped me patch him up. Didn't blink an eye."

Lowell stared at Leonie. "I don't think I could do that."

"Of course you couldn't," Zara said. She was watching the doctor carefully. "How is my aunt?"

"She's not at all well. I'm going to keep her confined to her room. No one should go in but Miss Dousett and myself."

"Should we get another doctor?" Zara said.

"If you would like. Two doctors are probably better than one."

"Why, that's ridiculous, Zara," Lowell said. "We have a doctor here."

Nora began serving dinner. It was an excellent meal consisting of crawfish casserole and crawfish bisque.

Lowell seemed very interested in Dr. Sheffield and peppered him with questions.

Sheffield answered easily and seemed to be studying the two cousins. Leonie was fairly sure he was trying to figure out the family situation.

After the meal was over, the doctor excused himself, and Leonie went back with him to check on the patient. As soon as they were gone, Lowell said, "It's a good thing that Leonie is here. You wouldn't want to be in a sick room with scarlet fever, would you, sister dear?"

"No more than you."

"I've been wondering about the will. You haven't seen it, have you?"

"No. She's very secretive about things like that."

The two sat talking in whispers, and finally Lowell said, "You know, it might be better if she didn't make it through this illness. I'm pretty sure she hasn't changed her will yet. I'd still be the heir."

The two stared at each other and Lowell laughed. "I didn't mean that, of course." The two got up and left the room, but Zara pondered what her brother had said.

⌒

"Well, I think the crisis has come."

Leonie had been sitting beside Lady Maria. She looked up quickly at Dr. Sheffield. "What do you mean?"

"I mean if she can make it through tonight, I think she'll be all right."

"She has to live. She just has to." She looked over at the woman whose lips were parched, although Leonie had kept them as moist as she could.

"Do you ever pray for your grandmother?"

Leonie was confused by the word "grandmother." "Yes, I do pray for her."

"You know the Bible says that it's better for two to pray than for one."

"I didn't know that."

"Yes. One of my favorite verses. 'If any two of you shall agree on anything, it shall be done.' Jesus said that Himself."

"I don't know that verse."

"It's given me a lot of comfort. I always like to find somebody to pray with me, to stand with me before God, so why don't you and I take our stand together?"

"All right," Leonie said rather breathlessly.

"Here. Give me your hand."

Leonie tentatively reached out, and he took her hand. "Now you put your hand on your grandmother's shoulder and I'll do the same on her head. The Bible says, 'Lay hands on the sick and they shall recover,' and that's what we're going to do—to pray that God will work." He bowed his head and said, "Lord, we remind You of Your promise, for You cannot lie. And You have said that if we will agree, You will do what we ask. So Miss Dousett and I agree that we want to see this woman made strong and well again. In the name of Jesus, we ask for this healing."

Leonie trembled. There was a unique power in the man's prayer. His hand was strong, and when finally he released hers, she looked up and said, "I feel the Spirit of the Lord here in a strange way."

"Nothing strange about it." The doctor's face changed, and he said, "God is going to do something in Lady Augustine's life." He added, "And I think in your life."

Leonie looked up at him. "I'm thankful that you came, Dr. Sheffield."

"Do you believe God's promise?"

"Yes, I do."

"Good. The two of us make a good team, don't we?"

Leonie suddenly felt warm and confident about the future. She looked at the face of the woman that now she was certain was her grandmother. The fever seemed to have gone down, and she turned and said, "Yes, Dr. Sheffield, we make a good team."

PART THREE
· NOVEMBER 1833–MARCH 1834 ·

Chapter fourteen

One of the heavy logs settled in the fireplace, making a hissing sound and sending a shower of golden sparks up the chimney. Lowell Augustine had been reading a book but looked up and watched the display for a moment. He got up and walked over to the fireplace. He picked up one of the logs, put it on top of the glowing embers, and then used the heavy poker to shove the log until more sparks flew upward. The tiny flames began to lick around the fresh fuel, and for a time Lowell stood soaking up the heat. It had been a cold November for New Orleans, and Lowell made a note to remind Julius to bring in more wood for the fireplaces.

From somewhere deep in the house, he could hear voices. Punctuating this noise, the grandfather clock began striking a slow, sonorous tune. Replacing the poker, Lowell walked over to the window and looked up at the leaden gray sky. The sun had been hiding itself for several days behind heavy gray clouds, and now the whole earth seemed cloaked in funeral garb.

Lowell's gaze fell upon a large red squirrel that scampered down the tree and dug industriously in the soil, then sat up. He folded his paws and for a moment looked like a priest engaged in his prayers.

"I wonder if squirrels ever pray," Lowell murmured, and then the foolishness of his thoughts made him grin. "I'm going crazy in this house. I've got to get away." He turned and walked around the room, looking at the covers of the books. His Uncle Ancel had been a collector of fine first editions, and Lowell had found great pleasure in going through the library. He remembered suddenly how grim life had been as he and Zara grew up. Their father had been a failure in business, and they had moved from one wretched house to another as he tried to eke out a living at various occupations. None of them had succeeded, and when he had finally died, Ancel Augustine had taken his family in.

Reaching up, Lowell took down a book and ran his hands over the fine leather cover, memories flooding him about the days that he, his sister, and his mother had first come to Belle Fleur. *It was like going to heaven,* he thought. *Plenty of food, warm rooms, no worry about how to pay the bills.*

He thought briefly of his mother, who had died only two years after they had moved to Belle Fleur. He still missed her, for he'd had a genuine affection for her. He replaced the book slowly, stood irresolutely before the books, and considered his future. He had tried several occupations. None of them seeming to suit, and he faced up to the fact that he was not by nature a driven individual as his Uncle Ancel had been. He loved the life of high society; parties, balls, and social events of all kinds were his delight. Zara was the same. Both of them had grown accustomed to an exorbitant style of living. Their Aunt Maria had been generous, far more so than Uncle Ancel had been. Since Ancel's death, she had given them everything they wanted, although at times she also delivered a lecture on wastefulness.

Footsteps coming down the broad hallway interrupted Lowell's thoughts, and he turned to see Julian Harcourt enter. "Hello, Julian," he said. "Foul weather, isn't it?"

"Yes, it is." Julian walked over and turned his back to the fireplace, spreading his hands out behind him. "I wouldn't be surprised if it snowed."

"Not in New Orleans. It's not our style." Lowell studied Julian carefully. At the age of twenty-seven, Harcourt was a fine-looking man, not more than average height and very trim. He had fair hair, bright blue eyes, and classic features. His family had a long and illustrious history, but Harcourt's grandfather had started dismantling the family fortune with his dissolute habits, especially gambling. Harcourt's father, Sir Ralph Harcourt, had done the same. He had finally killed himself rather than face poverty, leaving Julian, his mother, and two sisters practically penniless.

"Are you and Zara going out?"

"Yes. The McKays are having a ball. You're not going?"

"I think I will. Nothing to do around here particularly."

"How is Lady Maria?"

"She's getting better. That doctor seems to know his business."

"I never heard of him."

"No. He's new in practice here." The two men talked aimlessly for a while, and then Lowell said, "Maria's gotten very close to Leonie."

Harcourt shot a glance at his friend. "That's only natural, I suppose. She's taken care of her during this sickness."

"I'm not sure it's a good thing, Julian."

"What do you mean?"

"Oh, come now. You must know that we're on mighty shaky ground here. If that girl is really Ives's daughter, my aunt will make her the main heir of all of this."

"Well, there's nothing we can do about it, I suppose," Harcourt said gloomily.

"I suppose not. It scares me a little bit."

"What does?"

"The idea of having to go to work. I'm not fit for anything."

"Well, I'm not either, I suppose. Blast it!" Julian's countenance darkened, and he added vehemently, "All would have been fine if she hadn't shown up! Zara and I would have gotten married. The money would have eventually come to us. We could have gone on just like we have been."

"You'd better talk to Zara about it."

"What can she do?"

"She can be nicer to our aunt, for one thing. It's past time to use a little caution."

"All right. I'll try."

"I'm going up to get dressed. I'll ride with you, if it's all right, to the ball."

"That'll be fine."

⌒

Zara entered and twirled around. "How do you like my new dress?"

The dress was made out of a dark purple silk with a low neckline, tight-fitting bodice, and long sleeves. The neckline and the sleeves were trimmed with black lace with a row of tiny black bows running down the middle of the bodice to the cinched-in waist. A black silk sash was tied around to the back in a bow, and the full skirt featured black embroidered flowers with three rows of the same black lace along the bottom edge. She wore a black lace wrap around her shoulders and black shiny shoes peeked out from under the long skirt.

"You look beautiful as always, Zara." Julian went over and put his arms around Zara. She embraced him, received his kiss, and then stepped back, putting her hands on his chest. "Don't muss me up now. It took me two hours to get this way." She turned back to the mirror.

"Well, it was worth it. Oh, by the way, Lowell's going with us to the ball."

"I guess that's all right. It ought to be a fancy affair. The family has enough money to do it."

"I've got to talk to you, Zara."

Surprised at Julian's tone, Zara turned and studied him. "What is it?"

"It's about us, I suppose. Things are not going well."

"What do you mean, 'not going well'? You don't mean that girl?"

"Yes, I do. Lowell said he's talked to you about her."

"Oh, he has."

"Well, you should listen to him. I might as well spell it out." Harcourt grimaced. "We're in trouble here. You know I have no money. We've been depending on the estate coming to you. I feel bad enough about that."

Zara moved closer and looked up at him. "We've talked about that many times. When we're married, it won't be 'my money' or 'your money.' It'll just be the two of us sharing it."

"That may never happen. The old woman's getting mighty fond of Leonie."

"Well, what can I do about that, Julian?"

"You can do what Lowell says: be nicer to her."

"That girl! If only she hadn't shown up!"

"I know, but she did. And she's not going away."

Zara's face clouded. "We've got to get rid of her somehow."

Julian stared at Zara. "What do you mean by that?"

"I mean she doesn't deserve to be the heiress of Belle Fleur. Lowell and I are the family."

"Not if the courts declare her the daughter of Ives Augustine."

"There's not enough evidence for that!"

"I'm not sure about that. In any case, you be sweeter to your aunt."

Zara looked at Julian and nodded. "All right. Maybe you're right."

⌒

"My, you look like a young woman, Lady Maria."

Maria Augustine was sitting in a chair. The doctor had arrived that morning and was sitting across from her. He smiled and reached out and took her wrist. He felt the pulse, then nodded. "Running like a fine watch. I do pronounce you 'Out of danger.'"

"It's been a hard sickness," Maria murmured. "I don't remember a worse one."

"Scarlet fever's a terrible thing." Ransom shook his head. "I see sad things every day. Whole families decimated. There's not really much we can do."

"You did a great deal for me, Dr. Sheffield."

Ransom smiled. "You're a tough patient. Always questioning the doctor."

The two were sitting in Lady Maria's bedroom. Faint sunshine had broken through the clouds and threw its beams on the fine carpet. It also touched Maria's face, and Sheffield noticed that her color was much better. "I'm going to leave instructions for a special diet for you. I'm going to put some meat on your bones."

"Just give it to Leonie. She'll see to it." She looked at the doctor curiously. He had made three visits to Belle Fleur, staying overnight, and had been a comfort to Maria. She had actually been fearful for her life, but Ransom Sheffield's cheerful manner, his care, had been a comfort to her. She had watched him carefully, and being a good student of human nature, she knew that there was a chance he was just after a wealthy patient. She had, however, also listened as Sheffield had talked to Leonie about the work he did with the poor people of New Orleans, and now as she considered him, she asked, "What about your practice? You seem to be rather able to leave it."

"Well, my patients can't go anywhere else." Ransom grinned. He had a cheerful, open expression, and there was a winsomeness in the man that Maria liked. He was not handsome, but even the roughness of his features had a certain attraction. He had none of the classic good looks of Lowell or Julian Harcourt, but he had a strength that Maria admired.

"Couldn't you take over some of Dr. Duvall's practice?"

"He talked to me about it, but I couldn't see my way clear to doing that."

"Why not, Doctor?"

"Because I have another dream."

"What sort of dream?"

"I don't talk about it too much. I've told Leonie about it. My mother died because she couldn't get the proper medical care, and somehow God put a desire in my heart to become a doctor to help those who couldn't get help anywhere else. So, that's what I want to do."

"Couldn't you do that and carry on Dr. Duvall's practice at the same time?"

"I don't think so. I think God's calling me full-time to serve Him in this way."

Maria considered the young man thoughtfully, then said, "Leonie told me that your facilities are very limited."

"Oh yes, they are. Just a couple of rooms in a run-down house. It gets packed like sardines in a can sometimes, but I've done something now that'll make it better."

"And what is that?"

"Well, I've rented an old warehouse. It's right in the heart of one of the worst slums in New Orleans. It's a mess," he admitted ruefully. Then he laughed and said, "I've been working nights trying to make it presentable, but just hauling off the trash is pretty tiresome."

"And you're going to make some sort of a hospital out of it?"

"Well," Ransom answered, "I think that's a bit too ambitious. But I could make a clinic out of it. There are some rooms in the back that could be made into living quarters. I could cut expenses that way. But it's going to take a while just to get it prepared. It needs a lot of work."

Maria looked down at her hands and thought for a moment. Then she looked up and said, "I have an idea—something that might help with your work."

"And what's that, Lady Maria?"

"It's the middle of the winter, and there's nothing much for the slaves to do until spring planting. Why couldn't I send them down to help you with this renovation work?"

A pleased light came into Ransom Sheffield's eyes. "Why, that would be of immense help!"

"I'll do it then. I'll send Julius down the first thing in the morning, and you'll have all the help you want. Also, if you need supplies, I'll write a note to the supplier who furnishes that sort of thing for us here at Belle Fleur."

"Aren't you afraid I'll take advantage of you?" Ransom smiled.

"No, I'm not."

Ransom blinked. "Well, I'm glad you feel that way, Lady Maria, and I'll keep a strict account." He got up and began to pace around. "This is going to be great!" he said enthusiastically. "I can first—" He broke off when Leonie came into the room bearing a tray covered with a white cloth. "Leonie, guess what?"

"I guess it's time for Lady Maria's lunch."

"Yes. Here, let me help you." He walked over, picked up a small table, and put it in front of Lady Maria. Leonie put the tray down, uncovered it, and said, "I made you some candied sweet potatoes. I know you love that."

"Oh, Leonie, that smells so good!" Maria said. "And what's this?"

"Mushroom and eggs a la ritz. I learned to cook it for my employer when I was a seamstress."

Maria tasted it and said, "This is delicious. You're a fine cook."

"You eat, Lady Maria, and let me tell Leonie the good news." He turned to her, his face was alight with pleasure. "Lady Maria is going to send some of her slaves down with Julius to help with my new project. I haven't told you about it."

"What is it, Doctor?"

"I've rented a big warehouse, and I'm going to turn it into a clinic. There's nothing like it in New Orleans, and I've been working nights trying to get it ready. It was such slow work, it seemed almost hopeless." He turned to Lady Maria, reached over, and put his hand on her shoulder. "Now we're partners. She's also going to pay for some paint and some materials to put in walls for private rooms."

"Oh, Lady Maria!" Leonie exclaimed. She was pleased to see the color in her grandmother's cheeks and said, "I think it's wonderful to help like that. And I want to help, too, if you agree."

"Certainly," Lady Maria said.

"Come anytime, Leonie. I think it'll be pretty confusing for a while, trying to renovate that warehouse and see patients at the same time. I'm going to see if I can interest some of the other doctors in coming in and seeing a few patients."

"I'll drive in with Julius tomorrow," Leonie said. She went over and took her grandmother's hand and held it. "I'm so glad that you're willing to do this. It's very kind of you."

Lady Maria was not accustomed to being praised for her virtues. She flushed and said, "It's nothing, really."

"That's not so, Lady Maria," Leonie whispered. "It's something."

⌒

The work at the clinic had gone well. For three days Julius oversaw a dozen of the slaves there, and Leonie had made herself responsible for feeding them well. They had enjoyed the work, apparently, and the good food that she put before them.

The warehouse was a low-ceilinged, rambling sort of place, but Julius, who was a gifted carpenter, had thrown up extra walls, and some of the women had been painting. They had begun to sing during their work. Some of the songs were ones they sang while they were working in the fields. Once Ransom had come to stand beside Leonie, and the two of them had listened. "They sound happy, don't they?" Leonie said quietly.

"Yes, they do. They don't have much color and light in their lives. Slavery's a bad thing. It'll have to go one day. God willing, it will be soon."

"I don't see how that could happen."

"It's in God's hands, but the abolition movement in the North is very strong."

"Come along. I want to show you your office. We're all through with it." Leonie led the way, and when they stepped into one of the larger rooms, Ransom said, "Why, it's beautiful!"

"No, but it'll be handy. Notice you get lots of light from the sun through those windows."

One side of the large room was banked with three windows that admitted sunlight freely. The walls had been whitewashed, and Leonie had managed to scrounge some furniture from the attic back at Belle Fleur. Medical equipment was at a minimum, but at least there were chairs, tables, and cabinets to keep a spare store of medicine and equipment.

"Why, this is really fine! You've done wonders, Leonie," Ransom said, walking around the room, his eyes lighted with pleasure.

Leonie smiled. "I've enjoyed it, and Lady Maria is going to come and see it as soon as she gets better."

"I couldn't have done it without her and without you."

The two were talking about the improvements that still had to be made when suddenly a voice rang out. "Hello, Leonie!"

Leonie turned to see Jean Larue come through the door. She smiled. She had seen little of him since she had worked for Madam Honore, but he had visited the clinic a couple of times and met the doctor. He went to her and took her hand, leaned over, and kissed it. "There you are, my little seamstress."

"Not a seamstress anymore. She's my chief helper," Sheffield said.

Larue said quickly, "Doctor, I brought you a patient. I don't know what to do with her."

"What's wrong with her, Jean?" Sheffield asked.

"She has been badly beaten."

"Beaten! Who beat her?" Leonie asked, her face indignant.

"She worked for a man over in the Quarter. He misused her and beat her. I'll fix him, though. You wait and see."

"Where is she?"

"In my cab. Can I bring her in?"

"Of course. Bring her right in here."

Jean disappeared, and Leonie began to make a place for the new patient. "It's sad, isn't it, when things like this happen?"

"Yes, it is. I think Jean's mad enough to shoot somebody."

They waited until Jean came in, half supporting a young woman.

"Here. Put her right here in this chair."

"You take care of her, Doctor. I'll be back to see you later on, Leonie."

"Thank you," the injured young girl whispered to Jean. She was no more than seventeen or eighteen, Leonie figured. She had a beautiful, light-olive complexion. Her eyes were swollen nearly shut, her lips were cut, and there was a large bruise on the side of her cheek. She cried out when the doctor bent over and touched her.

"Here, why don't you lie down, Miss? What's your name?"

"My name is Lolean Delaughter."

"Would you stay with me, Miss Dousett? I may need some help."

Leonie said, "Yes, of course, Doctor." As Ransom began to examine the girl, she was shocked at the severe beating the girl had taken. She could barely move, and Sheffield murmured, "I think you've got some cracked ribs there. Nothing much I can do about that except try to make you comfortable, but we can take care of some of these cuts on your face."

After treating the girl, he asked, "Do you have a home to go to?"

"No. I have noplace."

"Well," Ransom said, "we've got a room practically ready, and I've got a cot we can put in there. You can stay there until you find someplace better."

"Thank you, Monsieur," the girl whispered. She lifted her eyes to the doctor and said, "I have no money."

"No money necessary. Why don't you take care of this young lady, Miss Dousett?"

"Come along, Lolean. Here. Let me help you." She assisted the young girl, who could barely walk, to one of the rooms and saw that she had all she needed. "I'll bring you something to help you sleep."

"Thank you, Mademoiselle."

Blaise Mignon appeared unexpectedly the next day. He greeted Leonie with a smile and said, "Maybe we can talk."

"Of course. Come over here where it's quiet."

Blaise followed her and looked around at the slaves who were banging away, putting up a new wall. "What is all this?" He listened as she told him the plan to make a clinic for poor people, and he said, "That doctor, he must be a nice fellow."

"He's a fine man."

Blaise said, "How are you getting along with your grand-mother?"

"She was very sick, but she's better now. Dr. Sheffield treated her, and she's paying for having this clinic refurbished."

"Has she said anything about you?"

"You mean has she admitted I'm her granddaughter? We haven't talked about it."

Suddenly a loud voice—an angry voice—sounded.

"Who's that yelling?" Blaise asked, looking toward the door.

"I don't know." Leonie quickly moved outside and saw a very large man towering over Sheffield. He was shouting, "I've come to get that girl! My name's Carl Hackman, and she's my property!"

"She's not a slave. You don't own her," Ransom said. He was as tall as Hackman but looked thin next to him.

Hackman had a blunt face, and his eyes were small and burning with rage. "You keep out of this! I'm taking her back!"

"No, you're not. She says she won't go back with you—that you abused her."

Hackman continued to shout, and then he looked up and saw that the young girl was watching him fearfully. "You come with me," he demanded.

"No. I will never go back with you," Lolean whispered.

"Then I'll take you!"

Hackman started for the girl, but as he did, Ransom reached out and caught his arm. "You can't take her. I'll have—" He had no time to finish, for Hackman had swung a fist and caught him right over the eyebrow. Sheffield reeled backward into the wall, and at once Hackman was at him, striking fierce blows at his body and face. Sheffield tried to defend himself, but he was no match for the bruiser.

Leonie cried out, but before she could do more than that, Blaise Mignon reached down and picked up a short length of timber. Swinging it like a bat, he caught the big man on the side of the head. Hackman staggered but did not go down. As coolly as a man casting a fly with a fishing pole, Blaise took another swing even more powerfully that hit the man again in the head. Hackman collapsed, blood streaming from his head.

"We'll have him arrested," Mignon said lightly.

"Is he dead?" Leonie whispered.

"Unfortunately not. He's got a hard head." He walked over to Sheffield, who had stumbled to his feet, and said, "You must be the good doctor."

Sheffield was dazed, and Leonie went to him and said, "Come and sit down, Dr. Sheffield."

Blaise left and returned shortly with two burly policemen. They hauled Hackman to his feet, and Blaise said, "I'll be down to press charges later."

"Your poor face," Leonie whispered to Ransom. "Let me put some cool compresses on it."

Slaves had gathered around to watch, and Julius said with indignation, "If I'd been here, I could have hit him my own self!"

"Just do that the next time he comes in," Blaise said with a smile.

"Are you hurt badly?" Leonie whispered to Ransom.

Ransom Sheffield reached up and touched his bruised face.

She said, "Where are you hurting most?"

"I guess I hurt all over more than I do any particular place." He tried to smile and said, "Ouch!" He looked up at Blaise and said, "Thank you, sir."

"Anytime. Come to think of it, maybe I can make a living as a tough guy."

"You need a doctor to put you together," Leonie said to Ransom. "That eyebrow. That cut's going to take some stitches. I'll go down the street and get Dr. Roberts."

As soon as she left, Blaise said, "That's a fine young woman."

"Yes, she is. I don't believe we've met."

"I'm Blaise Mignon, an old friend of Miss Dousett."

"I hope that fellow doesn't come back."

"I don't think he will. A few days in jail may cool him off. I'll go along now. Tell Leonie I'll be back later."

"Yes, sir, and thanks for your help." As Blaise Mignon left, Sheffield got slowly to his feet. His ribs hurt, and as he went over to look in a mirror, he said, "You were ugly enough to begin with, and you're going to look like a gorilla now."

"Are you all right, Doctor?"

He turned around and saw the young Creole woman, Lolean. Concern was in her face.

"I guess we're about the same. Both of us had a beating."

She reached up and touched his face. "I am so sorry. He is a cruel man."

"He won't be back anymore. I promise you." He looked down at the young woman and smiled. "I guess we could hire a bodyguard to take care of both of us."

Tears came to her eyes, and she said, "Thank you for taking care of me."

Ransom Sheffield had a tender heart. "Why, that's what I'm here for, Lolean."

Chapter fifteen

February had passed away, taking with it the worst of the cold weather. March came in like the proverbial lamb, with warm days of sunshine and even breezes loaded with warmth from the South. The beaches of the Gulf Coast were filled with bathers, and the streets of New Orleans were packed with visitors.

Leonie had just returned from a trip into town. She greeted Lady Maria, who asked, "How was the clinic doing?"

"Dr. Sheffield looks so weary," Leonie answered, a troubled look in her eyes. "He's lost weight, and he works day and night. I'm afraid for him."

"You've grown very fond of that physician, haven't you?"

"Yes, I have. He's such a good man."

Maria sent more funds to help with the clinic and to pay for medicine for those who could not afford it.

As the weeks passed, Leonie stayed close to home, but she had little to do except take care of her duties in the house. As a result of this, she spent a great deal of time out-of-doors, wandering through the bayous. She had been confined to a city most of her life, and it began to delight her to watch the reptiles, birds, and mammals of the swamp. She became familiar with the staccato *quock* of the stubby black-crowned night heron, and she loved to watch the great space-loving egrets as they came to fish and nest in the swamps. She grew familiar with the small mammals, such as squirrels and swamp rabbits, who inhabited the solid land. The shy otter and the gregarious raccoons fed on the banks of the swamp, their diet fish, crawfish, and young amphibians. Once she saw a pair of black bears, shy creatures that usually stayed deep in the swamp. Many days she went out to roam the land whose only significant rises were natural ridges called *levees*. The cypress and tupelo gum trees were everywhere, and a green gloom in the depth of the bayous gave it a romantic image.

Flowers, even in early March, were a delight. Hibiscus, wild iris, spider lilies, and pond lilies decorated the freshwater marshes, and Leonie delighted in gathering them and taking them into the house. Sometimes a solid layer of hyacinths stretched from bank to bank on the surface of the bayou.

"You better watch yourself in that bayou, Miss Leonie," Julius warned as she began spending more time there. "There's bad things there. There's alligators that could swallow you in one bite and cottonmouths most thick as my leg." He shook his head and frowned. "It's a beautiful place, but it's full of death."

Leonie was careful, and many times she did see the monstrous leviathans looking like logs for all the world. She also was careful to stay away from anything that looked like one of the cottonmouths that pervaded the swamp.

One late afternoon, as she was walking home from her wanderings, she passed through hackberry trees and live oaks and white oaks towering seventy feet above the earth. The live oaks were not as tall, but they made up for it in breadth, stretching out their branches to make crowns a hundred feet or more across.

As she made her way back to the house, she noted that the streams were muddy, the color of milk chocolate, as if the earth had melted and begun to ooze. The broad streams were lined with the oaks, and there were enormous patches of long, yellow-spiked cane and green palmettos rearing up from the banks like oversize hands, motionless in the shade. Finally she passed out of the bayou, walking down a long, winding road that led to the plantation itself. Some of the hands were out, and as she passed, she gave them a cheerful call, and they looked up from their plows to wave back at her. She had become acquainted with most of the slaves and felt a great sorrow at the plight that most of them endured.

Finally she reached the house, and when she entered, she found Mrs. Danvers in the kitchen working with the cooks. The older woman looked up and smiled. "You've been out in that bayou again."

"Yes, I have. It's such a wonderful place."

"It ain't wonderful to me," Opal Dupre snorted. Opal was the cook, a heavy woman with green eyes and thick brown hair. She was superstitious. "I dreamed about that place once. I wouldn't go out there if you gave me the city of New Orleans."

"Oh, don't be foolish, Opal," Leonie replied with a smile. "As long as you stay away from the alligators and the snakes, it's a beautiful place. What can I do to help you?"

"You can peel these potatoes."

"All right." Leonie sat down on a high stool and began peeling. As she did, the three women talked about the plantation, and Leonie thought again how Mrs. Danvers had become far more friendly than she had dreamed could happen. The older woman had been antagonistic when she had first come, but Leonie understood that. Mrs. Danvers now was as friendly as it was in her to be. And as she peeled the potatoes, Leonie asked, "What was Mr. Ives like growing up?"

"He was a good boy but mischievous. Always pulling a practical joke," Mrs. Danvers answered. She was carefully shelling crawdads and preparing them for the pot. She smiled unexpectedly then and shook her head. "He was one for practical jokes. I had his mother paddle him more than once for some of his wild tricks."

"Tell me about them." Leonie listened as the older woman began to relate stories, and finally, when all the potatoes were done, she sighed, "I wish I could have known him."

Mrs. Danvers suddenly looked at her. "He would have been proud of you, Leonie, very proud."

Leonie's face colored as it always did at praise. "Do you think I am his daughter, Mrs. Danvers?"

Mrs. Danvers looked at her for a long moment silently, then nodded. "You are very like him. I think you have the Augustine blood."

"My grandmother never says anything."

"She's afraid of being deceived. She has been fooled many times by people, some of them in her own family."

Leonie did not ask more, for she knew that Mrs. Danvers would never go into detail. "I'm going up to see how she is." She left the kitchen, walked upstairs, and found Lady Maria sitting out on the balcony.

"It's too brisk out here for you, Lady Maria."

"No, it feels good. It'll be sultry and hot soon enough. Where have you been? I saw you coming down the road."

"Oh, I just went out to the bayou. I like it so much out there."

"You be careful. That's a dangerous place."

"I am."

"What have you heard about the clinic? Anything more?" Lady Maria asked.

"I got a letter from Dr. Sheffield this morning," she said. "The clinic is full, and he's working full-time there."

"I don't see how he does it. The people can't pay."

"He's mentioned the money you sent, and he says he's writing you, too, to thank you."

"Yes, I got his letter. He writes very well for a Kaintock. He says business is slowing somewhat now."

"Yes, so he says." Leonie hesitated, then said, "Mrs. Danvers was telling me about my father when he was a boy."

It was the first time that Leonie had had the courage to call Ives "my father." She saw Lady Maria's eyes fly wide open and expected her to protest, but she said only, "He was a good boy. What did she tell you?"

"She said when he was a boy, he played practical jokes."

Lady Maria smiled. "Yes. Even on me. Not on his father so much."

"Didn't they get along?"

"My husband was too strict with Ives. I always told him that, but he would never listen."

"That's sad. A boy should be close to his father."

"So I always thought, but they didn't have the same sort of personality. My husband was a strict man, not one given to levity, but Ives was full of fun."

"Tell me more about him."

For a time Maria described her son and his escapades. Then Leonie asked, "Did you like my mother?"

"I didn't at first, but I probably wouldn't have liked any young woman Ives chose. I was very possessive of him. I see that now."

"What was she like?"

"You've seen her picture. It's very like her. I know now that she was one of the sweetest young women I ever met. But my husband was proud, and he wouldn't listen to Ives. Ives loved her very much; he told me that many times."

"I wonder what I would have been like if they had lived."

"Probably as you are now. Perhaps a little more so." Suddenly Maria asked, "What is it you want out of life, Leonie?"

"Why, to be a good woman, to serve God."

"What about a husband and children?"

Leonie flushed slightly. "That will come if God's wills it."

"A good answer. I'm going to give a party for you!" she said abruptly.

"For me! What kind of party?"

"We'll have a ball here at Belle Fleur. We'll invite the neighbors."

"Oh, you don't have to do that, Lady Maria."

"It's something I've been thinking about. I want to do it."

"But I have nothing to wear."

Maria laughed. "You're a seamstress, aren't you? We'll buy some attractive material, and you can make your own dress."

⌒

The conversation at dinner had been fairly friendly, but it fell off abruptly when Lady Maria said, "I've decided to give a ball for Leonie."

Instantly Zara and Lowell glanced at each other, and then Lowell said quickly, "Why, I think that's a wonderful idea."

Zara quickly masked her displeasure and said, "Yes, it is. I'll be glad to help you with a dress, Leonie."

"That's good of you, Zara," Maria said, "but Leonie's going to make her own dress. I have a feeling she can do a better job than any of those French dressmakers in town."

Leonie said only, "It seems like a lot of trouble." But Lady Maria affirmed again, "This is the right thing to do. It's good for our neighbors and our acquaintances to meet you."

⌒

Lowell and Zara met briefly after dinner outside in the garden. Lowell said, "This isn't good, Zara. There's only one reason why Maria would want to give a party."

"Yes, I think you're right."

"If she introduces Leonie as her granddaughter, we're sunk."

"I know. We'll have to do something about it."

"I don't know what we can do," Lowell said miserably. "It's out of our hands now."

Zara was silent, and there was a steely flicker in her eyes. "We've got to do something, Lowell," she repeated. "We *can't* lose all this."

Mrs. Danvers looked out the window and said, "There's that lawyer again."

"Lawyer?" Leonie was sewing her dress and did not get up, although she looked across the room at Mrs. Danvers.

"It's Mr. Mignon."

"Really? I'm surprised."

"So am I."

"I know for a fact that Lady Maria told him not to come back."

Leonie was aware of this as well, and she put her sewing down saying, "I'll let him in."

"You better not let Lady Maria know. She'll be displeased."

Leonie nodded, then went to the door. She opened it and waited until Blaise came up the steps. He was wearing the suit that she had made for him, and it looked a little bit worse for the wear. He was clean-shaven, his eyes were bright, and she couldn't smell liquor on him. "Hello, Blaise," she said.

"Well, greetings, my dear. I suppose you're surprised to see me."

"To be truthful, I am."

"Lady Augustine sent for me."

Surprise washed across Leonie's face. "She did? Well, come in then."

Mignon stepped inside the door and gave her his hat. She hung it on the hall tree and said, "I'm glad to see you again."

"Let me look at you. Why, you're blooming. A flower on the bayou." He took her hands and smiled broadly. "I know someone else who would like to see you."

"Who is that?"

"That doctor friend of yours. He told me to tell you he can hardly run the clinic without you. Wants to know when you're coming back."

"I think I can come fairly soon."

"Good."

"How is he, Blaise?"

"Worn down, as usual. Of course, he's got Lolean to take care of him. That young woman has taken over like a mother hen with one chick. I wish a beautiful woman like that would decide to take care of me."

"She's still there?"

"Yes, she works at the clinic now. She's gotten to be very handy. Almost like a nurse."

"Oh."

Blaise gave her a wise glance. "What do you mean, 'Oh'?"

"Nothing. I'm glad he's got someone to look after him," she said stiffly. "Come along. I'll take you to my grandmother."

"Do you call her that?"

"Not when I'm around her."

"I'm curious as to why she sent for me."

"I am too. She was very suspicious of you before."

They had reached the second floor and stopped outside of Lady Maria's door. After Leonie knocked, they heard her say, "Come in," and Leonie opened the door and went inside. "Monsieur Mignon is here to see you, Lady."

"Come in, Monsieur."

Blaise came in, stopped in the middle of the floor, and made a quick bow. "You sent for me, Lady Augustine?"

"Yes. Have a chair. Leonie, would you mind bringing refreshments for us all? I will have café au lait."

"That will do fine for me as well, Lady Augustine."

Filled with curiosity, Leonie went downstairs, fixed the thick coffee laced with milk, and took it back upstairs. She found Blaise telling her grandmother about Dr. Sheffield and his clinic. He seemed excited about it. "To tell the truth, no one thought it would work. And, of course, the poor chap was overflowing from the very first. So many poor people and so many sick people. He's made quite a name for himself, and I know some of the wealthier people have made contributions to the clinic. He's thinking now of expanding. About all he talks about."

"I would like to see him again."

"I'll tell him you said so, Lady Augustine."

Leonie took a chair and sat quietly as her grandmother and the lawyer talked for some time. Finally Lady Augustine said, "I feel that I have not been just to you, Blaise."

Blaise was obviously surprised. "Why, what do you mean?"

"I mean that I was very suspicious when you brought Leonie here. I didn't trust you."

"There was no reason why you should."

"Perhaps not, but I have now decided that you are to be trusted. I am wondering if you would like to be my man of business, as you used to be."

Blaise's face suddenly went pale. "Why—why, nothing would please me better, Lady Augustine."

"Good. It's settled then. We'll talk about terms later."

Blaise glanced quickly at Leonie and said, "Well, if I'm now officially your man of business, there's one question I would like an answer to."

"And what is that?"

"How do you feel now about this young woman? In other words, do you feel that she is Ives's daughter?"

Silence filled the room, and for a moment Leonie could not breathe. She saw her grandmother's eyes were resting on her. She could not imagine what the older woman was going to say, but her eyes were kind. Leonie's whole life seemed to be resting on a pair of balance scales, and Lady Augustine's words would decide her fate.

"I am convinced that she is." Maria rose from her chair, and Leonie rose as well, feeling faint. Lady Augustine reached out, embraced the young woman, and said, "Granddaughter, it is good to have you here in your home, where you belong."

Blaise Mignon expelled a deep breath of relief. He smiled broadly as he saw tears come to the young woman's eyes, and she held fiercely to the older woman. *Well,* he thought with pride, *at least I've done one thing right in this sorry life of mine!* In his satisfaction, he announced, "A regular job is much better than a monetary reward! Therefore, I will forego financial remuneration for delivering your grandchild. Thank you, Lady Augustine."

Chapter sixteen

Luke Benteen took a sip out of the whiskey bottle, gasped as it hit his stomach, and then leaned back against the post that supported the roof over the small porch. His tiny shack sat on a piece of the bayou just outside the plantation. He had been drinking steadily all afternoon. He looked up and saw the moon begin to rise, covered with stains of clouds. Discontentment filled him, and he had an impulse to go visit the next plantation, where he could have a liaison with one of the slave women. He knew better than to have any such encounter with the slaves on Belle Fleur; nothing happened in the slave quarters there without everyone knowing about it.

From far off in the swamp came the sound of a bull gator grunting, and Luke listened to it with half his attention. He had been working at Belle Fleur for two years. He was well enough paid for his position, which mostly involved caring for the horses. He had come from New Orleans after experiencing some unpleasantness with the police, and as he sat in the bright moonlight, he longed for the city again. At the age of twenty-eight, he felt his life had gone nowhere.

A slight sound caught his quick ear, and as he turned, he saw a glimpse of white. "Who can that be?" he muttered. He strained his eyes and then suddenly saw Zara Augustine walking toward him. He had quietly admired her beauty many times but knew nothing could ever come of it. *What can she want with me?*

It was not usual for one of the family to be roaming around servant quarters, and curiosity began to fill him.

"Luke," she said, coming closer, "is that you?"

Luke put the whiskey bottle down on the porch. "Yes, ma'am, it is."

"Stand up. I want to talk to you."

Luke jumped up to face Zara. She looked strangely determined—but about what? "Don't see you here often, Miss Augustine."

Zara ignored his remark. She was looking at him steadily, and Luke frantically tried to think what he might have done that she had come to scold him about it. "Anything wrong, ma'am?"

"No. Not yet, but I've come to ask you to do something."

Luke grew wary. *What would this woman be coming to ask me?* "I'm surprised, but I'll do what I can."

"You haven't heard what it is yet."

Luke grinned. "Well, I reckon you wouldn't want it known or you wouldn't be comin' like this, Miss Zara."

Zara's face was fixed. She had thought of nothing else but a way to get rid of Leonie, and now there was a frightening rigidity in her body, and her eyes seemed almost to glitter. "Do you like money, Luke?"

"I reckon I like it as well as the next."

Zara was carrying something in her hand. She held up a handful of bills and said, "This is for you if you do what I ask." She handed the bills over, and Luke took them. He didn't count them but saw that it was a considerable sum. He held the bills tightly in his hand and asked, "What is it you want me to do?"

"Something that isn't honest or honorable."

Luke Benteen laughed. "I don't reckon we need to worry about that."

"You understand if you ever breathe a word of this, I have ways of making you wish you hadn't."

"For this kind of money, no problem about that. What is it you want? This ain't enough to hire me to kill somebody."

"You don't have to kill anybody." She took a step forward and said, "Here is what I want you to do . . ."

⌢

At dinner that evening, Zara seemed brighter and more cheerful than usual. Leonie thought she looked nervous, but she could not think why that would be. It was just the usual family: Leonie, Lady Maria, Hugh, Lowell, and Zara. The talk had been mostly of the ball that was coming. Lady Maria spoke of it with great anticipation, saying, "We're going to spare no expense on this, Lowell. I'll expect you to help with the preparation. You, too, Zara."

"Why, of course, Aunt," Lowell said at once. "It'll be a pleasure. We'll do it up right."

"How's your dress coming, Leonie?" Zara asked, fixing her eyes on Leonie.

"It's nearly finished."

"I'm sure it'll be beautiful," Lady Maria said.

"I feel odd about all this," Leonie said.

"Why 'odd'?"

"Because I'm not using to having a fuss made over me."

Hugh smiled and said, "Then it's time, isn't it? After all, we can't have a second-rate ball for Lady Maria's granddaughter."

Lowell and Zara seemed to have frozen in position. Finally Lowell said, "You've decided that, have you, Aunt?"

"Yes, I have. The more I thought about it, the more I saw Ives in Leonie. She resembles him greatly physically, and her ways are like his. And besides, there's the evidence. I told Hugh of my decision this afternoon."

"Well, welcome to the family, cousin," Lowell said. He moved his foot to touch Zara's under the table.

"Yes. Welcome to the Augustines," Zara said. She held her glass high and said, "A toast to our new cousin."

Leonie took the glass and drank. Her face was pale, and she

could not take her eyes off her grandmother. She said, "Thank you, Grandmother."

"I wish your father were here to see this," Maria said. "But at least we have you."

⌒

Zara had watched Leonie carefully for several weeks, and she had learned that every night Leonie went to the kitchen and drank a large glass of buttermilk. She had asked Leonie once why she did this, and Leonie had said, "Oh, I love buttermilk, and it seems to make me sleep better."

The house was still as Zara made her way to the kitchen. She opened the cabinet where a quart of buttermilk was kept, removed the top, then poured the contents of a brown bottle into the milk. Quickly she replaced the top, put the jar back into the cabinet, and left the kitchen.

She barely managed to conceal herself behind the door that led to the dining room when she heard steps. Peering out, she saw Leonie enter the kitchen. She watched as the young woman poured a glass of buttermilk and drank it with obvious enjoyment. Relief came to her, then, for she had not been certain that the sour taste of the buttermilk would conceal the taste of the laudanum.

As soon as Leonie left, Zara quickly moved to take the tainted buttermilk from the cabinet. She stepped outside, poured the contents of the jar on the ground, and then filled the jar with fresh buttermilk from the springhouse. Moving inside, she put the jar into the cabinet, and as she turned to leave, a smile was on her lips.

⌒

Benteen stood waiting in the darkness. He hid behind one of the large live oak trees, his eyes fixed on the light just over the back porch. It threw its feeble yellow gleam over the yard, and he felt nervous. There was never a thought in his mind of refusing Zara Augustine's offer. He had done worse things for less money.

Suddenly a noise caught Benteen's attention, and he straightened up. He saw Zara Augustine step out on the porch. At once he slipped out from behind the tree and approached the house. He asked, "Is it time?"

"Yes. You'll have to be quick."

Luke Benteen, of course, had never been in the big house. It was late, nearly midnight, and the house was quiet. "Don't make any noise," Zara said.

"No, ma'am."

Benteen followed her through the kitchen, down a hall, and then up to the third floor. She stood outside the door and said, "Go in, and do as I told you."

"What if she's awake and makes a holler?"

"She won't be," Zara said flatly. "You go in now. You know what to do when someone comes."

"I reckon so."

"You'd better be sure of it. You're getting well paid enough."

"I know what to do," Benteen said and stepped inside the door, closing it behind him. The silver moonlight came through a window, illuminating the room. His eyes went to the young woman lying asleep on the bed. Moving quietly, he went to stand over her. She was lying on her back, and her face was placid and still. He knew her name and that she was reputed to be Lady Augustine's granddaughter. *Too bad for you, Miss,* he thought, *but I've got to get out of this place, and you're my ticket!*

Maria looked up, surprised, at the door. It was late, and she had been unable to sleep. She could not imagine who would knock at that time of the night. "Who is it?"

The door opened, and Zara came in. Her face was fixed. She said, "Aunt, something terrible has happened."

Instantly Maria threw the cover off. "What is it? Is someone injured?"

"No. It's worse than that."

"What is it, girl? Tell me!"

Zara had practiced this scene many times. She swallowed hard and tried to make the words come out as if they were bitter. "I hate to tell you this, Aunt, but it's about Leonie."

Maria flinched. "What is it? Is something wrong? Is she sick?"

"I wish it were only that." Zara was a good actress. "It's so hard," she said. "I know how much you care for her, and I've tried to keep you from finding out."

"From finding out what? For heaven's sake, child, tell me."

"Well, Leonie's been having an affair with one of the servants."

Maria's eyes flew open. "That can't be true!" she exclaimed. "It's impossible."

"I thought so too. She fooled me for a long time, but it's true enough."

"Which servant? Who is it?"

"Luke Benteen."

"Why, he's nothing but a rascal!"

"I know, but I got suspicious some time ago, and I began watching them. I hate a sneak as much as you do, but I felt that I had to find out if it was true."

"What did you do?"

"I followed her. She goes to his room at night after everyone's in bed, and lately he's come to her room more than once." She hesitated, then said, "He's there now, Aunt Maria."

"I don't believe it."

"I didn't want to either. That's not all. I've been missing things, some valuable jewelry, and I believe she's been stealing from me. She's helped me clean it. She's the only one that could have taken it."

The missing jewelry did not seem to disturb Lady Maria as much as the charge of a liaison with one of the servants. "I'll have to see it."

"I knew you would. That's why I waited. He's there now."

"Show me."

The two women left the room and walked down the hall. They ascended the steps to the third floor where Leonie's room was, and Maria's face was pale. She watched as Zara opened the door and stepped inside with her.

She saw Luke Benteen jump out of the bed half-dressed. He scrambled into his clothes, and her heart seemed to grow cold. He began to babble something, but she did not hear it. "Get out of here!" she shouted. "Right now!"

Benteen grabbed his shoes and scurried out of the door, and Maria stood looking in disbelief at the girl in the bed. She was lying still, and Zara said, "She's drunk, Auntie. Here. See this bottle." She reached on the table and picked up a whiskey bottle. "She pretends not to drink, but I know she does."

Maria Augustine stood looking at the face of Leonie Dousett. Her heart seemed to have stopped, and she turned and walked out in silence. Like a sleepwalker, she went down the stairs and back to her own room. She sat down heavily in a chair. All strength seemed drained from her. She did not move and could not think straight.

Finally she looked up and saw that Zara had entered. "I found the jewelry," she said stiffly. "It was under her things in a drawer of the chest in her room." She held out her hand with the jewelry in it.

Silence filled the room them, and Maria heard herself speaking as if a stranger. "Get rid of that man."

"Yes, Auntie. Anything else?"

"I will tend to the rest."

Leonie's head seemed to be splitting as she woke up. She had never had a headache in her life, but she felt as though someone were putting a red-hot ice pick through her temples. She heard a voice, but for a moment she could not make it out. When she opened her eyes, the room was blurred, and finally her eyes focused and she saw Mrs. Danvers.

"Lady Augustine wants to see you right away."

Leonie sat up and had to pause. She felt sick, and the pain in her head was terrible. Her tongue seemed thick. "What did you say?"

"You heard me," Mrs. Danvers said coldly. "I suggest you go to her right away." She turned and walked out of the room without another word.

Leonie could not put things together. She looked in confusion, then slowly began to remove her night dress and to put on her clothes. It was difficult. She thought, *I must be coming down with a fever. I've never felt this bad before.*

Finally she was dressed, and she made her way to Lady Maria's door. She knocked, then she stepped inside and saw Lady Maria standing over by a window.

"You wanted to see me, Grandmother?"

Lady Augustine turned, and a glare was never fiercer. "Do you have anything to say for yourself?"

"About—about what, Grandmother?"

"Do I have to spell it out? Do you have to hear it? I'm talking about the man you had in your room last night. A servant, and a bad one at that!"

"No. That's not true!"

"I saw it myself, Leonie." She repeated what had taken place, and Leonie's mind seemed to be whirling.

"I don't know what's going on. I'm sick."

"I wanted you to be my granddaughter and perhaps you are, but the bloodline does not run true. You're not what I thought you were. I expect you to be out of this house today, as quickly as possible."

Leonie stared at Lady Maria, then she turned woodenly and left the room. Her mind would not seem to function. She went upstairs to her room and sat down. Her legs felt weak, and the headache continued to rage. Finally she fell on her knees and said, "God, I don't know what's happening, but I know one thing. I don't have any money and no place to go, but I have You, Lord, and I believe that You'll take care of me."

For a long time Leonie Dousett remained on her knees. Finally the headache seemed to grow less violent and then passed away. She thought about all that had happened and knew that she had no choice. She felt a touch and looked down to see Louis pressing against her. She picked up the large cat and hugged him, pressing her face against the fur. "We've got to leave this place, Louis, but God will take care of us."

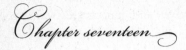

Chapter seventeen

Ransom Sheffield slumped down in a chair and let the weariness fill his body. He had worked steadily for almost twenty-four hours, having missed a night's sleep because of the demands of the clinic. For a moment he felt completely and utterly drained, unable to do more than listen to the hum of voices that came from the outer offices.

The door opened, and he looked up to see Lolean enter carrying a tray. "What's this, Lolean?"

"You must eat something, Doctor."

"I'm not very hungry."

Lolean set the tray down on the desk in front of him. "Sometimes when we get very tired we don't know we're hungry, but you must eat. You can't keep going like this."

Ransom looked up and managed a weary grin. "I don't know what I'd do without you to take care of me, Lolean."

The young woman flushed at his praise and said quickly, "I made you some bouillabaisse."

"What's that? It smells delicious."

"It's mostly fish. I made a lot, so it will last."

"What's in it?"

Lolean smiled. "A whole redfish, a whole red snapper, a whole blackfish, and a whole sheepshead. And shrimp and crawfish tails."

"Well, Lord, for what I'm about to receive, make me truly grateful." Ransom dipped into the soup with the large spoon she had provided, took a sip, and blinked. "That's hot."

"Bouillabaisse is supposed to be hot. I added some hot peppers. I always like it that way myself."

"I think you could get a job cooking at a fancy restaurant."

"No, men do all that. Here, I think you'll like this, Doctor."

"What is it?"

"Creole lamb chops."

Ransom cut off a bite of the meat and tasted it. "Why, this is great! I'm going to weigh three hundred pounds if you don't stop stuffing me."

"No, you never will. You're not one of those men that gets fat."

"No, I guess I'll be tall and skinny all of my life."

"You're not skinny," Lolean said. "You're lean and trim."

"I guess 'lean' sounds better than 'skinny.' How many patients are out there now?"

"They're all gone except three, and I asked Dr. Roberts if he would see them. You've worked hard enough today. Two days, really."

"I guess I'd have to agree with you."

"I don't know how long you're going to keep this up. You're doing too much."

"It's what I set out to do, Lolean—to help people who couldn't help themselves."

Ransom ate steadily, his hunger aroused by the good food, and finally she took a napkin off of yet another plate and said, "Here. You will like this."

"What is it?"

"Gateaux galore."

"Always loved chocolate. How'd you learn to cook, Lolean?"

"My mother taught me how. Now, drink your coffee."

"You're up awfully late, Lolean. You'd better go to bed."

"I'll go later after you."

"I'm so grateful for your help," Ransom said, sighing with contentment. "It's almost like having a wife. No, it's better than that. Most wives don't take care of their husbands as well as you look after me."

The young woman did not speak, and when Ransom glanced up, he saw an odd expression on her face. "Why, what's the matter?"

"Nothing," Lolean said quickly. "It's just that I don't know what I would have done if you hadn't taken me in."

"Well, I guess the Lord knew that you needed me and that I needed you. God always puts things together exactly right."

"You really believe that, don't you?"

"Of course I do."

"I hope you always will."

"You know, Lolean, there are beautiful simplicities in every life. Oh, there are mixed-up things, too, but basically we need to love God and love each other."

Lolean sat down, seeing that despite his fatigue, Sheffield wanted to talk. It had occurred to her more than once that he really had no one to talk to, at least not on an intimate basis. She loved listening to him, and as he began to describe his dream of a hospital, she was happy to draw up a chair.

"You know, sometimes I wonder if I'm crazy, Lolean. I feel as if I'm a man in the middle of a bridge who forgets both its ends and just stands there, looking down at the water flowing below."

"That is not what you're like, Doctor."

He looked at her, thinking again what a beautiful young woman she was. He had been surprised when she seemed to have no interest in the many men who were certainly interested in her. He took in the ripe and self-possessed curve of her mouth, her wide-spaced eyes colored a golden brown that seemed to have no bottom, and the pale olive shading of her skin—a beautiful complexion. He could not help also but notice the shape of her body: slim and tall. The light from the lamps were kind to Lolean, showing the soft lines of her body and the womanliness in her breast and shoulder.

"You're a comfort, Lolean," he said. "I don't know why you sit here in the middle of the night, listening to my rambling."

"I like it," she said simply. "And you are going to have your hospital one of these days."

"I hope you're right." He leaned back, closed his eyes, and locked his fingers behind his head.

"Have you ever had a sweetheart?" Lolean asked abruptly.

Startled, Ransom opened his eyes and took in the expression on her face. "Not really. Women seem to play a game, and I never learned the rules of it."

Lolean studied him, saying little for a while. "I feel like an orphan, Ransom: too young to die and too old to play, and I'm always losing people. Beloved people push off from my life like boats on the shore, and they disappear."

Ransom Sheffield felt compassion for the lovely, lonely young woman before him. He leaned forward and took her hand. "Don't be sad," he said quietly. "You have many wonderful qualities."

"No, not really."

The two looked at each other, and her lips parted in wonder. She had never been as attractive to him as she was at that moment, and he suddenly realized that she was looking at him the way a woman looks at a man. He knew she admired him, and he had come to feel a great affection for her. He opened his mouth to speak, but as he did, the door suddenly resounded from a knock. Quickly he drew his hand back and said, "Come in." When the door opened, he jumped to his feet. "Why, Leonie, what are you doing here this late?"

Leonie's face was strained, and her eyes were filled with misery of some sort. "Could I—could I talk with you, Dr. Sheffield?"

"Of course. Come in."

Lolean stood and gave a half-resentful glance at Leonie. "I'll be going now." She picked up the tray and said, "Go to bed as soon as you can. You won't be fit for work tomorrow."

"I will, Lolean. Thanks for the supper." As soon as the door closed, he turned and said, "What's the matter?"

"Something terrible has happened, Dr. Sheffield."

"Look, I think we're good enough friends we can be on a first-name basis. Leonie and Ransom, all right? Now, what's happened? Is Lady Maria ill again?"

"No, it's not that. I had to leave Belle Fleur."

"Had to leave? Why?" He listened as she repeated the story, and he saw the despair etched on her face and deep in her eyes. "I can't believe it, and I don't see how Lady Maria could believe it."

"The man was in my room. Something was wrong with me. I don't even remember any of it."

"You were obviously drugged, Leonie."

"And the jewelry. Zara says I stole the pieces from her and she found them in my room."

Anger began to build in Ransom. His face grew stern. "I think Lady Maria's lost something somewhere along the line—compassion or common sense. She knows you well enough to know better."

"She couldn't deny the evidence."

"Well, we're going to look into this. Don't worry about it."

"How can I help it?" Leonie said, tears tingeing her voice. "I have no place to go, Ransom, except back to the convent."

"Nonsense. You're not going there. We'll fix up a room here at the clinic, and you can work here. Not much money for anybody, but it'll be a place to stay, and I can certainly use the help."

Relief flooded Leonie, and she said simply, "I knew I could come to you. You were the first one I thought of."

"I'm glad you did."

"You're so kind. I don't know what I would have done if I hadn't had you to turn to."

Ransom put his hand on her shoulder. She seemed very small and vulnerable. "People have to learn to serve each other. We live on credit, balances of little favors we give, and one day we have to return. If you meet someone in trouble, you stop. Another time he may stop for you. One of these days you may pull me out of trouble."

"I can't imagine that."

"The first thing is to get you settled. Come on. Let's get that room fixed up."

Leonie's life took such an abrupt turn at times that it left her breathless. The room in the back of the clinic was small, but she made it functional and attractive. She hung the tapestry she had been working on on the wall, and it gave her comfort to look at it. Some of it she had done before she had left the convent, some while she was working for Madam Honore, and some at Belle Fleur. She thought often that the tapestry was like herself, the fabric of her life woven into it.

She was sitting in her room early in the morning before breakfast. She had been reading her Bible, and it came to her suddenly that her life had a vastly different shape from anything she had imagined. It had new branches, and some of the old branches were dead. It had followed the constant pattern of discard and growth that all lives follow. Things passed, and she had confidence that new things would come. She got up, washed her face, and walked outside. It was too early for patients to begin to gather, so she went to the small kitchen and began cooking breakfast.

She thought of Lolean and knew that the girl resented her. She also had learned during the days she had been there that Lolean had eyes for Dr. Ransom Sheffield. This came as no surprise to Leonie; the girl had come in pitiful condition, and it was Ransom who had pulled her out of it. It was obvious he was a hero to her. Quickly she made eggs, fried ham, and coffee. She had just finished eating when a knock on the clinic's front door startled her. She got up and walked to the front. When she unbolted the door and opened it, she found Blaise Mignon. "Blaise," she said, "come in."

"Good morning. Am I too early?"

"No. Have you had breakfast?"

"Not yet," he said. He was wearing a new suit, not the one she had made for him, and looked altogether more prosperous.

"Come in. I'll fix you something. Will eggs and ham be all right?"

"What could be better?"

He followed her into the little kitchenette and sat down. She poured him a cup of coffee and then began to prepare the food. "I've done nothing but think about what happened," Blaise said.

"It doesn't do much good to think about it, does it?" She tried to smile, but the pain of her separation from her grandmother was keen. "When I didn't have any relatives, I had nothing to lose. But I was just beginning to feel that I was a part of Lady Maria's life."

"You were. She was very fond of you. Everybody could see it." Blaise sipped his coffee, then shook his head. "Something is wrong, and I'm going to find out what it is."

She finished preparing the breakfast, and when she sat down, he began to eat. But his eyes were fixed on her. "Are you very unhappy, my dear?"

"I have a hurt in my heart, for I hate to disappoint my grandmother."

"This place isn't much," Blaise noted. "I'm being paid now. If you'd like to move to a better place—"

"Oh no, this is fine. I have work to do here."

"It's not a paying proposition, is it?"

"No, not for anyone. I suppose that's why I admire Dr. Sheffield so much. He could be making a lot of money in practice. He's such a fine doctor."

"I admire him, too, although sometimes I think he's a fool for turning down prosperity. I think of my own life and the mistakes I made. They were the worst kind. You know, sometimes I think we're made of memories. They say 95 percent of us is water, but that's wrong. It's 95 percent memories." He took a bite of toast, chewed it thoughtfully, and shrugged. "My memories are all snarled and tangled like a line on a reel that had to be cut away. I'll never get them straightened out."

"God could straighten them out for you, Blaise."

He smiled. "You're going to preach at me. I can feel it coming. Well, I'm eating your food, so preach away."

"I've become very fond of you, and I want to see you safe."

The simple declaration made Blaise stop midchew. He said, "I believe you mean that. Well, don't give up on me, Leonie. I've thought about God more since I met you than I have in my whole life."

At that moment Lolean entered the kitchen. She was startled to see Leonie and Blaise there.

"Let me fix you some breakfast, Lolean," Leonie offered.

"No, thank you," she said, backing toward the door. "I'll eat later. Good morning, Monsieur."

"Good morning, Miss."

Lolean disappeared, and Blaise lifted one eyebrow. "What a beautiful girl."

"She is very pretty."

"The doctor's doing all right. Two beautiful women to take care of him."

"It's not like that, Blaise," Leonie protested, "and I'm not beautiful the way she is."

"We won't argue about that." He finished his breakfast and said, "Do you need any money? I just got paid."

"No, I'm fine."

"All right. I've got to go." He reached out and took her hand and kissed it. "You're going to find your place. I'm going to see to it."

"As God wills."

"I don't know much about God, but I think it's always His will that a family be together. Good-bye." He left abruptly, and Leonie stood thinking what a strange man he was.

⌒

"We worked too hard. We've got to have a break."

Leonie looked up. She had been mopping the floor, and Ransom had come in, his face determined.

"You work harder than anyone," she said.

"Well, I need a break then. Tonight we're going out on the town."

"Going out? Where?"

"We'll go out and have dinner at an expensive restaurant. Then we'll go to either the circus or an opera. They are both in town. I'll let you choose."

"I'd rather go to the opera, but isn't it expensive?"

"I got a new contribution for the clinic. We'll take a little out of it. We owe ourselves a night out."

"If you say so!"

The two looked at each other like conspirators, and he said, "You know, we ought to ask Lolean to go."

"Oh, that would be very nice."

Lolean, when Ransom mentioned it, brightened up at first, but then her face fell when he said, "Just the three of us."

"Leonie is going?"

"Yes. It'll be fun, Lolean."

"I'd rather not. I don't care for operas."

"We'll be disappointed."

She did not answer, and Ransom could not persuade her to go. He mentioned this to Leonie, who looked at him oddly. "Don't you know why she won't go?"

"She says she doesn't like operas."

"Ransom, she's a woman, and you practically saved her life. It's only natural she would attach herself to you."

"Well, nothing can come of that."

"Why not?"

"Well, I don't know why not. It's just not to be."

"Be very careful, Ransom."

Ransom stared at her. "What do you mean, 'Be careful'?"

"I mean she's a beautiful young woman, and you're often alone with her. You could make a big mistake and hurt her very badly—yourself too."

Ransom looked confused. "That won't happen, but I'll be careful. Another night I'll take her somewhere else—just she and I will go."

"That's a good idea. What time shall we leave?"

"As early as we can. I want to make this a night to remember."

⌒

The meal had been excellent, and the opera had been fun. Leonie had been pleased to see her old schoolmate Damita Madariaga there, and the two had had time for a brief visit.

Driving home in a carriage that one of Ransom's doctor friends had offered, Leonie and Ransom carried on an animated conversation punctuated by laughter. When they reached the clinic, he unhitched the horse, and the two went inside. The clinic was silent. A single lantern hung on the wall threw its amber corona through the room, twisting shadows into shapes and shedding yellow on the walls and on the floor.

"I'm tired, but I hate to go to bed," Leonie said with a sigh.

Ransom turned to her and asked, "Did you have a good time, really?"

"Oh yes!"

"I wanted to make you forget some of your problems. I had some things I needed to forget myself."

"What would you want to forget?"

"Oh, we all have things that need to be shoved into a box and locked up."

The two stood talking in low voices, and as Leonie stood looking up at Ransom, he recognized a deep and well-guarded interest. He was aware that something warm and real lay between them, strong and unsettling, and he gave way to a smiling restlessness. She spoke in a detached and unstirred voice, but somehow Ransom knew she was not as cool as she seemed, for somewhere within, an emotion worked and left its fugitive expression on her face.

Then suddenly, without really meaning to, he leaned forward to see more of what was in her face. He caught the smell of her perfume, lavender, and as he drew even closer, he put his hands on her shoulders. He saw that she had not moved but was looking at him with her face lifted, her eyes motionless. He saw the quick rise and fall of her bosom, and he leaned forward and kissed her. At each moment he waited for her protest and was astonished when it did not come. He felt her hands go to his shoulders, and she did not pull away.

For a moment, as his lips lay on hers, there was a sweetness in them for him. Then the heat of something rash and timeless touched him. She had the power, he discovered with a start, to deepen his sense of loneliness and his hungers.

Leonie knew she was trembling, and she was enormously aware of the strength of Ransom's arms as they pulled her closer and even more aware of the pressure of his lips on hers. It was like a tall fire springing up through a black sky, and she knew somehow she had crossed a boundary that she had set for herself. She pulled him closer for a moment, and then with a sob pushed him away.

"Don't cry, Leonie, it was my fault. I'm sorry."

"Don't be sorry," she whispered. "Please don't be sorry."

"Then I won't be." Faint color stained her cheeks, and she looked at him with a glance that he could not really understand. She was like a strong presence, like a fragrance riding the night air, like a melody coming from a great distance. Ransom said, "We better say good night."

"Yes. Good night, Ransom. It was a lovely evening." Turning, she walked quickly away, but he stood for a long time in the yellow light of the lantern.

"What did I mean by that?" he whispered. And he found that he did not know.

Something had changed. He knew that the two of them had turned a corner, had touched the mystery that lies between a man and a woman, and could never be again what they had been before that night.

Chapter eighteen

Two weeks had passed since Leonie's trip to the opera with Ransom, and every day and every night she was conscious that something new and different had touched her life. It was not the memory of the opera or the fine meal at the restaurant that she dwelt upon but the moments when the two were alone, and Ransom had put his arms around her and kissed her. She had no experience with men and was not sure what he meant by it. She had listened to other young women talk about their romances, but that was of no help to her.

Late one Thursday afternoon she had taken a few moments off from her work in the clinic to walk around the city. She walked aimlessly for a while and found herself on St. Peters Street, walking through the cemetery. She knew that burials in New Orleans were different from those in other places. New Orleans was built on low and swampy ground—the area surrounded by ditches and the earth from the ditches used to raise the level of the land. All of the plots were aboveground, and the cemetery was fenced partly by a wood palisade and partly by a brick wall. She knew that the cemeteries in the city were called Cities of the Dead, and somehow the walk troubled her.

She remembered that on All Saint's Day, the relatives came to decorate the cemeteries. She had joined the sisters and the students at the convent in this ceremony. They cut down weeds that grew rank in some of the cemeteries, and they patched and freshly white-washed tombs.

Always one could hear the *tap-tap* of the marble cutters' mallets on the tombs of those who had recently been interred. People brought vases of marble and cement and glass and thousands and thousands of chrysanthemums to the cemeteries and placed them at the tombs. Leonie saw that many of the burial sites were graced not with flowers but with funeral ornaments that consisted of floral emblems called *immortelles*. They were made of wire, beads, and glass. She had heard someone say that Mark Twain, the writer, had said on a visit, "The immortelle requires no attention; you just hang it up, and there you are. Just leave it alone; it will take care of your grief for you and keep it in mind better than you can."

This had seemed callous to Leonie, and she had resented its seeming indifference to genuine grief. Finally she left the cemetery, disturbed for some reason, and walked down toward the river. For a long time she walked along the banks of the Mississippi, watching the steamboats as they moved in a stately fashion up- and down-stream. All the time, she was thinking about her grandmother and Belle Fleur. She had had to remain in prayer almost constantly to keep her spirit sweet, for a bitterness would rise in her, and she would have to struggle against her natural instinct to strike out. When not thinking of this, she was thinking of Ransom Sheffield and what his caresses meant.

Finally she decided to go see the sisters. She made her way through the city until she reached the convent. As soon as she went in, Sister Margaret greeted her. Surprised, Leonie asked, "Where is Sister Agnes?" Agnes usually met all visitors.

"You have not heard?" asked Sister Margaret.

"Why, no. What is it?"

"She's very ill," Sister Margaret said, shaking her head sadly. "The doctor says she can't live long."

Leonie stared at the nun, filled with shock. Sister Agnes had not been a favorite with most of the students; she was a hard taskmaker. But lately, since she had left the convent and been out on her own, Leonie had discovered another side to the woman. She asked, "Could I see her?"

"I think it would be very good. She may not know you, however."

Leonie followed Sister Margaret to the infirmary. She walked into the room and was stunned to see Sister Agnes's emaciated form.

"She can't eat. The doctors have tried everything. There's nothing they can do," Sister Margaret whispered.

"I'll just sit by her."

Sister Margaret left, and Leonie stood over the bed of the dying woman. Sister Agnes's face was merely the outline of a skull. Her lips were drawn back, and she moaned slightly in her sleep. Leonie took a chair and drew up closer. Sister Agnes moved occasionally, as if in pain. Finally she opened her eyes, and her lips moved slightly. "Leonie," she whispered.

"Sister Agnes," Leonie said. She reached over and took the hand that was nothing but skin and bones. "I'm so sorry to find you like this."

"Don't be sorry. I'm going to be with my Lord soon." The voice was weak and thin, and speaking seemed to take all of her effort.

"Is there anything I can do for you? Anything?"

"No. At a time like this we can only go so far with our friends."

Leonie held onto the woman's hand, and Agnes wanted to know what was happening in her life. Leonie did not tell her about leaving Belle Fleur. She spoke mostly of helping Dr. Sheffield in the clinic.

Sister Agnes listened, sometimes seeming to doze off. Leonie's heart gave a little lurch each time, for she thought the woman might be dying that moment.

Suddenly Agnes seemed to gather strength. She turned her head, and her eyes seemed enormous in her shrunken face. She began to speak of her childhood. "I was in love once. You didn't know that, did you?"

"No, I didn't."

"I was very much in love, but I couldn't make up my mind

whether God was calling me to be a nun or to be a wife and mother." She lay very still, and finally she whispered, "I made a mistake. My calling was to be a wife and a mother, not a nun."

"Oh, I can't believe that, Sister Agnes! You've served God so faithfully."

"I've tried to." Agnes seemed to struggle for breath, then whispered, "God uses people who make mistakes. Now I'll never know what could have happened if I'd married Joel."

"God will honor you, for you served Him faithfully."

Sister Agnes had no strength in her hand, but she tried to squeeze Leonie's. "Don't make the mistake I made, Leonie."

That was the last word she spoke to Leonie. Then she drifted off into what seemed to be a coma. Leonie was alarmed, and she called Sister Margaret to the bedside. "She does this. The doctor says she can't last more than a few days, if that long."

Leonie stayed at the convent for the rest of the day. Sister Agnes did not awaken again. When Leonie decided to leave, she stopped at the mother superior's office. The two women were grieved, and Leonie said, "I didn't show Sister Agnes the love that I should have."

"She was a very strict woman and didn't make friends easily, but the Lord Jesus is her friend, and she'll be with Him soon."

Leonie hesitated, then decided to tell the mother superior her entire story. The older nun listened without a word. Finally, when Leonie had finished, she said, "You mustn't try to defend yourself, and you mustn't grow bitter. Those are the two worst things you could do. God knows all of this, my child, and His hand is on you."

Leonie listened as the mother superior spoke for some time, and finally she said, "I'll come back and see Sister Agnes every day."

"That won't be many days, for she's on her way to the other world."

⌒

Sister Agnes died two days later, and Leonie attended the funeral. It was a grievous time for her, and she was quiet for several days.

Somehow the death of Sister Agnes had touched her in a way that she had not anticipated. She could not figure out why it so affected her. She kept thinking back over the words, "Don't make the mistake I made."

One night Leonie Dousett sat trying to pray, and finally she fell on her knees beside her bed and said, "I don't want to make a mistake in my life, Lord. You know I love You, but I can go wrong. So I'm asking You for wisdom."

She prayed for a long time, and she thought of the intimate prayers of certain individuals she had met. They had seemed to have a closer relationship with Jesus than she had.

Finally she began to pray in desperation. "Lord Jesus, I want to know You better than I know anyone else. I want to love You more than anyone on this earth, so I ask You to come into my heart in a new and fresh way. Give me Your Spirit that I may walk free from bitterness and free from anger, filled with love as You were filled with love."

For hours Leonie struggled in prayer, but she was not conscious of the passage of time. She was locked in a struggle with God, and once she thought, *This is like Jacob struggling with God all night.*

Finally, near midnight, she suddenly relaxed, and she felt something change within her. She did not know what it was, but she knew that somehow God was in it. She cried out softly, "Lord Jesus, I give You my life. Whatever You want me to do, I will do. I only ask that You be with me."

Joy suddenly flooded her heart, and she began to weep. As she wept, she managed to say, "I'll serve You, God, any way that You choose."

Finally the dawn came, and Leonie Dousett got up. She knew somehow that never again would she be the same.

PART FOUR
· March–July 1834 ·

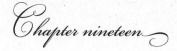

Chapter nineteen

"Oh, it's you, Leonie! Come right in."

Leonie smiled at Susan Barnes's greeting. The woman had always been fond of her, and now she grinned broadly as she reached out and drew Leonie into the interior of the small house. She gave her a hug and a kiss on the cheek then exclaimed, "Where have you been? We've missed you so much!"

"I've been away for a time, but I'm back now." Leonie had time to say no more before the four Barnes children came flowing in, two from a back room and the others from outside. They pulled at Leonie, all vying for her attention, and finally Susan cried, "Now, you children leave the poor woman alone! You're going to have to be quiet."

"It's all right, Susan. I'm so glad to see all of you." She spoke to them, each one in turn. When she had greeted them all, Susan said firmly, "Now, you come and sit yourself down right here. I made a new prune cake just this morning. I had a feeling we'd have visitors. While you eat it, you can tell us all you've been doing."

For the next twenty minutes Leonie alternated between small bites of cake and answering the questions that the children fired at her. They were naturally interested in what she had been doing, and finally she laughed and said, "You are all far too curious."

At that moment the outer door opened, and William Barnes entered. He was wearing his working clothes, his face was sunburned, and he looked healthy and strong. "Who is this come to the Barnes house?" he cried and went at once to shake hands with Leonie, who rose to greet him. "It's about time you made your way back to our humble abode," he said.

"I'm so glad to see you, Sir. You look fine."

"The good Lord's given me good strength and health. It's another miracle. Now let me sit myself down and eat some of that cake my dear wife has made, and you can tell me all you've been doing."

Nothing would do but that Leonie would have to go over her activities again. She was discreet about the trouble she had undergone and did not mention the circumstances that had caused her to leave the Augustine estate. Finally she said, "So I've come back now, and I'm living at the clinic and helping Dr. Sheffield."

"Oh, you're a nurse! How wonderful!" Susan exclaimed.

"Oh, I'm not really a nurse. I don't have that kind of training. I just help as I can."

"That man is a saint," William Barnes said, thumping the table with the flat of his hard hand. "Only God above knows the good he's done for the poor people in this section. He's an angel. I wouldn't be surprised to see wings sprout from his shoulders one day."

Leonie laughed. "He's not an angel, Sir, I'm afraid. But he is a good man."

"In any case I revere the man, I truly do," William Barnes said, winking at her.

For the next twenty minutes Leonie enjoyed her visit with the family, and finally she rose saying, "I really must go."

"No. Stay and tell us stories!" Annie begged.

"Now don't pester the lady," William said gently. "She has work to do."

"I'll come back another time, Annie, and tell you stories."

Leonie had to promise faithfully. Before she left, she knew she had to say something about the new walk she had with God. "Mr. Barnes and Susan, I need to tell you something," she said. "I learned so much about trusting in God from watching you two. When things were bad you never doubted, and God has been speaking to me lately. I don't know what to call it—a second conversion or what—but I have learned to trust in the Lord for everything."

"Well, bless the Lord!" William Barnes exclaimed loudly. "Glory be to God and the Lamb forever! I rejoice with you, Leonie."

"I'm so happy for you," Susan said, and tears were in her eyes. "You have always been so good to us, and it's good to know that you're walking closer to God now."

Leonie left the house, and on her way back to the clinic, she thought of how those poor people had such happiness and joy while there was such unhappiness in those who had much more materially. She thought of this all the way home, and going to her room, she sat down in a straight-backed chair, and Louis jumped up into her lap. "Well, what have you been doing, Louis?"

"Yow!"

"You always say that. What does it mean? And by the way, I don't want you bringing me any more presents, no more mice or birds. You hear me?"

"Yow!"

Leonie laughed and squeezed the cat and stroked his silky fur, and for a time she sat thinking about where her life had come in such a short time. She had thought she would stay permanently with her grandmother, but somehow that had not happened. She could not understand it at all, and she reached over and picked up the Bible. Louis was protesting, but she put him on the floor.

She opened it up to the book of Romans and searched for the verse that had been coming back to her again and again. It was in the eighth chapter of Romans, the twenty-eighth verse: "All things work together for good to them that love God, to them who are the called according to his purpose." She closed the Bible and put her hands on the cover. Her head was bowed, and she did what she had been doing of late:

simply meditating on the Word of God. No one had taught her, but she had read in the First Psalm that those who did mediate were blessed. She thought about the verse and how strange it was. *How can it be good when bad things happen? And yet God says that it is. That all things are working together for good. I don't understand it, but I believe it.*

For a long time she sat thinking about what God was doing in her life, and more than once she thought of what a tremendous effect Ransom Sheffield had had on her. She had not given much thought to young men or to marriage while a student at the convent, but lately she had wondered about such things. What would she do with the rest of her life? She knew deep within her heart that she wanted a husband and children, a home based on love between a man and a woman. But which man?

Finally she knelt down and began to pray. Her prayers until recently had been rote, going over a rosary and repeating the same prayers without giving them much thought. Now, however, when she talked to God, she simply spoke to Him as a woman talked to her friend. She poured her heart out to God, and when she finally rose, she felt a warmth and a sense of having met with the Lord.

Leaving the room, she went at once to the main part of the clinic where a large number of patients were waiting. Many of them she knew and spoke to, stopping to chat for a moment. When she went into the main examining room, Dr. Sheffield was treating an older man. He was a small man, shrunken, but his eyes were an amazing bright blue, electric and alert. They were almost hidden in their sockets, and his face was lined and tanned a deep mahogany. "This is Mr. Griffith, nurse," Dr. Sheffield said cheerfully. "He's having a little trouble with his rheumatism, so we're going to give him something to make it better."

The patient smiled and bobbed his head. He had an odd habit of keeping his head turned sideways and squinting upward. "How you be, Miss?"

"Very well, thank you, Mr. Griffith. I hope this treatment will help you."

"Not much can help rheumatism. Too many nights at sea, wearing wet clothes."

"You were a sailor, sir?"

"All my days, from the time I was five years old. I went out with my dad, I did. Still miss the sea, I do." He winked and took the bottle that Dr. Sheffield gave to him. "What be this, Doctor?"

"Something that'll make the pain a little bit more bearable."

"Thank ye, Doctor." The old man held it and looked at it carefully. "I'm short of money right now, but I'll have some next week from my son."

"Don't you worry about it, Mr. Griffith. Come back if you have any more trouble."

"That I will. That I will. Good-bye, Missy. Good-bye, Doctor."

"Good-bye, Mr. Griffith," Leonie said. After he left she said, "He's very lively for his age, isn't he?"

"Yes. I wish I could do more, but laudanum is about the only thing we have that'll help, and it's temporary. Maybe someday one of the real doctors will discover a cure for rheumatism."

Leonie looked puzzled. "What do you mean, 'real doctors'?"

"Oh, I mean those that find the causes of disease. The rest of us struggle along, giving laudanum and half a dozen other remedies, and that's about all we can do."

"I won't have you talk about yourself like that, Ransom Sheffield!" Leonie stared at him, her face flushed. "You help these people every day, and I don't want to hear you put yourself down again!"

"Whoa, don't shoot!" Ransom laughed and held up his hands in mock defense. "Maybe I'm more wonderful than I think."

"You may make fun, but that old man didn't have anybody. He's probably pretty much alone in the world, but now he knows there's one man he can come to."

"You really think our work is that good?"

"Of course I do!"

"Well," Ransom said slowly and thoughtfully, "I'm glad to hear you say that. It's always what I wanted, to be a help to people, and I've asked God to put me in that position."

"He's answered your prayer."

Suddenly the door opened, and Lolean came in. She was wearing a white dress much like a uniform. When her eyes went to Leonie, there was a hardness there. "Shall I show the next patient in, Doctor?"

"In a minute. First I've got a surprise for you two."

"A surprise?" Lolean asked. Leonie could see the devotion in her eyes. She could not hide her love for the doctor any more than she could hide her dislike for Leonie. "What kind of a surprise?"

"We've been working hard, and I think we deserve a reward," Sheffield said. "Tonight we're going out to Antoine's for dinner."

"But that's so expensive!" Lolean gasped.

"Hang the expense!" Sheffield waved his hand in the air airily. "We're going out on the town, so you two have your best dresses on at seven o'clock. I'll put on my ratty old suit. But people won't be looking at me anyway. We'll go out and have ourselves a time."

"It sounds wonderful, doctor," Leonie said. "We'll enjoy it, won't we, Lolean?"

Lolean did not even answer. "I'll send the next patient in," she said.

"What's the matter with her? She seems grumpy," Ransom said.

Leonie almost burst out, "She wants to be alone with you—can't you see it?" but she caught herself just in time. "I think she's all right. She just works hard."

The two women and the doctor all worked long hours that day. It was late in the afternoon when the younger woman confronted Leonie. Leonie had gone to the room where they kept their meager supplies, and as she turned to leave, suddenly Lolean came in. "Hi, Lolean," she said, smiling. "We're going to have a good time tonight, aren't we?"

Loleen did not smile but said abruptly, "I know you think you're in love with Dr. Sheffield, but you don't love him like I do. You couldn't."

Leonie had known for some time of the girl's affection for the doctor but was surprised at the bluntness of her words. "What are you talking about?"

"You're in love with him. I can see it."

"No, you mustn't say that."

"Don't bother to deny it," Lolean said scathingly. "I know it's true. But I love him more than anyone else, and I just want you to know that you couldn't make him happy." She turned and left the room, leaving Leonie staring after her. "The poor girl," she said, "but she's wrong."

The rest of the day was unpleasant since the two women had to work closely together, and Leonie could feel the hard feelings that Lolean had for her.

About four o'clock she heard a voice and looked over to see that Blaise Mignon had entered the clinic. He rushed up to her, and she saw that his face was flushed. He had been drinking, she realized, but his eyes were alert. "Hello, Blaise," she said. "What brings you here?"

"A little business. I've got some bad news from the house." Seeing the quick look of worry on Leonie's face, he said, "It's Hugh. He's very ill. Dr. Sheffield needs to take a look at him."

"What's wrong with him, Blaise?"

"I don't have a clue," he said. "What with the scarlet fever floating around New Orleans, every time anybody coughs it scares us a bit. I'm quite fond of Hugh."

"I'm sure the doctor will want to go."

"Well, this won't be a charity call. He'll be well-paid for his trouble."

The two chatted for a moment, then Blaise said, "I've been poking around a little bit, and I think I may have a line on why you had to leave the house."

"What is it?" Leonie asked.

"I won't say much about it now, but you keep your faith up, for one of these days Lady Maria is going to know the truth about all this. I'll be going now, but I'll probably see you at the house. You be sure Dr. Sheffield gets the message."

"I will, Blaise."

She quickly found Ransom and told him what Blaise had said. He said, "We'll have to go out as soon as we get the patients all seen. You'd better go with me."

"I'm not sure I'd be welcome."

"You're my nurse," he said. "You'll be welcome enough."

As the horses pulled the buggy along at a fast clip, Ransom spoke with obvious excitement of the plans he had for the clinic. The buggy was one of his recent purchases, made possible by the donations from wealthy patrons.

Leonie listened, giving him a smile and an encouraging word from time to time.

Finally he said, "If we expand like I'd like to, we'd have to get some more help. You and Lolean won't be enough." One of the horses suddenly reared up and threw the other horse out of step. It took some time for Ransom to get them quiet, and he shook his head. "Must have been a snake or something. Jack's not usually that spooky. Come on, Jack, calm down now. It's all right." When he got the horses under control, he was quiet for a time, and then he said, "I've been a little bit worried about Lolean."

"Why is that, Ransom?"

"She seems sort of—oh, I don't know, hard to get along with. No, that's not right. She's very affectionate, but she's moody."

"Don't you really know what's wrong with her, Ransom?" Leonie asked. She knew him, she suddenly realized, better than she had known any man, and now she studied the familiar features of his face. Although he was not at all handsome, something in him strongly appealed to her. He had almost a fanatical streak in him when it came to doing the right thing. She had never known a man so concerned with being fair and honest. The patients sensed this and clung to it, and now, as she studied the rugged terrain of his features, she knew that somehow he had a lack of confidence in himself where women were concerned, which surprised her.

"I suppose she's just not feeling well."

"Oh, Ransom, she's in love with you! Surely you can see that."

Suddenly Ransom Sheffield he turned and looked at her, his eyes wide. "Oh, don't be foolish, Leonie!"

"Why would it be foolish?"

"Why, she can't be in love with me. She's just a child."

"She's not a child. She's a woman, and you came to her aid when nobody else would, Ransom. She's with you almost constantly. The fact that you're a doctor has an appeal for some women. You're not handsome, but women like you. I've seen that."

Ransom grinned wryly. "I'm not handsome."

"No more than I'm pretty."

"Well, there's two opinions about that. But you're wrong about Lolean—at least, I hope you are."

"I don't think I am."

"But, dash it all, that's going to complicate everything!"

"Why is it?"

"Because I'm not in love with her. I have no idea of being in love with a child like that."

"Stop referring to her as 'a child'!" Leonie said sharply.

"Well, don't snap my head off! But you can see how difficult it would make things."

"I don't know what you can do about it."

"Why, I can talk to her."

"And what would you say?"

"I would say—let me see—I would say, 'Don't be in love with me.'"

Leonie laughed. "Oh, Ransom, you can't say that! You'd hurt her feelings. But you've got to say *something*."

"I know. Why don't you talk with her, Leonie? You're good with talking with women patients."

The idea was so ridiculous that Leonie could not help but laugh again. "I can't talk to her."

"Why not?"

"Don't you see? She's jealous of me."

Once again Ransom was taken aback. "Did she tell you that?"

"She would be jealous of any woman you paid attention to."

Ransom was quiet for a time. Finally he turned and said, "Well, we'll just have to work it out, you and I. I don't want to hurt the girl."

"Of course you don't. You don't want to hurt anybody."

Ransom did not answer. They pulled up at the door of the house, and Julius came out at once to take the team away. "Good day, Sir, and to you, Miss."

"I probably won't be staying too long, Julius, but you might feed the horses a little bit."

"Yes, Sir, I will do that."

The two went up the steps. When they rang the bell, it was Zara who answered the door. She gave Leonie a frigid glance and nodded without enthusiasm at the doctor. "I suppose you've come to see Hugh."

"Yes, I have, Miss Zara. How is he?"

"Not too well."

"Then we'll go up right away."

"Hello, Zara," Leonie said. She received only a brief nod in reply, and the two went up to the sick man's room. Hugh was lying in bed, his face twisted with pain. "Hello, Doctor. Hello, Leonie," he said in a strained voice.

"What's the trouble, Hugh?"

"It's my gut. It feels like I'm being stabbed with a sword."

"Well, we'll have to find out about that. Let's take a look . . ."

⁓

"It's appendicitis, Lady Maria." Sheffield stood alone in the parlor with the older woman. Leonie had stayed to try to comfort Hugh.

"Oh dear!" Maria said, alarm washing across her face. "What can you do?"

"We'll have to operate. No time to go to the hospital. We'll have to do it here."

"Will he be all right?"

"If nothing goes wrong. Operations are always dangerous, but I have Leonie to help me. We should do fine."

"What will you need?" Lady Maria listened as Sheffield outlined his needs. Then she said, "I'll see that it's all done."

"He's going to do fine, isn't he, Ransom?"

The two had were sitting in rocking chairs on the porch. The operation had been much briefer than Leonie, who had never seen such a thing, had expected.

"I think he is, but it would have been dangerous if we had waited much longer." He turned and smiled. "I couldn't have done it without you."

"I'll bet you could," Leonie said, "but I'm glad I was able to help."

"I'm sorry that Lady Maria feels the way she does about you. It's not right."

"It will come out all right."

"You think so? You really do?"

"I was reading in the Bible today. All things work together for good to those that love the Lord."

"I've always loved that verse, but it's hard to understand sometimes. When a terrible thing happens, how can we apply that verse?"

"I don't really know, except it doesn't say 'All things *are* good.' It says 'All things *work together* for good.' That's a little bit different."

"I don't understand. What do you mean?"

"Well, I was reading the story of Abraham in the Old Testament last week. You remember God told him to go out and make a sacrifice of his only son, the one he had waited for all of his life."

"That was a terrible command, wasn't it?"

"It seemed to be, but Abraham obeyed. But God let him keep his son, and when it was over, Abraham was a better man. God knew that he wouldn't withhold anything from him. So while it was all going on it didn't seem good, but it worked for good, just as the Bible says."

"You're becoming quite a Bible scholar." Ransom leaned over and put his hand on her shoulder. She was startled at his touch, and she turned and saw that he was smiling at her. He had heavy lips and his features were plain enough, but there was a light in his eyes now that caught her attention. "You're a fine young woman. God's going to do great things in your life."

Leonie could not answer. The touch of his hand was warm on her shoulder, and the approval in his eyes meant more to her than she could say. She tried to express herself, but she could only say, "I try to do what I can."

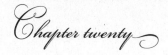

Chapter twenty

Leonie looked up, and when she saw Lowell enter, she grew nervous. She had been walking through the garden, thinking mostly of Hugh and how miraculously he had recovered from the operation. Ransom had gone back to town but had asked her to stay and be sure that Hugh suffered no aftereffects.

"Hello," Lowell said, and he came over and stood beside her. He was studying her as if he was not quite sure how to approach her, and finally he asked, "How did the operation go?"

"It went fine. He's much better."

"That's good. I've always been fond of Hugh."

"I think he's going to be all right. Dr. Sheffield is a wonderful surgeon."

"I'm sure he is." A silence fell between the two, and finally Lowell said, "I always feel a little bit protective toward Hugh."

"Protective—why is that?"

"Well, I've always felt that he missed out on life somehow. He could have done a lot more with his life than he did. He could have made something of himself."

The remark did not sit well with Leonie. She was a quiet, modest girl not given to making judgments, but as she looked at the tall young man who stood beside her and thought of what his life was, she could not help remarking, "What about you?"

The simple question seemed to put Lowell on the defensive. "What do you mean, 'What about me'?"

"I mean you could have made something of your life, too."

"There's nothing wrong with my life."

Leonie did not answer. She only looked at him, and something in her gaze struck Lowell. He said stiffly, "Are you trying to tell me that my life isn't right?"

"Well, is it?"

Lowell's face flushed a dusky red. He was an easygoing young man, but Leonie's questions obviously disturbed him. "I don't do any harm to anyone."

"Life's more than that, I think," Leonie said. "I'm sure you don't harm anyone, but do you help anyone?"

"That's none of your business!" Lowell snapped.

"I suppose not, but you were the one who brought it up, speaking of Hugh. I felt sorry for him, but I don't feel sorry for you. At least he has some reason for having missed out, as you put it, on life. He lost the one he loved very dearly, but your own losses have never crippled your penchant for laziness and luxury. Your life isn't making anyone else's better."

"I don't appreciate your comments," Lowell said angrily. He turned without another word and stalked away. His back was stiff, and as he entered the house, he slammed the door behind him.

"Well," Leonie said, not at all disturbed by his anger. "We are a little touchy about it, aren't we?" She walked for another half hour in the garden and then reentered the house. Climbing the stairs, she went up to Hugh's room, and when she stepped inside, she halted suddenly. Lady Maria was sitting in a chair beside Hugh's bed. "Excuse me," she said, "I didn't know you were here."

"Come in, Leonie," Hugh said. His head was propped up with a pillow, and his color was much better. He smiled, and his voice was weak but stronger than it had been. "Come in and take care of your patient."

Leonie smiled and walked over to his bedside. "You don't need much care," she said. "You're looking fine."

"I feel pretty washed out, but I think I would have died if you and Dr. Sheffield hadn't come."

"I think you might. Dr. Sheffield said he got to you just in time."

"Sit down, Leonie. I was just talking to my sister about what happened to me."

Somewhat hesitant, Leonie sat down. She felt Lady Maria's eyes on her and met them. The older woman was studying her carefully, and there was something in her gaze that was cryptic. She turned again to face Hugh, finding his smile ready. "What is it you've been telling her?"

"I've heard all my life that when someone is drowning, just before he dies, his whole life flashes before him."

"I heard that too."

"Well, it's true enough, or at least it was for me." Hugh lay quietly in the bed. His hands were folded together, and there was a thoughtful expression on his face. "I really thought I was going to die, and the thing that came to me was what a waste I've made of my life."

"I wouldn't say that," Maria said suddenly. She leaned forward and put her hand over Hugh's, and her voice was gentle. "You've been a help to me."

"No, I haven't, but you've been a help to me," Hugh said. "Ever since I lost my wife, I just haven't cared about living. I just gave up. But when I lay here thinking I was going to die, it came to me that that was the last thing Autumn would have wanted for me. She wasn't a quitter, but I have been."

"You loved her very much, didn't you?" Leonie said quietly.

"More than anything else. You know, I just wonder, from time to time, if I didn't love her too much."

"I don't think it's possible to love anyone too much," Maria murmured.

"I don't know about things like that, but I thought maybe God took her because I loved her more than I loved Him."

The three were silent, and finally Maria said, "I don't think that's the way it was. We can't explain why we lose those we love." The sunlight filtered down through the window, and millions of tiny dust motes danced and fluttered in the yellow beams. The beams touched the carpet and brought out the rich colors of the oriental rug, and from outside a bird, lifting his voice in a chorus, sounded joyful and full of hope.

Hugh turned his head. "Listen to that bird. He sounds happy, doesn't he? That's what I'd like to be like. What I used to be like."

"We can't sing like birds all the time," Leonie smiled. She leaned forward and studied Hugh's face. "But I'm glad you're feeling better."

"I've always had kind of a contempt for those who made New Year's resolutions," Hugh said. "I've always thought, *Why fool with such things? Just do what you intend every day*. But I made a resolution while I thought I was not going to make it."

"What was it?" Maria asked.

"I resolved that if I got well, I was going to go back to work. I was going to start painting again. I was going to make myself of some use in the world."

Immediately Leonie thought of Lowell's words about Hugh's uselessness, and it pleased her that Hugh had come to this conclusion. "I think that's wonderful," she said. "I've seen some of your early work—you're very talented. In a way it's sort of cheating not to paint."

"What do you mean?" Hugh asked curiously.

"I mean when we have a gift God gives us, we're obligated to use it to help others."

"I think you're right about that," Maria said, "and you do have a great gift, Hugh. Your work gives pleasure to so many."

"I don't know about that, but I know I'm going to try. I've probably forgotten all about how to paint, it's been so long."

The sound of horse hooves caught the attention of the three. Leonie rose and went to the window. "It's Dr. Sheffield," she said. "He's probably come to check on his patient."

That proved to be the truth. Ransom came through the door smiling and spoke to the two women, then examined Hugh. "Why, you're going to be able to get out of this bed pretty soon."

"I don't know how to thank you, Dr. Sheffield."

"You don't have to do that. Why, that's what I do."

Ransom gave a few instructions to Lady Maria, then said, "I suppose you are about ready to go back, Leonie?"

"Unless you think I should stay."

"You know, that might not be a bad idea." Ransom nodded. "At least for a couple of days."

"I really would feel better if you stayed," Maria said quickly.

"Well, then I will," Leonie said.

"Good. I like being waited on," Hugh said.

"Come along, Doctor. I have your fee in the study."

"I'll come back the day after tomorrow, Leonie. Take good care of this fellow."

"I will, Doctor."

"Thanks for coming, Dr. Sheffield," Hugh said.

After the doctor had left, Hugh said, "That's one fine fellow." He turned his head and studied Leonie. "He might be good material for a husband there."

Leonie flushed. "I suppose so."

"On the other hand, doctors may be very poor husbands. They stay busy all the time."

Leonie didn't answer. "I think Dr. Sheffield's calling is going to keep him busy, but a good wife would understand that."

Hugh studied her carefully, then smiled. "I believe she would," he said. "How about reading to me for a while?"

The dinner was excellent, as usual, consisting of a jellied veal consommé, a French bean salad, and beef bordelaise. Leonie ate hungrily, for the cooking was very good. She said very little but listened carefully. Zara did most of the talking. Her eyes went, from time to time, to Leonie, and while she never specifically accused her of anything, she hinted strongly that Leonie had come simply to ingratiate herself with Lady Maria. Suddenly she said, "Aunt Maria, Julian and I have decided we want to get married."

"I thought you decided that a long time ago," Maria said quietly. Her eyes were fixed on Zara in an odd sort of expression. "What's the urgency?"

"We've waited a long time," Zara said. Her manner was nervous, and with her fork she pushed a grape around her plate. She had something on her mind, they could all see, and finally she said, "Julian and I have wanted to get married for a long time, but things were so—so unsettled."

"Unsettled in what way?"

"Oh, you know," Zara said, shrugging her shoulders.

Lowell laughed. "Yes, I suppose we do know. You mean you want to confirm how much money you are going to get and when."

Zara was furious. "That's unkind, Lowell."

"I'm sorry. I didn't mean to be."

Zara got up and swept out of the room without another word, her face livid with anger.

"You shouldn't have said that, Lowell."

"It's true enough, Aunt Maria."

"It may be true, but we shouldn't be unkind to one another."

"Zara has always been selfish."

Maria Augustine straightened up. She looked at Lowell and said, "She's not the only one, Lowell."

Lowell flinched, and his face turned slightly pale. He could not answer but looked down at his plate.

"I think that it's time you did something with your life."

Lowell's gaze went instantly to Leonie. "Leonie said the same thing," he said.

"She's a wise young woman," Maria said. "I think you ought to pay attention to her."

The tension grew in the room, and Leonie longed to say that strangers should not be included in family arguments. She excused herself and went to her room.

Later that evening, Leonie was sitting with Hugh. He had gotten out of bed, and she had fed him his supper off a tray. When she had taken the tray away, he had asked her to bring him some paper and a pencil.

"Are you sure you feel up to going to work? It's very soon."

"I'm just going to try a few scribbles," he said. Leonie brought the tools he requested.

"Now," he said, "sit right over there where the light from the lamp strikes you."

Leonie was startled. "What for?" she asked.

"Because I'm going to sketch your picture."

"Oh, no, I don't—"

"Don't argue with the patient. You'll aggravate me, and it'll be bad for my condition. Now sit down."

Hugh was happy, she saw, and she went to sit down. He propped the tablet up on his lap, holding it with one hand at the right angle, and his hand moved rapidly. He did not speak, and his eyes studied her from time to time. "Tell me about yourself, Leonie," he said.

"Tell you what?"

"Oh, about what you've done, what you're going to do."

Leonie hesitantly began to speak of her life. She did not dwell on the past but spoke mostly about her work at the clinic. He kept her sitting still for a long time, and then finally he said, "Come and see."

Rising from her chair, she went over and stood over him and looked down. "Why, that doesn't look like me."

"Yes, it does, and it'll look even more like you when I transfer the sketch to canvas and the paint goes on. I'll start that in the morning. You know, I'm really excited about beginning to paint again."

"Did you sell many paintings back in the earlier days?"

"Quite a few. I could have made a good living at it, but there didn't seem any point. I was depending on Maria. I was a parasite, I suppose, just like Lowell and Zara."

"Oh, I wouldn't call them that."

"Well, that's what we are or were. But no more for me." He looked up and said with a teasing grin, "Leonie, how about marrying me?"

Leonie knew he was joking. She smiled and said, "I don't think so, Hugh."

"I know your secret."

"What kind of a secret? I don't have any secrets."

"Yes, you do. You're in love with Dr. Ransom Sheffield."

"No, I'm not."

"Ah, your answer was too quick, but I believe you are."

It was the second time someone had pointed out that she was in love with Ransom. She had paid little attention to Lolean's charge, but Hugh was a man of some observation, and Leonie suddenly realized that he was right!

"He'll marry someone from a higher social standing than I've got," she said weakly.

"You think he's looking for a fancy bride from the social register? You know better than that, Leonie."

Leonie was too confused. She shook her head and was glad when suddenly the door opened and Maria walked in.

"Why, sister, I've begun my new work. What do you think of it?"

Maria went over and looked at the paper. "Why, it's Leonie," she said. "What a fine sketch."

"The painting will be even finer. I'm going back to work with a vengeance. Tomorrow the painting starts."

"You are looking fine, Hugh. I'm so pleased."

Hugh grinned and winked at Leonie. "I feel so good at getting a new lease on life. And I'm so grateful to you, Leonie, and to Dr. Sheffield, of course."

For one horrible moment, Leonie was afraid that he was going to say something about her being in love with the doctor. She did not want to hear it, so she got up and said, "I'll leave you two alone."

As soon as she was out of the room, Maria said, "You are really fond of her aren't you, Hugh?"

"Of course. She's a fine young woman."

Maria hesitated, then said, "You know, you say that knowing what went on here between her and that stable hand."

"I never believed a word of that."

"But we had evidence."

"I don't care about the evidence. I know she's not the kind of girl who would do a thing like that, and that's all there is to it."

"You're not very logical."

"No. We artists aren't," Hugh said cheerfully. "Now, I want you to stop being logical and start thinking with your heart. That girl is Ives's daughter. There's no question in my mind."

Maria began to tremble. "I know that she is, but she did a terrible thing. I was about to put my whole heart and trust into her when this came along, and now—"

"And now you've lost her. What if you're wrong?"

Maria stared at her brother. She had no answer for that question had echoed in her own heart. "I can't help it," she said. "It's hard for me to let myself love someone unconditionally."

"That's the only real kind of love there is, sister," Hugh said gently. "I hope you find out about it."

Zara had greeted Lowell with a harsh word when he had gone to her. She was still angry at him for his remarks, but he was always able to talk her out of her fits of anger. Zara finally said, "That girl is here to wind herself back into Maria's good graces, but I'm not going to let that happen. You have to help me discredit her."

"I won't do it, Zara, and I think you're behaving badly too."

"Have you lost your mind?" Zara cried, staring at Lowell in angry disbelief. "If she comes back here, you'll having nothing, and neither will I."

"Nothing? Well, to tell the truth, that's about what I've got now, Zara." He looked at her and said, "I've been thinking what a sorry way it is to live, to sit around for years, waiting for someone to die. I've about had it with that kind of life."

"What are you going to do? You're pretty old to start in a profession."

"I'm pretty old to be acting like a child, too," Lowell said. His own remark seemed to surprise him, and he said, "I think I'll have to do a little rearranging in my life, and I think you'd better do the same."

Zara glared at him, but he only laughed and left the room. Zara shook her head, "You fool! You'll throw everything away because that girl came back, but I won't!"

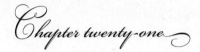

Chapter twenty-one

Sunday morning was a beautiful day—the bright sun was shining and a cooling breeze made everything comfortable. Leonie had gotten up early and gone to Mass. When she had arrived back at the clinic, which was closed on Sundays, she encountered Ransom, who was just leaving. He was wearing a white suit and a black string tie, and he removed his hat with a sweep of his hand. "Good morning to you. Been to Mass?"

"Yes, I have."

"Well, I'm going to church. Why don't you go along with me?" He saw her hesitate, so he said, "I think it would be interesting for you."

For one moment Leonie struggled with herself. She had known nothing but Mass all of her life. Then something stirred within her, and she suddenly smiled. "I think I'll go with you then."

"Fine. It's a small church, but I like the preacher very much. Come along. I'll hitch up the buggy, and we'll get started."

The church was on the outskirts of New Orleans, set back in a field under several huge live oak trees. Buggies and horses tied to racks announced that a crowd was beginning to gather, and as they approached, several people spoke to Ransom, addressing him formally as "Dr. Sheffield."

"I feel so odd," Leonie whispered.

"I stopped paying attention to the signs on the outside of church buildings," Ransom said easily.

"What do you mean?"

"I mean it doesn't matter whether a church is Baptist or Catholic or Presbyterian. What matters to me is one thing: the Spirit of the Lord in the service."

"I never thought of it like that."

"Well, it's natural you wouldn't, since you grew up in a convent. Let's go while there's still a seat."

They entered the small church, and Leonie looked around curiously. It was a small church with plain wooden benches and at one end, a raised platform with a pulpit right in the center. Behind the pulpit were two rows of benches where a group of plainly dressed people had already assembled. She assumed that was the choir.

"I see two seats up close to the front," Ransom said.

Leonie felt that everyone in the church was looking at her as she walked down to the front. She would have preferred a less-prominent place, but every bench seemed to be filled. When they got to the row, people had to stand to let them in. When they sat down, Leonie saw that she was seated directly in front of the pulpit.

"Best seats in the house," Ransom said with a smile. He saw she was nervous and reached over and touched her shoulder. "Don't worry. The Spirit of the Lord will be here. You will enjoy it."

While they waited for the service to begin, Leonie looked around. It was a poor group of people for the most part, many of the men wearing overalls and some plain denim trousers, but nearly all of them wore a white shirt with a tie. The women wore their best dresses. All of them wore hats, it seemed, and they all seemed happy and pleased to be there.

Leonie thought about how different the atmosphere at the

church was from Mass. People were whispering to their neighbors, some, perhaps, a little too loudly, but it was nothing at all like the Catholic church that she was accustomed to attending.

A tall man with a string tie and his black hair slicked back stood and said in a high tenor voice, "Well, folks, it's time to begin. We'll start by singing the doxology."

The crowd rose to its feet, and an organist hit a note. The congregation sang loudly and enthusiastically:

Praise God from whom all blessings flow
Praise Him all creatures here below
Praise Him above, ye heavenly hosts
Praise Father, Son, and Holy Ghost.

The tall man bowed his head and prayed fervently that the Spirit of God would be present at the service. Then he said, "Now we're going to praise God with all of our hearts. You will remember that the psalm says, 'Let everything that hath breath praise the LORD.'" A smile split his wide lips, and he shook his head. "I sure would admire to see everything in creation praising God like that. Well, maybe the forests and fields won't sing, but we can—with all of our might. We'll sing a good old song written by Charles Wesley himself: 'O for a Thousand Tongues.'"

The organ boomed forth, and the congregation lifted its voice. Leonie did not know the song, had never heard it, but she listened carefully to the words:

O for a thousand tongues to sing
My great Redeemer's praise
The glories of my God and King
The triumphs of His grace.

My gracious Master and my God
Assist me to proclaim

To spread through all the earth abroad
The honors of Thy name.

Leonie had never heard such singing! It was not that the worshipers were skilled or that their voices were excellent. Indeed, it was nothing like the trained choir she was accustomed to, but excitement and sincerity marked not only the voices, but the faces she glimpsed around her. They sang one song that touched her heart particularly:

Holy, holy, holy, Lord God Almighty!
Early in the morning our song shall rise to Thee
Holy, holy, holy! Merciful and mighty!
God in Three Persons, blessed Trinity!

As Leonie began to follow in the hymnal and sing, feelings swept over her in a way she could not define. The hymns all exalted the holiness of God or the sacrifice of Jesus on the cross. She longed to know the words by heart, so she might join more freely in the worship of these simple people. Finally they sang a song that she had never heard before but whose words seemed to ring her heart.

Alas! and did my Savior bleed?
And did my Sovereign die?
Would He devote that sacred head
For such a worm as I?

Was it for crimes that I have done
He groaned upon the tree?
Amazing pity! Grace unknown!
And love beyond degree!

Well might the sun in darkness hide
And shut His glories in

When Christ, the mighty Maker, died
For man the creature's sin.

But drops of grief can ne'er repay
The debt of love I owe
Here, Lord, I give myself to Thee
'Tis all that I can do.

As the last verse echoed through the small chapel, Leonie suddenly felt that Jesus Christ had entered into the building. She saw Him in her mind's eye on the cross, and she thought of her own sins, and tears rolled down her cheeks. Taking out her handkerchief, she tried to wipe them away without being seen, but she knew that Ransom, standing beside her, had noticed.

After the song service, a short, muscular man got up. He was wearing a black suit and a white shirt, and he was bald except for a fringe of hair around his head. He wore a winning smile, however, and he preached a sermon such as Leonie had never heard. It exalted the name of Jesus and held him up as the Lamb of God. A hundred times, it seemed, he said during the sermon, "Behold the Lamb of God, that taketh away the sin of the world." At other times he said with excitement lighting his face, "Blessed be the Lord God and the Lamb forever."

At the end of the service, the minister gave an invitation, and several went down to kneel at the front and pray. Leonie did not understand any of this, but she knew that God had touched her. When the service was over, the minister said, "We have eight candidates to be baptized. We invite you all to the river."

"Would you like to go to the baptism, Leonie?" Ransom asked.

"I think I would."

"It's not far. I always enjoy baptism. There's something especially holy about it."

"I was baptized when I was an infant. I don't even remember it."

Ransom smiled and squeezed her arm. "I think you'd remember it if you ever got baptized like this. Come along."

The tributary that fed into the Mississippi was small, no more than fifteen feet across, but it had cut a deep channel. Most of the congregation, Leonie saw, had come to the river and now lined the eastern bank. The preacher and those he was to baptize had donned plain work clothes. Leonie watched as the preacher waded out until he was nearly waist deep and said, "Come along, brother Ed. You'll be the first."

The man walked forward and stood almost directly in front of the minister. He was somewhat taller, and the preacher put his hands on his shoulders and looked at the congregation. He raised his voice, saying, "Jesus died and was put into the earth, but on the third day He rose from the tomb. Baptism is a picture of that. When an individual stands in this water, he's alive to the world, but then when he is put under the water, he dies to the world. He's a dead man. But when he comes up out of the water, he shows that he is no longer the man he used to be. Let me make it clear: this is a picture of the death, the burial, and the resurrection of Jesus. Baptism never saved anybody. Only the blood of Christ can do that, but the Lord has told us to go into the world, preaching the gospel and baptizing those who believe. When a person is baptized, he is saying to the world, 'Look at me. I'm a new man. I'm a new woman. I'm a new young person.'"

All of this was foreign to Leonie. She watched, fascinated, as the minister put his hand on the back of the tall man's neck while the man clasped his arm. Then the minister leaned him back and slowly lowered him into the water. He went down deep, deep, deep, completely submerged, and when he came up, people along the bank cried, "Glory!" "Praise God!" "Hallelujah!" The man wiped his eyes, and Leonie could see he was weeping. He said in a broken voice, "Praise the Lord!"

As Leonie watched the procession of people being baptized, something was happening inside of her. She could not describe it exactly, and it frightened her, for it was like nothing she had ever known. She closed her eyes for a moment, wondering what was wrong with her, but whatever the emotion, it was intensified.

Suddenly she was aware of a great desire being born in her heart to be baptized. This startled her, for she had known only sprinkling as a mode of baptism. But something about this service seemed to draw her spirit, and she felt that God was speaking to her.

The thought of God Himself speaking to her was a fearful thought. She had spoken often to Him, but now she knew that the Creator of heaven and earth was communicating with her. It did not come in words, but in human speech it would have been, "I want you to announce your love for Me to the world, publicly undergoing baptism."

Leonie began to tremble, and she knew that this was a turning point in her life. She wanted to turn and flee and wipe all of it out of her mind, for it broke the tradition that she had been born into, all that she had ever known. But the ceremony had been so powerful, she knew she could not run.

Vaguely she was aware that the service was over. A hymn was being sung, and then when it ended, she felt Ransom's eyes on her. "Is something wrong, Leonie?" he asked quietly as he led her away toward the buggy.

"I don't know."

"Don't you feel well?"

She did not answer until they got to the buggy, and then she turned to face him. "I have the feeling that God is telling me that He wants me to . . ."

When she broke off, Ransom said gently, "What is it? You can tell me."

"I have the feeling that I need to be baptized as those people were, but if I do, it will cut me off from all my friends."

"Not if they're your real friends. We're all just Christians, whether we're sprinkled or immersed. That's not the test of whether people are converted or not. It's a sign, a symbol, a picture, as the preacher said. It's just a declaration that you are a follower of Jesus."

"I don't know what to do," Leonie said helplessly. She felt weak and faint, and he put his arm around her. "You need to pray about it, and I'll pray with you. You'll do what God tells you to do, I'm sure. Come along now. We'll talk about it some more."

For the next two weeks, Leonie thought every day of her desire to be baptized. She grew calmer about it and searched the Scriptures to find guidance. Daily she prayed, "God, show me the way," and always the answer came back in one form or another. "I want you to announce your discipleship."

On a Thursday, Hugh came to see her, bringing her the picture he had finished. "Here it is!" he announced when she greeted him. "Hope you like it." He stripped off the paper that protected the painting and held it up. He watched her expression and then smiled. "What do you think?"

"Why, it's beautiful. But I never looked like that!"

"Yes, you do. Don't insult the artist in me now."

The picture was expertly done. She exclaimed, "You're such a wonderful painter!"

"Come along. Let's show it to the doctor."

They went at once to the inside office where Ransom was seated at his desk, studying a medical book. He looked up and smiled. "Well, hello. How's my patient?"

"Completely cured and gone back to work." He held up the painting and said, "Here's your favorite nurse."

Ransom stood and exclaimed, "Why, that's marvelous, Hugh! You've done a wonderful job." He walked over and examined the painting. "I'll buy it."

"No sale. It's for you, Leonie." Hugh gave it to her, and she stood speechless.

"You mean I can keep it?"

"Yes. A small token of appreciation from a grateful patient."

Hugh soon left. Ransom would not let Leonie leave with the

painting. He kept admiring it, and he suggested, "I tell you what: let's hang it on the wall here. It'll be yours, but I can look at it."

At that instant Lolean walked in and stopped abruptly when she saw the painting.

"Look at this, Lolean. Isn't it a marvel?" Ransom asked.

Lolean stared at the painting and then said in a toneless expression, "It's very nice."

"It's better than that. Here—let's hang it right here where we can all look at it."

Lolean did not respond, but she watched as Ransom hung the picture on the wall.

"Now," he said, "that adds a little color to this drab office."

Leonie knew that it was a bitter thing for the girl, but she could not think of a thing to say to her.

The patients had come and gone, and the clinic was closed. Ransom Sheffield had stayed late in his office, preparing for the next day. He was startled when the door opened and Lolean stepped inside. "I thought you'd gone to bed, Lolean."

"No. I wanted to talk to you."

"Is something wrong?"

Lolean had prepared herself for this moment. She said, "I have to tell you something, Dr. Sheffield."

"You're not ill, are you?"

"No, nothing like that." Lolean's face was tense, her eyes were wide, and she breathed quickly as if she had been walking very fast. "Don't you know I care for you, Dr. Sheffield?"

Ransom suddenly knew that Leonie had been right about the girl. He had thought about her and hoped that the situation would never come to a confrontation. Now he felt helpless as he faced the young woman. "Why, of course, we're fond of each other. That's the way it should be."

"That's not what I'm talking about," Lolean whispered. "I mean I love you." She watched his face, and the light went out of her eyes. "But you don't care for me. I can see it."

Clearing his throat, Ransom said, "You're such a lovely young woman, and you're going to find a man one day. For him you'll be everything."

"But not for you," Lolean said flatly.

"I don't think I'll be getting married for a long time. I have a lot of work to do with building a new clinic."

Lolean watched him as he faltered for words, and then she said, "I'll be leaving tomorrow."

"Leaving! Where are you going?"

"Away from here. Thank you for all you've done for me." She turned and left before Ransom could move. When the door closed behind her, he stared at it and said, "Blast, why did this have to happen?" He knew she would be gone the next morning, for she was a very strong-willed young woman, and he was grieved for her. *I'll have to see what I can do for her. Maybe I can find her work somewhere else.* But he knew that she was dreadfully hurt and in all probability would accept no help from him.

"Lolean left this morning."

Startled, Leonie looked up. She had been arranging the equipment and supplies for the day's work. She had noticed that Ransom had been very quiet, and now he was pale.

"What do you mean, she left?"

"We—we had a talk last night, and she decided to leave."

"Did you quarrel?"

"No . . . well, I guess we did in a way. You were right, Leonie. She came and told me that she cared for me. And when I couldn't return her affection, she said she'd find work elsewhere."

Leonie felt great pity for Ransom. "I'm sorry," she said quietly.

"I don't think there was any way you could have avoided it."

"I feel rotten."

"You didn't do anything wrong, Ransom."

He looked at her quickly. "Don't you talk about leaving me now."

Leonie stared at him. *He has no idea that I care for him.* She said, "No, I won't be leaving, Ransom."

The mother superior sat listening as Leonie spoke. She did not say a word until Leonie had completely finished. Then she asked, "Why are you telling me this, Leonie?"

"Because you've always been so good to me, and whenever I had troubles, I came to you with them, and you always listened. And I'm troubled about what I feel. I feel that I need to be immersed, baptized the way the Protestants do it, but that's not what I was taught. That's not what I have always believed."

"Catholics and Protestants differ, but they're not the only ones. Methodists don't immerse either—they sprinkle or pour. Episcopalians do the same. The only question is this: is God telling you to do this?"

"I've prayed and prayed, and the feeling won't go away. Every night I go to sleep thinking that God is telling me to be immersed, and then the next morning, that is the first thing I think of." Leonie's face was twisted with anxiety. "Tell me what to do, Reverend Mother, please."

"I can only tell you to follow the Spirit of God. And I can assure you of this: if you do decide to leave the Catholic church and go another way, I will still love you as much as ever. We will be on different paths, but they lead to the same destination."

"Pray for me, Reverend Mother."

"I have prayed for you since you appeared on my doorstep," the mother superior said kindly. "But there comes a time when each of us must make her own decision. You listen to the voice of God. Be sure that it's God who is speaking, and then you do exactly what He says. That's the only road to happiness."

Chapter twenty-two

Carefully Leonie stitched on the tapestry. She had gotten up before dawn, and now yellow sunlight streamed in through her window. Stitch by stitch she made the pattern come alive, and finally she straightened up, took a deep breath, and smiled. "It isn't bad," she said aloud. "Not bad at all."

She had been working on the tapestry now for longer than she had ever worked on any of her projects. It was a large wall hanging, and she had woven into it things that had been meaningful to her. There had been times when she had had no money for thread or materials, but for the last two months she had been able to make considerable progress.

Running her hand over the silken surface, she took a deep pleasure in what she had created. She didn't know why it was, but making something seemed to be an act that relieved her from the pressures of the world. Ransom had told her it was therapeutic. She knew it was good for her to work, for as she put herself into the cloth and the thread and the materials of the tapestry, somehow the world seemed to fade away, and she could concentrate solely on the project.

Finally she heard the sounds from the street outside and rose to put the tapestry away. Carefully she folded it and put it into a large box that she had saved for that purpose. Then after looking in the mirror and fixing her hair, she left her room.

She began making a breakfast, for she knew Ransom liked to have a large morning meal. She had just begun stirring the beaten eggs in a frying pan when he came in, his cheeks rosy from a shave and his eyes bright. "Another good day, Leonie," he said cheerfully and sat down at the table.

"It is a good day." She smiled. "I fixed you a double portion of eggs and bacon this morning. I didn't make biscuits, though. You'll have to eat yesterday's."

"That'll be fine."

Leonie set the table for the two of them and poured fresh coffee into the large cups and then sat down. They bowed their heads, and he asked a quick blessing. And then he tipped a bottle of hot sauce and literally baptized his eggs.

"You shouldn't do that, Ransom."

"Makes them taste better. Good old hot sauce!"

"You've destroyed your taste buds," she scolded, but she knew it was useless. He liked hot sauce on practically everything he ate.

The two of them talked easily, and she realized, *Why, we're like a husband and wife in the morning.* The thought caused her cheeks to flush slightly, and she said quickly to cover her embarrassment, "Hugh came in yesterday while you were gone."

"How's he doing?"

"Very well. He's sold four paintings, and he's happier than I've ever seen him. He lives in a house in town now and has asked us to visit soon."

Ransom applied a fresh layer of hot sauce to his eggs and then spilled a few drops on the bacon. "He's a good man, I think."

Impulsively Leonie said, "Did you know he asked me to marry him?"

Leonie's words caught Ransom off guard. He had just placed an enormous forkful of scrambled eggs in his mouth, and he couldn't speak for a moment. Hastily he swallowed and nearly choked. He grabbed the coffee and drained the cup, then put it down and stared at her. "You never told me that," he said accusingly.

"I don't tell you everything, Dr. Sheffield," Leonie said, smiling.

"Well, you could have told me something as important as that." He leaned forward and studied her carefully. The light of her eyes held laughter, and he noticed, not for the first time, that she had a pleasantly expressive mouth—a woman's lovely lips.

Light danced in her eyes. "Did you think I should have sent him to ask your permission to marry me?"

Ransom said casually, "Well, since you don't have any parents, I think it might have been appropriate."

"What would you ask him?"

"Oh, the usual stuff. 'Are you able to support a wife? Do you love her with all your heart? Will you promise never to be short or angry with her?'"

"And what if he passed the test?"

"Leonie, why did he bring that up? It's an odd topic for the two of you to discuss."

"I think he's just lonely and—"

When she broke off Ransom studied her more carefully. "You're lonely too, I suppose."

"I'm very happy, Ransom. Much happier than I was when I was younger."

Ransom watched her face and said, "Well, if any young men come calling, I insist on interviewing them."

"You'd scare them off. You have a formidable manner at times."

"Me? I'm as mild as Louis."

Louis had been sitting on the floor, looking up, hoping for a bite of something. "You are gentle, aren't you, Louis?" Ransom said. He broke off a piece of bacon, leaned over, and gave it to the cat, who promptly devoured it.

"You can be stern sometimes."

"Not with you, I hope, Leonie."

"No. Never with me."

It was a pleasant breakfast, and finally Leonie rose, saying, "I've got to go to the market. Do you need anything particularly?"

"Why don't you get some fresh jumbo shrimp?"

"You'd have those every night. You need a change."

"Just tonight. We can have what you want tomorrow night."

"All right. I'll see what I can do."

⟶

Jean Larue was sitting in his carriage half-asleep, but as Leonie emerged from the clinic, he straightened up and pulled at his mustache. His bright blue eyes lit up, and he whipped off his cap, exposing his bald head. "Good morning, Mademoiselle. Where can I take you?"

"Oh, I'm just going to the market, Jean."

"Get in. A young lady needs to go in style."

Leonie got into the carriage and said, "Let's go by the Barneses' house, Jean. I want to check on the children."

"*Oui.* I will take you there."

They arrived at the Barnes home a few moments later, and Jean said, "Take your time. I'm not anxious to work much today."

"All right, Jean." Leonie dismounted, stepped to the pavement, and knocked on the door. Susan opened it and greeted her warmly. "You're up early. Come in!"

"I can't, Susan. I'm going to market. I thought perhaps you might need something."

"No, but thank you for stopping. Why don't you come for supper tonight?"

"Oh, I've promised to cook Dr. Sheffield a special dinner. He loves shrimp."

Susan Barnes smiled and shook her head. "You're getting good practice for marriage," she observed. "You're learning how to take care of a man."

Leonie looked up quickly, embarrassed. "Well, I'll be going. If I see anything particularly good, I'll drop it off on the way home."

"Thank you, dear. You're always good to look out for us like that."

Leonie got back into the carriage, and Jean said, "To the market now, I take it?"

"Yes. And hurry, if you please. I need to be back before the patients start coming in."

⌒

The market was not busy, and Leonie made her purchases quickly. Jean had gone along with her, insisting on carrying the heavy parcels. Back at the carriage, Jean helped her in and seated himself. Suddenly the horse reared up, and he said loudly, "Stop that, you stubborn creature!"

"What's the matter with him? That's not your usual horse, is it?"

"No. My horse had a sore fetlock. I had to borrow one from my friend. This one is young and not ready to work. He thinks only of running. Stop that, you!"

Jean finally managed to pull the young horse around until he headed back toward the clinic. They had gone only a block when suddenly a bunch of youngsters ran toward them down the street, yelling happily. They were young boys who had obtained some firecrackers. They threw one with a yell, and it landed almost under the feet of Jean's horse.

When the firecracker exploded, the horse uttered a wild cry, screamed, reared up, and then dashed down the street at full speed. Jean hauled at the reins, but the horse was strong and had the bit in his teeth.

Leonie tried to hold on, but when the wheel of the carriage fell into a large pothole, the jolt threw her to the side. She made a wild grab but missed her hold and was thrown abruptly out of the carriage. For her the world seemed to go around, and then as her head struck the hard cobblestone street, it seemed to dissolve in a shower of brilliant stars.

Ransom heard the sound of pounding feet in the outer office and looked up from the patient he was treating. The door burst open, and Jean Larue ran in, his eyes wild. "Doctor, come at once!"

"What's wrong, Jean?" Ransom demanded. He headed for the door toward the older man and said, "Somebody hurt?"

"It is the Mademoiselle Leonie."

"Leonie! What's happened?" Ransom demanded.

"My horse, he ran away, and she was thrown. She struck her head on the pavement."

"Where is she?"

"Outside in the carriage."

Ransom did not ask more questions but dashed outside. He saw at once the wound on her head and her swollen face. Her eyes were closed, and she was pale. Quickly he reached in, picked her up, and shoved Jean aside. Going into the office, he told the patient, "Just take two spoons of that medicine every day, then come back in a week. I'm sorry, but right now I've got to tend to this young woman."

Placing Leonie on the table, he quickly examined her injuries. She seemed to have no broken bones, but the head injury troubled him. It looked serious, and he said, "Jean, do you know where Dr. McDowell's office is?"

"*Oui*, I know him."

"Go at once," he said. "I need him here immediately. Don't take no for an answer. Then get Lady Augustine here."

"I bring him, you bet!"

⌒

"Dr. Sheffield—is he hurt?" Maria asked.

"No, it is not him. It is the young lady Leonie. She has had a bad accident." After delivering McDowell to the clinic, Jean had raced to the Augustine estate.

At once Maria Augustine jumped to her feet. "What happened?" She listened as the cab driver explained the accident. He spoke rapidly and nervously and said, "The doctor, he says you come quick!"

⌒

Dr. Jamie McDowell stood looking down at the pale face of the patient. He leaned over, examined the head injury, and said nothing.

Ransom could not keep still. He desperately wanted to help Leonie, but he knew that McDowell was a far more experienced doctor in cases like this. "What do you think, Doctor?"

"You know these cases as well as I."

"No, I don't. What's your opinion?"

McDowell was a small man of Scottish descent. He had a full set of side whiskers, and his eyes were green. "I wish we could look inside her skull and see. Someday we may be able to do that, but for now," he said, looking down at Leonie, "it's in God's hands."

"I wish we could do *something!* It's hard to just stand here."

"I know, lad. This young lady—is she your fiancée?"

"Why, no. What makes you ask?"

"You've lost your calm spirit. It's easy to see you have feelings for her."

"I have a great respect for her."

"Indeed?"

"Yes. She's had a hard life, and I would like to make it easier."

"Well," McDowell said, shrugging his thin shoulders, "again, it's in God's hands."

⌒

"I may be some time, Julius. You'll have to wait."

"Yes, Madam, I will be here." Julius helped his mistress down and said, "You tell the young lady I'll be praying for her."

"I'll tell her that."

Maria reached the door just at the same instant that a woman in a habit arrived. The two paused. "You go first, please," Maria said.

"You are Lady Augustine, are you not?"

"Why, yes I am."

"I am the reverend mother at the convent."

"You've come about Leonie."

"Yes, I have."

"So have I. Perhaps we could go in together."

The two women entered, and Dr. Sheffield met them. "Reverend Mother, Lady Augustine, I'm glad you could come, both of you."

"How is she, Doctor?" the mother superior asked quickly.

"Not as well as we'd like."

"How badly was she hurt? What's her condition exactly?" Lady Augustine asked.

The two women listened as Ransom Sheffield described Leonie's fall and injury. He took a deep breath, and they saw how serious he was. "Head injuries are always more difficult than any other kind. She's been unconscious since she was brought in. I've had another doctor in who is very good in such cases. He'll be back later this afternoon."

"Could we see her?"

"Of course. I'll take you to her."

The two women followed Ransom Sheffield into an inner room. Leonie lay on a single narrow bed with a blanket over her, her bandaged head resting on a pillow. Lady Augustine whispered, "She looks so pale."

"We're doing everything we can," Ransom said, then added bitterly, "which isn't much, I'm afraid. These cases are very hard."

"We'll sit with her while you treat your other patients, Doctor," the mother superior said.

"That's kind of you. If you see any change, please come for me at once."

"Of course."

As soon as Sheffield left, the two women sat down in chairs next to Leonie's bedside. The room was silent, and finally the mother superior said, "Leonie was with us from the time she was born."

"Yes, I know."

"She is your granddaughter, I understand."

Lady Maria hesitated, then nodded. "Yes. It's a very complicated story."

"I think I know most of it. Leonie told me. When she discovered her identity, I was very happy for her. I was the one who found her, you know."

"You?"

"Yes. She was left at the convent, and I discovered her that morning. Somehow it made me feel closer to her. In all of the years that she was growing up, I did the best I could for her." She looked down at the silent young woman and whispered, "She has always been such a fine girl. A fine child at first and then an exemplary young woman. The best that I have ever known."

"I haven't known her long, but I had the same impression. But—" Maria bit her lip. "I don't know how much you know about the problem we had."

"I think I know most of it. She told me the story."

"I've been so disturbed about it, Reverend Mother," Lady Maria said. "She seems such a sweet child, so much like her father, Ives. He had a sweetness himself, but then—"

"I know the story, but I don't believe a word of it."

Lady Maria stared at the nun. "But we have evidence."

"And I have Leonie. I've know her all her life. Such a thing as she's been accused of, it is not possible."

Lady Maria did not answer. Finally she bowed her head. The mother superior started to speak, but then she reconsidered. She had learned that the power of conscience often had more impact than the spoken word of another. She prayed silently, "Work on her, God. Let her see that this child is not what she thinks."

Ransom came often into the room and once brought Dr.

McDowell with him. The two physicians removed bandages from the wound and reexamined and redressed it. Dr. McDowell turned to the two women and said, "There's little change. I think it's a time for prayer."

The mother superior asked, "Would you object if we prayed for her now?"

"No, certainly not," Ransom said quickly.

"I think we should anoint her with oil, and then all four of us should agree in prayer."

"Aye, that's what the Bible says," McDowell said.

"What kind of oil?" Ransom asked quickly.

"It doesn't matter. Olive oil will do."

"I'll get some from the kitchen."

In a few moments Ransom was back with a small bottle of olive oil. The reverend mother took the oil, let a few drops roll out on her palm, and then handed the bottle back. With her other hand, she dipped the tips of her fingers in, and walking over, she touched the head of the young woman and began to pray. It was not a formal prayer, but all three of those that gathered around the mother superior heard the pain in her voice.

Maria began to weep. She reached out and put her hand on Leonie's head and held it there. She felt light-headed, and her knees felt weak, and when the woman ceased praying, tears were running down Maria's face. She looked up at the three who were watching her closely. "She is of my blood. This is my granddaughter, and I love her. She must get well!"

The Mother superior said, her face beaming. "She is blood of your blood, and she needs you at this time. God will give her back to you. I know it!"

Chapter twenty-three

Everything seemed to be clothed with clouds. All were scenes from the past, at least she remembered that much. She saw herself dressed in her white dress as she made her First Communion, and standing close to her were Sister Agnes and Reverend Mother and her friends. It was as if she were seeing it through a veil of some sort, and she strained to see more clearly.

The scene changed, and she saw herself with her friends from the convent on a picnic. In this scene she was older, and she remembered that it was on the day of this picnic that she had experienced the primary signs of a young girl turning into a young woman. She had been so frightened. It had been Simone d'Or who had taken her to the mother superior, and the older woman had explained what was happening to her.

The clouds seemed to swirl around the scene, and she saw herself working in the clinic with Dr. Sheffield. The scene was clearer this time, and she watched his face, noting the seriousness of it. And then in the dream he looked up, smiled at her, and said, "You're going to be a fine nurse." She remembered that day. It had not been long ago.

But then abruptly she felt a sharp pain in her head and the clouds dissipated, and she felt the firmness of the mattress supporting her. She smelled the acrid odor of antiseptic and was conscious of a terrible thirst.

The sounds of voices from far away came to her then, and she could not distinguish any of them. But there was someone singing, and she knew she had heard the song before. Slowly she opened her eyes, and at first the light overhead blinded her and added to the pain. She closed them quickly and memory came swirling back. *I was in an accident. I fell out of the carriage, but where am I now?*

Cautiously she reopened her eyes and allowed them to become accustomed to the light. She knew then that she was in the room where Dr. Sheffield treated patients who came in from accidents. A fly buzzed in her ear, and she shook her head, but that was a mistake. The movement sent pain like a dagger running from temple to temple. She moaned slightly and lay very still. Finally the pain left her, and she turned her head slightly. There beside her in a chair, Dr. Ransom Sheffield slumped, his head back and his mouth open. He was snoring slightly, and the sight of him made Leonie feel better. She watched him as he breathed and finally settled himself into a more comfortable position.

For some time Leonie lay there, letting herself savor consciousness. Some of the dreams had not been particularly pleasant, although some had. Now she was back in her own world, and Ransom was there, and she was alive.

Slowly she raised her hand, touched her head, and her fingers felt the bandage that swathed her. She touched an area that brought a cry of pain from her, and when she did she saw Ransom's eyes open. When he saw her face, he jumped out of the chair instantly and cried with a glad voice, "Leonie, you're awake!"

"Yes," she whispered faintly. "Could—could I have some water?"

"Of course you can."

Leonie watched as he quickly moved to the table beside the bed and poured water from a pitcher into a glass. He went to her side and put his arm behind her. "I'm going to lift you up, so you can drink. I know you're dry as a bone."

Leonie felt the strength of his arms as he pulled her up. His arm behind her gave her a feeling of safety. When he lifted the glass to her lips, she gulped thirstily.

"Take it easy now. Just a sip at a time. You can have all you want, but a little now and a little later."

The tepid water was the best drink Leonie had ever had, but even better were the safety and security she felt in Ransom's embrace. He held her as if she were a child, and she rested against him. Looking up, she whispered between sips of water, "How long have I been here?"

"Two days. You've been unconscious the whole time."

"What's wrong with me, Ransom?"

"You got a nasty crack on the head, but you're going to be all right now. Here, have a little more water."

For some time Ransom held her, giving her sips of water, and he said, "The mother superior was here, and so was your grandmother."

"Grandmother was here?"

"Yes. She and the mother superior seemed to become quite good friends. They've both left for a while, but they'll be back later to see you."

Leonie could not think very clearly. She knew that her grand-mother was highly displeased with her, and finally she said, "Did Grandmother say anything?"

"She said you were of her blood and that she loved you."

"Really, Ransom?"

"Yes, really." His arm tightened about her, and he set the glass down for a moment and put his hand on her cheek. "My heaven, I thought I'd lost you," he said softly. "You gave me quite a scare." He leaned forward then, kissed her forehead, and when he saw the look on her face, he said, "Here I am, taking advantage of a helpless young girl. Just the sort of a rascal I am!"

"I don't mind," Leonie managed to whisper, and then she felt herself retreating somehow. "I don't mind at all," she whispered and lost consciousness.

"Well, it's very good news, Lady Maria," Ransom said cheerfully. He had greeted Maria when she had come back from taking a rest, and he had taken her hand and said, "I know you've been terribly worried, but she woke up about two hours ago."

"Is she all right? Why didn't you send for me?"

"I thought you needed the rest. You've slept hardly at all. But yes, she's all right. Her eyes are clear. She's weak, but I think she should be awake now. Come along."

Ransom led Lady Maria into the room where Leonie still lay in the bed. Her eyes were open and she smiled when she saw her grandmother. "You have a visitor," Ransom said cheerfully. "You think you feel up to a little talk?"

"Oh yes," Leonie said. She tried to struggle to a sitting position, but Ransom at once went to her, reached down, pulled her up, put a pillow behind her back, and then said, "I'll just leave you two to catch up." He looked at Maria and said, "God has been good to us, hasn't He?"

Maria Augustine could not speak for a moment. Relief had flooded through her when she had heard the good news, and now, seeing Leonie sitting up with some color in her cheeks . . . Then she gathered herself together and said, "Indeed He has, Doctor. Indeed He has."

Ransom left the room, and Leonie said, "Dr. Sheffield told me how you came at once when you heard I'd been hurt."

"Yes, and Reverend Mother was here, too." Maria sat in a chair at Leonie's bedside. She struggled to put into words what she felt. She thought again how very much Leonie looked like her father, Ives. Ives had had that same shape of eye, dimple, hairline. It was amazing now that she had accepted the fact that Ives's daughter was alive and well, and she saw freshly how much the girl resembled him. *How did I ever miss it before!* she cried to herself.

"I have something to say to you, Leonie."

"Yes, Grandmother."

Taking a deep breath, Lady Maria said, "I have failed you, and I failed Ives, and I failed myself."

"Oh no, don't say that!"

"Yes, I must. I should have ignored the stories I heard and trusted my heart. I know now, although I don't have any evidence, that you are innocent of those things I was told about you. I don't understand what happened, but I'm going to get to the bottom of it."

Leonie's face glowed, and she held her hand out, but Maria did not take it. Instead she leaned forward, embraced Leonie, and held her tightly. "Can you forgive me, my dear, for doubting you?"

"Oh yes. Certainly I can."

"Good. Then welcome to the family, and I will never doubt you again—not ever!"

Chapter twenty-four

"Oh, Louis, what have you done?"

Louis looked up with satisfaction at Leonie and said, "Yow!" He held the baby rabbit that he had brought into Leonie's room between his paws, and his golden eyes glowed with pleasure.

"You're a bad cat, Louis!" Leonie cried as she bent over. "Turn it loose." She freed the tiny rabbit from Louis's grasp and cuddled it in her hands. "You poor little thing," she said. "Now I'll have to take care of you."

For the next fifteen minutes, Leonie busied herself with making a home for the tiny rabbit, which was uninjured. She had made a nest in a large box by lining it with an old blanket and put a small saucer of water inside. "I'll go get you some milk," she whispered to the rabbit. With her forefinger she stroked the soft, silky fur and cast a disgusted look at Louis, who had watched all of this. "Now you'll have to stay out of my room until he's old enough to turn loose. It serves you right, Louis."

Louis stared at her but did not seem in the least repentant.

She left, then returned with some milk and an eyedropper. Carefully she fed the tiny creature until he would take no more. "You stay here now, and I'll be back and feed you a little more later. Come along, Louis. You can't stay in here."

As she left her room, she met Mrs. Danvers. "What are you doing, Leonie?"

"Oh, that cat of mine brought a baby rabbit in, and I had to make a home for it."

Mrs. Danvers smiled. "That's the nature of cats. I used to keep cats, but I loved the birds too, so it was a constant battle to save the birds and keep the cats. I don't think you can do both successfully, not all the time. Was the rabbit all right?"

"Oh, he's so tiny, but I fed him some milk with an eyedropper and made him a little nest. Louis will have to stay out, though, until he's old enough to turn loose."

Mrs. Danvers studied Leonie's face. The young woman had been back at her home now for five weeks. The injury to her head had given her little trouble, although Dr. Sheffield had insisted that she take things very easy. Slowly she had recovered her strength, and it had been a joy to watch her blossom.

"Your grandmother wants to see you as soon as you can find time."

"Oh, I'll go now."

"It's been a good thing for you to be here for everyone, Leonie," she said, "but especially for Lady Maria. She was so lonely, and now you and she are almost like a couple of schoolgirls. I've never seen her laugh or enjoy life so much."

Indeed, this had been the case. Lady Maria Augustine had blossomed as her relationship with Leonie deepened. The two of them spent hours together. Much of it consisted of Maria's telling Leonie about her father's early years. The two also had taken great pleasure in the tapestry that Leonie was making. Lady Maria was an expert seamstress herself, and the two had worked on the tapestry for hours at a time, sometimes in silence, sometimes laughing and talking.

"She's so sweet to me and so very good—as you all are, Mrs. Danvers."

"Well, we're glad to have you here."

Leonie smiled. "I've never had such a good time. It's so different from any kind of life I've ever had."

"Well, everyone's happy then."

"Except Zara. She doesn't like me."

Mrs. Danvers's countenance darkened. "She's jealous. That's what it is. She's always been first, but now she's not. It's understandable, I suppose. But she'll have to change. Now, you'd better get along to see your grandmother."

"I will, but I want to come and help work on the dinner tonight."

"All right, but your grandmother first."

Mrs. Danvers watched the girl as she stepped downstairs, then returned to the kitchen where the staff members were working—or at least talking about it. They were all sitting around the table, drinking café au lait, and Mrs. Danvers said in mock severity, "What's this? Have you all grown rich and retired?"

"Sit down and have some cake, Mrs. Danvers," Charles Dupre, the butler, said. He was a tall man with gray hair and brown eyes. "I couldn't have made better cake myself."

"I'm sure you couldn't," Mrs. Danvers agreed with a smile. She sat down and joined in the tea party. The talk and the laughter went back and forth, and Mrs. Danvers was very aware of the difference in the atmosphere of the house. Opal Dupre, Charles's wife and the cook, had always been a prophet of gloom, but now she seemed as cheerful as it was possible for a woman with her temperament to be.

"Well, I will say," Opal said between bites of the cake, "she'll be a good mistress, Miss Leonie will, when it's her turn."

"It's too soon to talk about that," Mrs. Danvers said.

"You never know," Opal said, frowning. "When we wake up in the morning, none of us know whether we'll be dead by nightfall."

A groan went around the table, and Olan Winters, the overseer who was rarely in such meetings as this, complained, "I wish you'd be a little bit more cheerful, woman. Charles, why don't you take a stick to her until she learns how to be more happy?"

"Yes, indeed," Charles said. "I will do that immediately."

"You will not!" Opal snapped. "It would worth your life."

"Well, I dare say that the day will come," Olan Winters said. "It comes to all of us, but you're right. She'll make a good mistress."

The party went on for some time until finally one of the maids heard the doorbell ring. "I'll answer it," Mrs. Danvers said. "The rest of you get on with your work."

Leaving the kitchen, Mrs. Danvers went to the door. When she opened it, she found Blaise Mignon standing on the porch. "Come in, Sir. I suppose you've come to see Madam?"

"Yes, I have, Mrs. Danvers."

"She's in the large parlor. Come with me, please."

Maria looked up as the lawyer entered and greeted him. "How are you, Blaise? Is it business that brings you here?"

"I have a rather important announcement to make, but I think I would like to make it, with your permission, before the entire family. It will save time."

"The whole family? You mean all of us?"

"Yes. It's very important. Critical, I would say."

"Very well." Lady Maria pulled the sash cord by her side, and Mrs. Danvers was back almost at once. "Would you go find Leonie, Zara, and Lowell, and tell them to come at once to me?"

"Yes, Madam, at once."

As soon as Mrs. Danvers closed the door, Lady Maria gave Blaise a careful look. "You're being very mysterious, and you look very pleased with yourself."

"I am both. More pleased than mysterious. How is the young lady doing?"

"Miss Leonie is completely recovered, I'm glad to say."

"That's good news indeed." Blaise studied the woman and said, "You two get along famously, do you not?"

"It has been a joy to have Leonie with me. It's almost like having Ives back. She is so much like him."

"She resembles him a great deal."

"But she's also like him in her ways. He was always sweet-tempered, and she has that same touch of humor that he always had."

The family began filing in. Lowell came first, a quizzical look in his eye. "What's going on, Blaise?"

"A matter of family business," Blaise said smoothly.

Zara was there almost at once, and she cast a cold look at Blaise Mignon. She had never liked the man or trusted him, and she barely gave him a nod when he greeted her. She went over to stand close to Lowell, looking suspicious.

Leonie entered then and went at once to Blaise with a smile. She extended her hand, and he kissed it and said, "Ah, Leonie, you look beautiful. All well now."

"Yes, indeed, Blaise."

"All right," Lady Maria said abruptly, "you've greeted everyone. Now, what is this all about?"

"It is a matter of business, Madam. I have two depositions here, and you will be very interested in both." Reaching into his pocket, Blaise pulled out an envelope and removed two sheets of paper. "The first is from a physician, Dr. Rupert Jones. He is semiretired now, but he is of high standing and of very good reputation among the medical community. It took some time for me to find Dr. Jones, for I had to check every doctor that was practicing in the area at the time that Leonie was born."

Every eye went to Leonie and then back to Blaise. He liked his drama, Blaise Mignon did, and held the paper high. "Dr. Jones vows in this deposition that he delivered a baby girl on the exact day before a child was found by the reverend mother of the convent."

"That proves nothing!" Zara said sharply. "It could have been anybody's child!"

"But according to the deposition, which you shall all read," Blaise said with some force, "the woman cried out in pain the name 'Ives' many times. And afterwards Dr. Jones does hereby avow she told him that her husband's name was Ives Augustine."

"My Ives!" Lady Maria exclaimed. "Let me see that, Blaise."

"Certainly, Madam."

Lady Maria took the paper, read through it quickly, and then looked across the room at Leonie. "I did not need this kind of evidence to know that you were my granddaughter. Nevertheless, it makes it more legally firm, does it not, Blaise?"

"Indeed, as firm as it can be. The evidence is irrefutable."

"Well, I don't believe it!" Zara said stubbornly. She was pale and glared across the room at Leonie. "Who knows whether that child even lived?"

"I think the courts would agree that in all probability the two infants were one and the same."

"Be still, Zara," Lowell said sharply. "It's obvious that Leonie is Ives's daughter."

"Yes, it is," Lady Maria said. "What is the other deposition?"

"The last, it is not such a happy one. I was never convinced that Leonie was guilty of having an affair with a servant, as someone accused her of doing, so I set out to find Luke Benteen."

Every eye then was riveted on Mignon, and he said, "It took some time, but I finally located him. He's serving a term in a prison in Tennessee—for assault and burglary. I went to Tennessee myself and spoke with him, and in the presence of another attorney I took this deposition."

He walked across the room and handed the paper to Lady Maria. As she read it, Leonie looked across at Zara and saw that her face had turned pale as paste and that she was trembling.

For a long time Lady Maria stared at the paper, and then she looked up and said, "I will deal with this, Monsieur Mignon."

"Yes, of course, Lady Augustine."

"You must stay for dinner. It's my granddaughter's birthday."

⁓

Leonie was puzzled about the contents of the second deposition. Finally she determined to ask no questions, but just before dinner, her grandmother called her into the study. When Leonie entered, Lady Maria said, "I didn't want Lowell to know about this unless it was necessary, but I want you to read the deposition that the lawyer brought."

Leonie took the paper and read it quickly. It was very brief, and she looked up in astonishment. "Why, can this be true?"

"The man would have no reason for lying. I am so ashamed of Zara. It's all her doing. She paid the man, and I've already spoken with her."

"What did she say?" Leonie whispered.

"She finally confessed it all." Maria shook her head. "She won't be at dinner. But I'm going to leave it to you, my dear, about what should be done. You would be totally just in demanding that Zara never show her face in this family again."

"Oh, we can't do that, Grandmother!" Leonie cried. "She did wrong, but we must show mercy."

Lady Maria's face softened. "I knew you'd say that, but I wanted to hear it. Very well. We will let her have some time to think about what she's done, and perhaps we can help her in some way."

Leonie left the room, and Lady Maria Augustine felt a tremendous satisfaction. *It's exactly,* she thought, *the sort of thing that Ives would have done. Zara deserves no consideration, but I'm glad that Leonie has the same quality of mercy as her father had.*

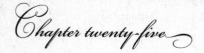

Chapter twenty-five

Hugh went to speak with his sister when she was in the rose garden. He stood talking with her for a moment and then said abruptly, "I've been somewhat surprised about Leonie."

Maria looked up quickly. "What do you mean?"

"Well, she's got what she wanted most. She has a family. She has security, but somehow, well, she just doesn't seem right."

"No, she's not entirely happy."

Hugh stood for a moment admiring one of the roses. He plucked it off and stuck it in his buttonhole. "I think I know what her problem is."

Maria looked at him. "What do you think is bothering her?"

"It's a secret, but let me work on it. I think I can help." He smiled, turned, and left the garden.

Maria stared after him and shook her head. "You always were a mysterious fellow, Hugh," she said, "but I hope you know what you're doing."

Hugh went at once into the house. He searched until he found Leonie in the library. She had pulled several books from a shelf and was poring over one of them. "Hello, Uncle Hugh," she said.

"I have to talk to you, my dear," Hugh said.

As Hugh came to stand over her, Leonie felt a moment's discomfort. "What is it? You sound serious."

"Well, it is serious," Hugh said. He studied the girl's face and said, "You're not as happy as you should be."

"Why, I'm perfectly happy," Leonie protested.

"No, you're not. It's been two months now since you've been proclaimed officially and proven to be, by our good lawyer, the granddaughter of Maria Augustine. So now here you are, Mademoiselle Leonie Augustine, heir to a prosperous plantation. But you stay in this house. You never go anywhere. You don't have any young men calling on you."

"I don't want any young men calling on me," Leonie said. "I'm happy enough as I am."

Hugh leaned forward and took her hand. "My dear," he said quietly, "you know my history. You know that I had a loss, and I allowed that loss to ruin much of my life. So I've come to beg you not to do the same as I did."

"I don't understand you, Hugh."

"You know, in a way Leonie, moments in time—that's all we have. We don't have yesterday. They are only memories. And no one is certain about tomorrow. But this very moment, right now, we have that. And I saw that I wasted many moments when I could have been doing something good and productive. I want to keep you from making that same mistake."

"You think I'm wasting my life?"

"I think there's something that you want very desperately, and you don't know how to get it. Therefore, think of me as your elderly uncle. Sit down, Leonie, and let me give you a push."

"A push? What do you mean?"

"I mean there are times in our lives when we need someone in our lives to help us get started when we are uncertain and unhappy. So I'm giving you a little push. Now sit down and listen to your Uncle Hugh!"

The day had been long, and Ransom slumped in his chair at his desk. He had seen many patients, and now that the day was over, he was drained. A knock on the door startled him.

Getting to his feet, he thought, *I thought I locked the outside door. How can anyone get in to my office?* He opened the door, and when he saw who was there, he exclaimed, "Why, Leonie!"

"Yes. I need to talk to you, Ransom."

"Well, come in." He stepped back, and when she stepped inside, he saw from her face how serious she was. Her lips were drawn tight. "Is someone ill?" he asked at once. "Lady Maria?"

"No. Everyone is fine—except me."

Ransom leaned closer and studied her face more intently. "You're not having headaches or any kind of aftereffects from that fall?"

"No, I'm not. Physically I'm all right, but I—I do have a problem, and you're the only one that can help me."

"Of course I will help in any way I can, Leonie," Ransom said at once.

The two were standing in the center of his office. The light cast a pale corona across her face, and he saw the tension and the strain there. "Come now, it can't be all that bad," Ransom said soothingly.

"I don't know how bad it is, but I will in a few minutes. I have something to confess."

"Confess? Why, I don't think it can be very bad, knowing you."

"I don't know if it's bad or good, but I've got to say it."

"Just say it then, Leonie." He reached out and took one of her hands and held it between both of his. The action seemed to encourage her, and she looked up into his face.

"I haven't had any experience in love, Ransom. I can only follow my heart."

Ransom was puzzled. "Well, I haven't had much experience myself." A thought came to him, and his brow wrinkled. "You haven't fallen in love with someone, have you?"

"Yes, I have."

Leonie felt his grasp tighten on her hand and saw that her words had shocked him.

"Who is it?" he demanded. "Who could you have met in this short length of time?"

"I met you, Ransom." He stared at her. Leonie knew she had to speak quickly, or she would never be able to express herself. "I have loved you for a long time. I know it's not proper for a woman to say this to a man. That men are supposed to make the first move. And I've been waiting for you to come, but—you never have, so I can only tell you what my heart is. I love you, and I want to be your wife. I know women aren't supposed to say this, but I have to, Ransom. I know I'll never love another man the way I love you."

As Ransom looked down, he saw the tears glimmering in Leonie's eyes, and her lips were trembling. She whispered, "Do you have any feelings at all for me?"

Ransom could not answer for a moment, but then he put his arms around her and drew her close. "Yes, I do, but I haven't come for a very good reason. You're going to be a wealthy woman. You'll be able to move in high society here. I'll never be rich. My heart is in serving poor people. You know that, Leonie. I couldn't ask a woman with money and position and all that goes with it to step down to my lifestyle."

"Oh, Ransom, I don't want those things! The money doesn't mean anything to me. I've already decided that whether you love me or not, when I get the inheritance it will go toward making your dream come true—for it's my dream too."

And then Leonie saw great happiness come to Ransom Sheffield's face. He pulled her forward and kissed her, and she surrendered to his embrace. She felt as if she were coming home as he held her. Leonie remembered how he had held her tenderly and gently when she had come out of her coma, and now she was not in a coma at all. She was strong and full of a woman's desires and dreams. She put her arms around him and held him close.

Finally he lifted his lips and said, "So you're determined to be the wife of a poor doctor."

"Yes," Leonie said, and her eyes sparkled. "Oh, we're going to have such a life together. And you're going to have to do one thing."

"What's that?"

"You're going to have to tell me every day that you love me. You'll never know how hard it was for me to come and say what I said. I felt so awful!"

"I do love you, Leonie, and we'll tell each other, every day."

And so they made the pact, and both of them knew as they stood there that they would be one, and they would never lose what they felt for each other at that moment.

THE EXILES: A NOVEL

BOOK ONE OF THE CREOLES SERIES

The Exiles, the first book of The Creoles Series, introduces Chantel Fontaine. Readers follow Chantel through the streets and swamps of Louisiana as she falls in love, faces the loss of both her parents, and searches for the baby sister she thought was lost forever.

The culture of the citizens of nineteenth-century New Orleans was as varied and intriguing as their complexions—French, Spanish, African, and American. As the layers of these cultures intertwine, a rich, entertaining story of love and faith emerges. It is the early 1800s, and Chantel Fountaine has finished her education at the Ursuline Convent. But the trials and tragedies that preceded her graduation have put her Christian beliefs to the test.

From bestselling authors Gilbert and Lynn Morris, this captivating novel offers a unique perspective in a distinct cultural setting that comes alive in the minds and hearts of readers.

ISBN: 0-7852-7002-7

THE IMMORTELLES: A NOVEL

BOOK TWO OF THE CREOLES SERIES

The Immortelles, the second book of The Creoles Series, follows the story of Damita De Salvedo, a fortunate young woman, born to a life of affluence and privilege in nineteenth-century New Orleans. Her beauty, accentuated with a wealth of glossy, jet-black hair, is exceeded only by her brashness. With a firm determination and willful disposition, Damita's spirit is not conducive to discipline, the one thing she desperately needs—and stubbornly resists.

With her family in crisis, Damita faces hardships she has never known. Does she have the character and fortitude to meet the responsibilities thrust upon her? Will she sacrifice body and soul to save her family's legacy?

ISBN: 0-7852-6806-5

Gilbert Morris & Lynn Morris

THE ALCHEMY: A NOVEL

BOOK THREE OF THE CREOLES SERIES

The Alchemy focuses on Simone d'Or, a vivacious young woman hardened by high society life, and Colin Seymour, a talented young man from humble beginnings. As the famed singer and composer Lord Beaufort nurtures Colin's singing voice, Colin rises to stardom in the opera world. At first, Simone judges Colin as a man beneath her standing, but after hearing Colin at the opera, she finds herself captivated by his talent and passion. Meanwhile, Simone's brother places the family name in jeopardy by his gambling debt, and she must face the possibility of marrying Vernay, a rigid young man of equal status who is feared for his skill in dueling others to the death.

ISBN: 0-7852-6806-5